LONG LIVE THE REPUBLIC

(All about me, and Julie, and
the end of the Great War)

Translated by Peter Kussi

Garden City, New York
1973

LONG LIVE
THE REPUBLIC

BY JAN PROCHÁZKA

DOUBLEDAY & COMPANY, INC.

ISBN: 0-385-04753-3 Trade
      0-385-05339-8 Prebound
Library of Congress Catalog Card Number 72–76183
Translation Copyright © 1973 by Doubleday & Company, Inc.
Printed in the United States of America
First Edition

This remembrance of native Moravia
and of my long-vanished childhood
is dedicated to Karel Kachyňa,
who provoked it
and for whose sensitive directorial talents
it was intended.

ABOUT JAN PROCHÁZKA

"When I really got to know my fellow citizens," said Jan Procházka, "my respect for some of them died and my respect for others was born."

Procházka himself was the kind of man who grows in stature on closer acquaintance.

The son of a small farmer, he spent his boyhood in the fertile Moravian countryside of wheat fields, meadows, white-steepled village churches, a land so lyrically described in this book.

In 1939, when Procházka was ten years old, Czechoslovakia lost its independence. Years of German occupation and war followed, dreary years of waiting and fear. Jewish families disappeared, now and then partisan shots rang through the woods. But the village felt the travails—and rewards—of war only toward the end, as the beaten German Army tried to stave off the pursuing Russians. These were the heady days of LONG LIVE THE REPUBLIC.

The post-war republic was not destined to live long at all. Within three years it was replaced by the communist regime of Klement Gottwald. By this time the undersized Pinda had grown into a stocky, vigorous young man with a zest for the new era. He became a youth leader, party worker, propagandist, an astonishingly versatile writer with the robust verve—if not the genius—of a Mayakovsky.

It is said that he owed his career to a bizarre misunderstanding. The story goes that the wife of the President of the Republic liked the way a certain Jan Procházka had talked about her husband on a Sunday-morning radio program. You should ask that man to visit us, she said. An invitation was duly dispatched. But both Jan and Procházka are extremely common Czech names. The appointment secretary made an understandable error of identification, and the Jan Procházka who appeared at the presidential palace had nothing in common with the Sunday radio commentator. The mix-up came to light only after the visitor had already succeeded in charming the President with his personality, his refreshingly novel combination of loyalty and outspoken directness.

Whether this anecdote is apocryphal or not, Procházka's rise was sudden and swift. The prolific but relatively obscure journalist, author, film-script writer became the government's chief literary spokesman and adviser; the still youthful activist rose to a succession of political posts culminating in appointment to the party's Central Committee.

Did Procházka sell out his integrity? There is no doubt that his pact with power tended to disarm him as a literary critic and to distract him as a writer. Much of his work became hurried, mediocre, even shabby. But Procházka was no tame poet laureate. With the uncouth tongue of a court jester he stung and derided the somber, prosaic men who ran the people's republic. He used his privileged position to ask subversive questions, to tell unpopular truths. This was notably true of the film scenarios which he wrote for the director Karel Kachyňa, including the script for the film version of LONG LIVE THE REPUBLIC.

Procházka's alliance with the men at the top ultimately proved to be as tenuous as Pinda's ties with his schoolmates portrayed in the pages of this book. There was much of the hard-headed farm boy in Pinda, but there was something else in him, too, a proud self-sufficiency akin to Cyril Vitlich, an alien sensitivity suggested by the itinerant puppet player. The schoolboy gang could neither ignore Pinda nor accept him; he was the scorned but pursued outsider, their elusive, troublesome conscience. And in his decisive moments, Pinda knew he could never jump to the safe shore along with the rest of the gang, but he had to remain alone, on the swaying ice floe, sailing on his lonely, perilous, blissful journey.

During the last part of the Novotný era Procházka had increasing doubts about the regime's desire and ability to respond to cultural values. Intercourse between power and culture, it seemed, would remain a monologue. The moment of revelation apparently came when Procházka convinced President Novotný to invite top political functionaries and representatives of Czechoslovak cultural life to spend a day together at the President's summer residence. The utter failure of communication that ensued was painfully evident. Thereafter, Procházka grew into an ever more hostile critic of the government. At the 1967 Writers' Congress, Procházka openly attacked Czechoslovak foreign policy, particularly its anti-Israeli position. He was expelled from the Central Committee, and after the Soviet invasion he became a hunted man. In 1971, the author died of cancer in a Prague hospital, under the watchful eyes of secret police.

LONG LIVE THE REPUBLIC concludes on the somber note that a single life means very little in this world; the enormous crowds that attended Procházka's memorable funeral clearly thought otherwise.

Jan Procházka's involvement in the repressive regimes of post-war Czechoslovakia is controversial; he has been accused of naïveté, political and artistic immaturity. But nobody can deny either his courage or his honesty. Both qualities speak eloquently from these remarks about his autobiographical novel:

"Long Live the Republic" describes how I saw and experienced the end of the great war. My mother is there, our small white-washed house, the river with its peculiar moist smell that clings to my nostrils to this day. My happy, painful, already so distant childhood . . . The book is about horses, too,

the yearning for horses which is the passionate dream of small farmers. I drank this longing with my mother's milk. My father's entire working life was spent in the pursuit of this equine fata morgana.

The Russian Army swept in on a flood of horses, compact horses with low bellies, tiny hooves, sad eyes. I was fascinated by this armada's exotic air, the tang of far-away places: Hungary, Carpathia, Ukraine . . .

During those exciting April days I lay stretched out on the roof of our house, eager to watch the war; I knew it was probably the last war I would ever see. Both armies had been bled white, they were staggering, resembling each other in their desperate exhaustion. They zig-zagged across the land through narrow country roads while flags of dust swirled overhead. And the guns had hardly stopped firing before my neighbors crept out into the streets to rummage through abandoned houses for a handy piece of property . . .

This was another reason why I wrote the book. Accounts of the war are usually full of laurel wreaths, lilac blossoms, bravely waving flags, and resounding anthems. Yes, there was reason for pride. But there was more to be told, too. And I believe that the greatest and most fundamental task of literature is to tell the truth.

Peter Kussi

LONG LIVE THE REPUBLIC

CHAPTER ONE

A Messerschmitt had been circling the sky, from early morning. Now it was tracing a thin white spiral, flying very high. At times it seemed to be headed right for the sun, but then it came back again. When it dived it whined like a buzz saw, and the engine knocked.

Dad was looking up, too. He squinted his eyes, his mouth open. He knew nothing about planes.

"It's way up there," I said. "Three or four thousand meters."

Sometimes I felt like chatting with Dad. But he always gave me a funny look, and I didn't want to go on talking anymore.

"It's a twin-engine job."

"Go over to Petrzela and get half a can of lime," he said. The Messerschmitt didn't exist for him any longer. He gave me a tin can for the lime, and shoved the bike at me. It was probably the first bicycle ever made. The wheels had no fenders, and about ten other parts were missing—maybe even the bearings. It looked like a pair of old grinding wheels.

I watched the plane going into a nose dive.

"The dumb things you worry about," Father said. He snorted contemptuously through his big nose. All my life he had treated me as if I was a big pain to him.

He opened the gate for me.

"And don't you dare waste time over at Vitlich's place!"

"No," I promised.

He gave me two crowns for the lime.

"Make sure you ask him for only half a can!" He raised his eyebrows for emphasis. Sometimes he treated me like a certified idiot.

Dad was rough and tough, but my mother was gentle.

I always wondered why she liked him.

"Ride carefully," she said. She always had a slight, almost invisible, smile on her face. "Don't fall off now!"

She spoke with a gentle voice.

"I won't fall, Mom."

Something flowed between us which Dad never noticed at all. "Don't worry, I know how to ride a bike."

Dad had already left, slamming the gate noisily behind him.

I knew Mother was watching me pedal off. It made me mad that I was still such a little runt. I tried to square my shoulders. For Mom's sake, I was sorry that I was so slow in growing bigger. I knew she worried about it. To show off, I started to whistle a loud tune. My legs weren't long enough to reach the pedals, so I had to ride the bike with one leg stuck through underneath the crossbar. My legs were quite thin; my thighs were no bigger than my calves.

At the bottom of the hill I saw the gang. It was a good thing I didn't have to pedal just then. I wouldn't have wanted them to see my awkward acrobatics underneath the crossbar, not for anything in the world. All four of them were there: Vyska, Rez, Kudera, Chumsky. Four of the dumbest jerks in the whole world. They had their mutts with them, leading them by ropes —anybody who ties a rope around a dog's neck has to be a superjerk.

The dogs turned their heads. They knew me. Unlike their owners, the dogs were bearable.

2

The boys were booting stones lying in the road. I whistled sharply to get their attention. The bike was rattling, dancing a jig, the empty can banged against the side.

They ran after me. That gave me a marvelous feeling.

"Your pins are too short, Pinda," they screamed. "They won't reach!"

"Nothing to it! Just watch me!" I yelled.

The bike flew like a rocket. Time to put on the brakes. I slid off the lumpy seat and parked my rear as far to the back as I could. I was sliding furiously from side to side, everything was going great. The speed was getting fantastic, out of this world. Whenever I hit a stone in the road the bike jumped a meter in the air.

"Break your ass, Pinda!" yelled Chumsky, laughing. I got a glimpse of them out of the corner of my eye, holding their bellies pretending to be dying of laughter. Then they started tossing rocks. They're always the first to start trouble.

"Vyska-Pisska! Koo-Koo-Kudera! Chumsky the Chump!" I yelled till my vocal cords started to pop. I had a million variations. "Here comes Rez the louse, let's fumigate the house!"

The curve by the Veterans' Monument was a suicide curve, pure and simple. In my panting fury at the gang I forgot about it, and at the speed I was going things couldn't end well, but they ended fast. Everything was over in a few seconds.

I got up very quickly, but something had to be broken. I licked my wrist; no big deal, just a little blood. Only a few drops. I sucked some more blood, spat it out. I heard the barking of dogs, the voices of the gang. The lime can was crushed as flat as a pancake, but it could be knocked back into shape. My front wheel looked like the figure eight; that I straightened between my knees.

Once more, I was dancing on the pedals. But no fancy stuff

this time. I just pedaled under the crossbar so I could get away as fast as possible. The smith had a sign written in chalk on his gate: WILL REOPEN AFTER THE WAR. I rode down to the stream, laid down the bike and washed my face, hands, and knees. The water burned like vinegar.

A bit further downstream was the sluice gate, where people went to fetch water. A long line was waiting, with buckets.

I could hear their voices. They were talking about the war, as usual. Somebody said he'd heard guns at night.

"Mark my words, the Russians will lob a few shells our way."

"The Germans, more likely. Before they pull out."

"Russians or Germans, the bombs are all the same. . . ."

At the narrowest part of the road I met old Kudera, Kudera's father. Whether in small or big size, they all looked the same. The Kuderas are the biggest show-offs in the whole village. Even my dad said so. Old Kudera always drove his animals as if the whole road belonged only to him. I had to glue myself to the fence, and even so the wheel of his wagon almost rolled over me. Kudera didn't give a damn. He wasn't going to pull his nags over to the side, not even a little bit, not for anybody. The outside horse snorted in my face, and stealthily I whacked it over the head. It had terribly stupid eyes.

"Good day, Mr. Kudera!" I always greet all grownups. If I didn't and my father found out, I'd get a licking. But for old Kudera I was just so much empty air. I might have been a gnat. As soon as he passed, I wheeled by the blacksmith's, and took a short cut through the back. I quickly circled the buildings, and hid my bike in the bushes. "Don, sit!" The dog obeyed my commands like a trooper.

My heart was in my mouth. I was hatching a plot against old Kudera. He had to pass by a certain wall, behind which I

4

was waiting. The cask on top of his wagon had a simple cast-iron stopcock in the back, a very primitive device. All you had to do was to kick one of the wing nuts—and water would come rushing out all over the road like a flood.

This was the right moment, first the horses were passing, then the peasant's smug profile, then his wagon. I jumped up, the trick was done in a single movement, and already I was behind the wall. I grabbed the bike and jogged through the bushes.

"Don, come on, let's go!" I called to the dog in a low voice. "Come on!"

"What the . . . ?" I heard Kudera. "Prrrrrrrrrr. Who the hell . . . !"

No doubt, I looked happy. I mounted the bike and took off, whistling cheerfully.

After that adventure, I kept on going until I reached Slejha's place. I could see into his yard. They had a big job to do before the war reached the village: They had to hide their pig. They were shoving it into a bunker made of wooden slats. The whole Slejha family was helping, and stationmaster Slejha had a double nelson on the pig's head.

"Won't it suffocate in there?" asked Mrs. Slejha. She weighed two tons. The fat jiggled on her arms and legs.

"It'll survive until the front passes by."

"It'll squeal," piped up their squeaky-voiced daughter, Andula.

"A pig never squeals in the dark," maintained Slejha.

The pig was already inside the enclosure, squealing furiously. Mrs. Slejha spotted me peering over their wall. She frowned, but I said hello to all of them anyway—Andula was my classmate. I thought I'd better get going, Mrs. Slejha seemed to be looking around for something to throw at me.

Petrzela lived at the end of the village. Very fancy house,

5

the prettiest in the village. MASTER BRICKLAYER. They say he built his place out of what he managed to steal on his jobs. Our people are a mean lot. I leaned the bike against the wall. Pieces of mica were embedded in the plaster, scales of shiny mica. When the sun shone, the house lit up with thousands of tiny mirrors.

"Sit!" I said to Don. I grabbed the can. I had to cross the garden, walk through the main door into the hall. In the hall Petrzela kept a small supply of building materials; wall tile, portland cement. The door to the kitchen was in the back. I could hear the chatter of a sewing machine. I knew who was sewing: Bertyna. Petrzela had no wife; only a daughter, Bertyna. I took a peek into the kitchen; she was pumping with her feet, her hands feeding the cloth. She was sewing a flag. Red-white-and-blue, beautiful, resplendent, Czechoslovak flag. It looked like silk. Bertyna seemed to be crying. I didn't know why. A flag is to be happy about. She should have been singing over the flag.

Now I could see Petrzela. He wasn't singing either. His face was the color of portland cement. When he talked his Adam's apple, as big as a spool of thread, ran up and down.

"You can sew a million of them," he was saying to Bertyna. "A million. But people will come and slap your face just the same."

Bertyna didn't answer, she just kept on sewing. I didn't understand why anybody would want to slap her face.

Bertyna was rather heavy and she was wearing a nightgown. Nobody else in our village wore a nightgown.

"Are you listening to me?" said Petrzela.

"I'm listening," said Bertyna. "I hear you. I have ears."

"Damn it all."

It was only then that he saw me. Bertyna turned, too, and smiled.

"Two crowns' worth of lime," I said. "Good day."

"How much?"

"Two crowns' worth."

"I'm surprised you didn't go to the pharmacist!"

I don't answer stupid jokes; I kept my mouth shut.

"Come on then," he said. And we crossed the yard. He had enough bricks there to build two castles. He saw the plane circling in the sky.

"German or Russian?"

"Messerschmitt," I said.

"Yeah?"

I bet he'd never heard the word before.

"A fighter."

"Where are those two crowns?"

I gave him the money. He took the coins with disgust, as if I had fished them out of the toilet. He reached for the can with the same expression. The lime was in a huge vat. I watched his hands; it seemed to me he was being a bit skimpy.

"Dad said half a can."

We looked each other in the eye.

The plane was climbing; I could hear the whine.

"If your dad lives long enough he'll become another Roth-schild." Petrzela was holding his bricklayer's spoon in one hand, in the other my can, he was picking up the white mass on the tip of the spoon. He knocked some into the can. He was trying to decide whether to add a bit more or not. He added a little, and then he gouged a smidgen back out again.

"Some business with you people," he said, contemptuously snorting out of his trumpet-like nose. "I'll get rich on people like you," he repeated.

I thanked him and walked out. I hung the can on the handle-bars by its wire loop. The weight of the lime pulled me over to the right.

Now I'd decided where I was going. I'd known from the very first that I'd end up there. I looked around to make sure nobody saw me. But people didn't wander around the streets; nobody left the house who didn't have to. I rode through the old brickyard; they'd stopped making bricks there, everything was overgrown with weeds and tall grass. There was a footbridge across the stream, actually just a single wooden plank. I risked it, pretending I was riding a tightrope. Vitlich's house came into view. A green walnut tree grew by the side of the house, the tallest one in the village. I reached the fence, and Don, who was still with me, started barking.

"Shut up, Don!"

Vitlich's mutt, Iza, answered from inside.

"Stop it, Iza!"

The gate was wired shut but I knew how to open it. I was on to all of Vitlich's little secrets. You simply took the gate off the hinges and then put it right back again. I went through it, and stared at the windows and the door.

"Cyril," I called out. "Cyril!"

Nothing. Not a voice, not a sound. I was surrounded by the oppressive air of the empty yard.

But I wasn't scared.

"Iza, Don, quiet!"

The landscape around there was rather strange—it looked a little like a cemetery.

I started to whistle quietly to myself. I walked over to the shed and knelt down. Three puppies were huddling together at the bottom of the old sugar crate.

Don and Iza were peering over the top of the crate, watching the pups with me.

I patted the little dogs, and played with them; they were the reason I loved to go there. I picked one up in my arms and walked all around the house.

"Cyril!" I called again. "Cyril!"

Not a sign of Vitlich. I dropped the pup back in the crate, I had no more time to waste. But I held out my arm and let Iza jump over it. Don couldn't do that. I picked up the bike, pedaled back across the bridge, through the brickyard; once again I was back on the road, the can banging against the handlebars. I was bobbing up and down. There was a sign stuck on the embankment: NESOVICE. I stopped—NESOVICE was our village. But over the Czech name there was a German inscription: NESSOWITZ. I looked around quickly, leaned the bike against a tree, and reached into the can, for a handful of white limey goo, and NESSOWITZ disappeared. I wiped my hand on the grass. Once again I was off like an Apache. I rubbed my hand on my pants.

Suddenly I almost fell off the bike, my heart stopped beating: the Germans were in the village! I could see them at the well. They were pumping water, the pipes were rattling, water was splashing the cobblestones and the rusty outflow gate. They were drinking and washing themselves. They were grimy, covered in dust. I freed my leg from under the crossbar, coasting along by standing on one pedal. And I kept on wiping my hand real hard against my trouser leg.

The soldiers were strung out along the whole road. Their bicycles were propped against the wall. It was a bicycle detachment. They looked like sixteen-year-olds, not like soldiers. Of course, they had no way of knowing that I had destroyed the

German road sign. They splashed each other like little boys. They were laughing and joking, you'd have thought they'd won the war. I knew how to splash just as well as they did: you press your palm against the pipe, you leave a little gap between your fingers, and the pressure of the pump creates a long piddle of water. Some were already soaked, they were clowning, shouting at one another, spraying water with their mouths like girls. The bicycles were shipshape. Every single one had an air pump, a bell, and a front brake.

Some of them were reading messages on the board attached to the wall of the town hall. I am no moron. I knew enough German to read the inscription too. THIS VILLAGE HAS FULFILLED ALL OF ITS OBLIGATIONS TO THE REICH!

Underneath, somebody had written a big letter V. I didn't know who.

One soldier leered at me. He asked if I was German.

I shook my head, meaning no.

"Czech?"

I nodded, meaning yes. He spoke Czech:

"Czech—you waiting for *Russki?*"

I didn't know what to say to him, but one of the non-coms told him to get going. They pulled out, riding two by two. The one who had talked to me was lagging behind. I didn't let him out of my sight. He had fallen behind on purpose. He pulled out a small pillow from inside his shirt, stuck it under his rear end, and gingerly mounted the bike using the little step by the side of the pump for support. He got on like a girl, first straddling the crossbar. He rode off in a wavy line, looking awfully tired.

As soon as the soldiers left, the people came out of their houses. They read the inscription.

"Who wrote that?" they asked.

"Shame," somebody said. "It's a disgrace to our village!"

"A wooden board can stand a lot," I heard them talking.

"Maybe they'll leave that much sooner."

But my eyes were glued to the road. I was looking at an object glistening in the dust. It looked like a silver rectangle. It was lying where the soldiers had stacked their coats, knapsacks, and weapons. Now I was right next to it. I made sure nobody was looking, and I covered the thing with my foot. Then I bent down, as if I was fixing the strap of my sandal. It was in my hand—a metallic, smooth, strangely cool object.

I spread my fingers just a little bit; it was a cigarette case, a silver case, fantastically shiny. I had never seen a case that beautiful.

I gulped with excitement, watching to see whether any of the soldiers were coming back. The road was deserted. The board on the town hall no longer interested me. Nor did the blabbing of the citizens. If they were really bothered about the inscription, they could erase it; they yapped and yapped, but left it on the wall.

Without opening my hand, I stuck the cigarette case in my pocket, hoping nobody saw me.

"Don, time to go home!" I chased the dog away. "Go home!" I knew that he would follow me all the way to my house, anyway—which he did. Dad was waiting at the gate.

"Where did you go for the lime? To the quarry?"

He walked up to me. When my dad walked up to me, and had that look like his teeth were hurting him—watch it!

"Petrzela wasn't home," I said. "I waited for him, but he wasn't home." I have had to lie quite often in my life; circumstances force me to do it.

"Yeah?" he said. He moved his hand a little and wham! I

got one hell of a slap. My dad could drive nails with his bare palm, I think he could kill an ox that way.

"I was all over the village looking for you! Where the hell have you been?"

Second slap. He must have found out about my little detour.

"Do me a favor, don't beat him on the street." My mother ran out. Mother always intervened just a fraction of a second before I was about to die. Dad calmed down, sulkily. But then he glanced into the can.

"That's what he gave you for two crowns?" he moaned. "That thimbleful of lime?"

He and Petrzela had pretty much the same temperament. For a while Dad yapped about Petrzela, then about me, and then he picked up a brush and rolled his sleeves up over his bronzed, veiny arms. His arms were tanned all year round. He stepped away from the gate, picked out a good spot, and then wrote in capital letters right across the brown boards—TYPHUS!

I stood a step or two behind Dad, my mouth wide open.

"Dad, who has typhus?"

"You'll get it," he said. "As soon as I pull down your pants and pick up a strap. You'll get typhus in no time."

"You're writing that so the soldiers keep away," I said. After all, I had a brain too. "Right? You don't want the Germans or Russians to come here, right?"

"Stop saying 'right' and get lost."

Streaks of lime seeped down to his elbow.

Nobody in the village was as tall as Dad, so it was a mystery why I turned out to be such a midget. I went inside the house, climbed the ladder to the loft. Once there I kicked the ladder to the opposite wall, so nobody would know where I was. I closed the trap door; I was alone.

Needles of light pierced through the chinks between the tiles.

I checked to see if Dad's smack had loosened my molar. My jaw was probably out of joint, I couldn't even spit, it was so painful. I pulled my valuable find from under my shirt. Maybe the case really was made out of silver. It was also inlaid with shiny black stripes. I wiped the silver on my pants, and I ran my hand over it to feel how smooth it was. But I couldn't open it. I pressed the catch, but nothing happened. Finally it opened, sharply, on a spring. It jumped out of my hands and fell to the floor, making a ringing sound.

I quickly picked it up.

It was stuffed with cigarettes, maybe thirty. One of them fell out, and I felt for it in the darkness. I lifted it to my nose, blew the dust off, sniffed the tobacco, and counted the cigarettes. Underneath, there was a picture. I put all the cigarettes in my palm and went to the little window. A strip of strong light was coming in.

Under the cigarettes a picture of a naked woman was glued to the metal. I snapped the case shut so quickly I almost caught my fingers. Suddenly my find seemed a lot more valuable. I opened the case again, squeezing against the windowpane to get as much light as possible. The woman in the picture was smiling, she was standing next to a bush in some photographic studio. Everything could be seen very clearly.

I closed the case again, breathing heavily, my hands almost shaking.

"Where is that brat?" I heard my father.

"Olda!" called Mother.

I started climbing the beams to the dormer.

"Olda," Mother called. "Olda!"

I opened the dormer to the roof.

CHAPTER TWO

I lifted the sheet-metal cover of the dormer with great care. In any escape attempt the most important thing is to keep quiet. Dad had tremendously sensitive ears. My hands were already feeling the roof. The sky was as blue as Mother's apron. The plane would probably be buzzing forever.

The neighbors had a German shepherd. He watched me, without barking, without snapping, not even when I jumped to the ground. He had been trained by me; an intelligent dog, never surprised by the weird situations I got into. He ran alongside of me, quietly, all the way to the garden. Through gooseberry bushes to the picket fence, to the spot where one of the planks was loose. I slipped through and put the plank back in place. I stuck my hand through the fence, patted the damp tip of the dog's snout, rubbed him between the eyes. He closed his lids, stuck out his tongue and licked my wrist.

"Go chase the chickens!" I said to him. "Give 'em a good run for their money, the lazy devils!"

And then I sprinted to the village green, sandals still in my hand, my feet plopping in the velvety dust. The dust on the roads of my childhood—I have never seen any like it since. Bits of hay and straw dotted the road, a shrub leaned across the ruts, a cat darted into the bushes. A certain flat stone was embedded in the road, and it was traditional to jump over it. Whenever I did, I had the feeling that I had performed an Olympic long jump. I picked up a stick, drew a line in the dust at the spot where my heels touched the ground. Several of my previous marks were still visible. I put on my sandals only after I reached the center of the village. The boys were there, under a porch. Chumsky, Kudera, Rez, Jozka, too, and Vyska. I pretended not to see them. Maybe I could walk right by them, but they seemed to be up to something. I lost interest in my cigarette case.

"Hey, Jozka!" I called out from a safe distance. I ignored Chumsky, Kudera, Rez. I wanted nothing to do with jerks. I ignored Vyska, too. In turn, Jozka completely ignored me. Chumsky flung a rock at me. But that's all you could expect from that moron, that's all he could ever do.

Calmly I kicked the rock aside with my sandal.

"Beat it, Pinda," said Chumsky. "Did you bust your ass falling off your bike?"

I stood my ground. "Did you bust your balls chasing me?"

They whistled sharply toward Miklik's house across the street. Miklik's dad came stomping out the gate.

"Lazy good-for-nothings! Get lost before I tan your hide! Rudy has no time now. Get going, you bunch of layabouts!"

Old Miklik spent his whole life yelling. At his horse, at his wife, at Rudy. All in vain. While he was shouting at us, Rudy was already climbing out the side window. All those years and Miklik had never discovered his son's trick.

"Yes, Mr. Miklik," we answered politely. "We are going, Mr. Miklik. Good-by, Mr. Miklik!"

We made a big show of leaving, hands in pockets, whistling to ourselves. The boys kicked at the pebbles, and I booted a few, too. Rudy crouched behind a pile of bricks, darted behind a row of carts, crawled through some shrubbery, hid under the terrace. We reached the next house. This was how we always went about calling a powwow.

I kept my distance, in case somebody happened to remember me. Jozka turned around and advised me to go to hell.

"Go back," he said. He wasn't yelling. Jozka never yelled like the other idiots. I'd like to have chatted with Jozka sometime. With him, yes.

"Beat it home to Mama, she's sewing you a doll," he said softly. He was the only one of them who had not only height and strength, but brains in his head. I knew that he was giving me a hard time only on their account. If he was the chief, he had to show his authority. I wasn't mad at Jozka, I understood his position.

"Come back in three years, Pinda," he said.

"You want your seat kicked in?" Chumsky butted in. That's all he could do, give himself airs.

"Don't fall out of your shorts, you tapeworm," I said. That was the worst insult I knew. He started throwing rocks. I expected that. He flung five or six, then lost interest.

The next stop was the game warden's. You could tell at a glance whose house it was. The gables inlaid with wood, antlers over the windows, big enough to hang the washing on, the yard full of firewood. The warden's son, a real Humpty Dumpty, was named Pepek, but we called him Puma. He was waiting for us, holding Zuza on a leather leash with silver metal tacks. Zuza came from a distinguished family; she had a pedigree. She recognized me and started barking. I whistled at her the way I always did. Puma knew nothing about animals. If he owned an orangutan, he'd lead it around on a leash just the same way.

"Stop whistling, fool," the boys hissed at me.

Puma called out toward the house, "Dad, I'm going out with the dog."

"Puma, you call that a dog?"

"Who asked Pinda to come along?" Puma was furious. "Who took him along?" I made donkey ears at him. "I'll box your ears till they fall off!" he threatened. "Jerk."

"Go jerk yourself," I answered. Nothing else occurred to me. Jozka asked Puma, "Have you got it?" He lowered his voice secretively. Almost to a whisper. At once the whole gang clustered around Humpty Dumpty.

Puma pointed at something hidden under his coat. "Yeah," he said. "I've got it."

"Jozka, let me come with you!" I begged, trying to be as humble as I could.

"You can't," he said curtly.

"Why not? I'm not afraid. That's a fact!" I followed Humpty Dumpty with my eyes; he was leading the dog behind the house. I knew right away where he was taking it; to the barn. The dog whined. He closed the gate, but the whining could be heard anyway. Puma kicked the gate. "Quiet! Shut up!" And suddenly he dashed right at me. I didn't expect it. The rest of the gang ran at me too, even Jozka. That surprised me most of all. I wouldn't have expected him to be so devious. I turned and took to my heels, but I couldn't run away from Rudy and Jozka, they had longer legs.

"Leave me alone!" I started yelling even before they reached me. "I didn't do anything to you!"

I tried to pull myself up on a branch of a tree, but they'd already got me. I could have known that Chumsky—that swine —would start pulling off my pants while I was hanging help-less! He pulled off my shorts too, and I had to let go. But I held on to my shirt. They knocked me to the ground, they were stronger and there were too many of them. I defended myself as best as I could, anything goes when the other side is

18

stronger. I bit Chumsky in the calf, he yelped and kicked me in the head.

I yelled much harder than necessary. It didn't really hurt all that much, but I squealed like a siren. "Aaa aauuuuuaaa!"

"Leave him alone," Jozka pushed them away. "He's had enough. You've had enough, right, Pinda?"

I stuck out my tongue at him, even Jozka was a moron. Now I could see that he was just as dumb as the rest of them. At the very end, after the tussle was over, Kudera kicked me. This always happened after a fracas, when peace had already been declared, Kudera couldn't resist kicking somebody. As the gang was leaving, I hit him in the back with a rock. Holding up my pants with one hand, I slunk away from the battlefield, spitting dust, my teeth full of sand. Someone else might have screamed with pain, but I didn't make a sound. Not a chance. I paused to think of revenge. Even from where I was I could hear Zuza whimpering. I walked back to the game warden's house; nobody was around. I opened the door of the barn without any trouble. Just as I'd thought, the poor dog was tied to a hook. It could only sit up, its nose against the wall.

First of all, I let the dog go, then it suddenly occurred to me where they'd most likely gone. I ran out between the barns, through the gardens, down the backyards to the big patch of clover, it was green and blue, and the dew dampened my knees. I reached the hollow. A meadow full of thyme, brambles, and coltsfoot sloped down to the hollow. I picked off a white, cottony coltsfoot leaf and put it over my head. Then I lay down and waited. I could see into the hollow, but from down there nobody could see me.

I raised myself on my elbows to make sure I could see the gang as they passed the curve in the road. But I heard them first, they were screaming like a bunch of wild monkeys. Five of them were carrying a ladder, it was the longest one they could get their hands on. They probably swiped it from Rapousek the roofer. Puma wasn't helping with the ladder, he was walking in front, holding a pair of binoculars. He was practically floating, he was so full of his own importance—he looked unbearable. Of course, I lay flat so nobody could see me, they'd have given me another beating if they'd spotted me.

"Hear that?" said Jozka, stopping. He lifted his head high. In my leafy hiding place, I could hear nothing. Just the buzzing of the plane.

"What?" asked Kudera. "What do you hear?"

"Guns," said Jozka. "Bombardment from the front!"

"No fooling?" said Rez in amazement. He was amazed at everything.

I stretched my neck to see what Chumsky was doing. He was lying in the grass, one ear to the ground.

"You can hear better on the ground!" he yelled.

Jozka pointed to his forehead, meaning that Chumsky was an idiot. I agreed with that.

"Are you on a railroad track?" asked Jozka. "You listening to a train?"

"I am serious," Chumsky said. He muttered for a little while more, but they'd already picked up the ladder and were moving on. And I moved like a shadow in their footsteps, they'd no idea I was watching their every move.

"How far does the sound of a gun carry?" I could hear them talking in the distance.

"About fifty kilometers," said Puma.

"Who said so?" asked Rez.

"Cmiral . . ."

"He's a jerk."

"He was in the war. He got a medal!"

"Big deal! Granddad got malaria!"

I couldn't resist it, I lay down and put my ear to the ground, like Chumsky. I listened for a few seconds, and when I lifted my head I saw they were on their way to the church. From where I was lying I could see in the distance the pigeons flying around the steeple. They circled the church like a living white cloud. There were always hundreds of them around our steeple. From where I was it seemed as if the plane was right over the steeple, too.

The gang had disappeared, and it was time for me to get going.

I took a short cut through the cemetery. First I heard the gang, then they came back into view. They were taking off their shoes, and they'd propped up the ladder against the lowest part of the church roof. I watched them through a crack in the cemetery wall. Jozka was first to climb the ladder. Barefoot he walked along the roof; it was the roof over the vestry. There was a round window over it that could be opened. They all climbed up after Jozka. Naturally, Rez almost fell off the ladder. They took Rez and rejected me! I was furious. I was a ten-times better climber than Rez. I can't stand injustice. Chumsky stumbled.

"Fall off," I said softly to myself. Nobody could hear me from behind the wall. "Break your neck!"

But the boys were already through the round window. I heard them, they trudged like a herd of elephants over the church attic and into the stone steeple.

They left their boots in a pile under the ladder. I didn't have to open the cemetery gate—they'd left it hanging wide open behind them.

"Don't touch the rope, or the bells will start up," I heard Jozka's voice from the steeple.

"Idiots," I said to myself. I was hiding behind a stone monument. I liked to read the inscriptions, some of them were wild! HERE REST IN PEACE ALOIS AND MARIE NAVRATIL. SLEEP WELL, ANNIE! An oval photograph behind glass. I bent down close to the girl's face, smiling up at me from the tombstone. I should have known they'd scare all the pigeons in the steeple. The birds were fluttering in terror around the dome, I could hear the rustle of their wings. There was a thud from the steeple, followed by: "Jerk!" They weren't talking church talk. I heard a few choice words which would sound interesting at confession. They appeared in the window by the bell. I could see them, but they still couldn't see me. Jozka had the binoculars, he was scanning the countryside.

"You can see all the way to the bridge!"

"It magnifies like crazy."

"The tanks are coming! Right under me, I could reach them they're so close. This thing sure magnifies!"

"Gimme," Puma wanted his binoculars. Then they took turns looking, one after the other.

I was stuck down on the ground, and I was as mad as a wild pig. I sat by the side of the church, my back leaning against the wall, my foot kicked at their ladder, I dug up handfuls of grass and scattered them all around. I kept on hearing their dumb remarks from the steeple.

"The plane is passing the bridge," yapped Kudera from up there.

I stopped pulling up the grass, I reached out into the pile of shoes and looked for his scuffed, down-at-the-heel clodhoppers. I found them, pulled out the laces.

"The Russians could blow it sky high . . ." the stupid prattle went on. I threw one shoe somewhere between the tombstones, the other one I heaved over the gate, into the shrubs.

22

"Maybe they'll level the village," said Chumsky, babbling as stupidly as the rest.

"I'd love to see that." I found his sandals, too. I looked around for another good spot.

"I'd never let them lock me in the cellar! When will we get another chance to see a war again!" That was Puma. His clogs were flying through the air. They made the longest arc yet. The pile of shoes was getting smaller.

"Maybe the school will burn down." That was Rudy. I was already holding his sandals, ready to fling them behind the wall. But he said something that caught my interest. "The principal might get frizzled to a crisp." I wouldn't throw his shoes away. I put them back. The vision he had expressed had my full sympathy. A sudden noise startled me. Somebody was urinating from the window in the steeple, smacking on the stones below. If the priest saw it, he'd have a stroke. The piss made an opalescent arc against the sun, which loomed behind the church like a yellow gourd.

I reached for the most beat up and shabby sandals. Once more I watched the arc of urine, to make sure they landed in the right place. Then I chose another pair, threw them way behind the gate. I got tired of sitting, so I got up, took all the remaining shoes except for Jozka's clumsy boots, and threw them into the briars by the side of the wall.

I came back, and touched the enormous ladder. I didn't want to knock it over, I just wanted to see if I could lay it down all by myself. Quietly. At the top, the ladder scratched against the eaves, but they didn't hear it, they were fighting for the binoculars. I couldn't hold it steady, it was heavier than I thought. I tried to catch it, but it turned over, fell down like a ton weight, and banged into the nearest tombstone. It made a racket that must have been heard even by those departed loved ones resting in peace. I was already behind the wall, with my eye glued to a crack. The boys were leaning way out; it was a wonder they didn't fall from the steeple. And then all their heads disappeared. I could hear them running down the stairs, across the church attic, to the round window. They were yelling about the ladder. What happened? How did it fall? They were hollering, one louder than the other. They climbed out onto the vestry roof.

"You must have stood it up all wrong," said Kudera to Jozka. Jozka didn't answer. He walked to the edge of the roof, and took a long careful look.

"He stuck it in the ground, I saw it," said Chumsky. But Jozka didn't answer Chumsky either. He was still looking down, to where the ladder had been standing.

It was as far down as from the top of a skyscraper.

An ant crawled up my calf, I scratched it with the instep of my other foot, the beast bit me, I had to put spit on the spot. I watched to see what the idiots would do next. I hadn't wanted to knock down their ladder, but now I was glad I had. Jozka was still searching all over the cemetery with his eyes. He couldn't see me behind the wall, but he looked that way too, as if he did see me. Jozka was the smartest of them all.

"Pinda!" he yelled loudly. "Olda!"

I was delighted to see Chumsky's face now. He was gaping like a roped cow. Amazement and surprise were pulling at his ears. Kudera leaned down.

"Hey, where are our shoes? That skunk's down there all right!"

"You're the skunk," I said to myself behind the wall.

"I see mine," said Rudy. "Mine and Jozka's."

Chumsky was looking for me through his binoculars. He cavorted over the cemetery with his glass eyes. He needled me.

I had an eight-strand slingshot in my pocket. There were plenty of small stones around. A small pancake-shaped pebble is best, and it's a good idea to spit on it so the leather won't slip when you aim. My hand was itching to nail Chumsky right between the eyes. But I didn't want to give myself away.

"Olda!" shouted Jozka. "Olda!"

"Pinda, come here, nothing will happen to you," called Jozka.

"I'll knock his teeth through his nose," said Chumsky.

"Me, too," said Humpty Dumpty.

"Don't be afraid, they won't do anything to you," repeated Jozka. "Come and fix the ladder."

"He can't lift it. He couldn't lift a donkey's tail." That's Rez. That kind of thing made me see red. When they talked like that, all self-control left me.

"Rez!" I screamed from behind the wall. "Rez, buy yourself a fez! You can be a Turk, you stupid little jerk!" I could have killed Rez on the spot.

I yelled till the veins stood out in my neck. I tried to outyell him so I couldn't hear his idiotic claptrap.

"We're counting to ten, Pinda," Kudera threatened from the roof. "Come out, you skunk, or you'll really get it."

"One."

I climbed up on the wall so they could see me. I didn't care. I'd just as soon risk my life. I guess I'm a little nutty like my father.

"Two, three, four, five, ten, fifty, hundred, thousand, million," I shouted. "I won't give you the ladder."

I sat down at the foot of the wall, leaned against it with my back. There they couldn't reach me. Rocks and pieces of tile rained on the shrubbery; some hit the top of the wall and bounced into the grass.

Then they stopped.

"He's gone," I heard them debating on the roof.

"He's still there."

"He could have slipped through the bushes."

"Olda!"

I pulled a few faces, just for myself, to calm myself down. I blew into my palm; there's an airmail message for you, you bastards!

"I'll give you my football!" called Humpty Dumpty.

But I could hear their whispers.

"You'd really give it to him?"

"Hell, no." And aloud: "You want a good football? Yes or no?" Puma must think I was born yesterday.

"We can go through the church," suggested one of them.

"The windows are barred."

"We'll break down the gate."

"Not a chance."

"Nobody might come around here," I heard Kudera, "till after the war."

I took a peek at the sky to see if the plane was still there. It kept on circling and purring; a calm, reassuring sound. I watched it for a while.

"I'm afraid of cemeteries at night," Chumsky tried to make a joke. But his voice sounded like his pants were full. They were acting cheery trying to give themselves courage.

"Listen, fellows, I can't stay here much longer," said Rez, getting to his feet.

Only now I remembered the cigarette case. I reached into my shirt. It was still there. I turned on my heel and trudged off. The gang no longer interested me. I was in a hurry to get where I wanted to go in the first place.

"Olda!" I heard them way behind me, after I'd been jogging a while. And then the whole choir: "Oooooooldaaaaa!"

"Piiiiiiiindaaaaaaa fooooooooool!"

I jogged through thick undergrowth, parting the brambles with my hands. I didn't have to climb a steeple to see far and wide. I knew which of the six linden trees standing on the opposite hill was the easiest to climb. Its trunk had big knobs I could brace my feet against, and slither up onto a bough. I grasped the limb with both arms. I didn't look down, not because I was afraid, but I'd rather not take a chance at slipping. I kept looking up at the very top of the tree. I swayed on thin, elastic branches, until I finally stuck my head out of the leafy crown.

It was like an observatory, I could see the whole countryside. It looked like a postcard: blue hills, green river, white bridge. I saw an army coming down from the hills, spilling over the bridge, hurrying along the road, raising a flag of dust. The wind was blowing in the opposite direction, hardly any sounds were to be heard. I watched the Germans patiently for a long time. But there were no tanks. Now I could see that the plane was circling right over the bridge. Always at the same height. Then I lost interest and slid down.

Once again I was jogging through the acacias between the walnut trees. The bank was sandy there, I slid down it standing up, the soles of my sandals turning into a pair of skis. They were full of sand. At the bottom, I shook them out. Suddenly I froze; forgot all about the sandals. From the nearest tree I broke off a branch for protection. The stick was quite strong and heavy. I turned around quickly, but it was only a rabbit jumping out of its hole. I walked in that direction, where two thick shrubs stood next to each other. I whacked the shrubbery with my stick, right over a thin, winding animal track, and right into a deer snare which somebody had set. The snare was attached

27

to a young tree that had been bent over; it freed itself, snapped through the air with a crack like a whip.

I hate poachers, and in our village they were all poachers. Even my dad went into the woods at night. I'll never forget one experience if I live to be a hundred. At that time the meadow was already yellow, drenched by wind-blown leaves; I trotted a few steps behind my father because I couldn't keep up with him. As he ran he was already opening a big knife. In the copse, a trapped doe was moaning like a human being, I could hear her thrashing on the ground. I lay down in the grass, closed my eyes, put my thumbs over my ears.

"Where are you?" he called out. "Olda, where are you?"

The doe was dead. I didn't see her, only a part of her head was sticking out of the undergrowth.

He wiped his knife on the grass. Then we carried the doe on a piece of canvas to the road. My mother was sitting on the cart, holding the mare's reins.

"Stop bawling, Goddamn it!" threatened Father, in a hissing voice, his eyes flashing angrily.

"Anybody'd think your mama died, carrying on like that!"

"Mom," I said later, when the cart was already rattling on the pavement and Dad was flicking our mare Julie with the whip. "Mom . . . !"

I put my face in her lap, hugging her with both arms. But when I looked up at her, she was staring watchfully into the countryside. She hoped that Father would succeed in bringing the catch safely home. In our village, even the women had some poacher blood in them. I jumped off the cart, and ran into the fields. I wanted to get away from my parents. Dad reined in the horse in surprise, stood on top of the bags of potatoes and shouted after me: "Olda!"

I ran all the way to the willow copse. There I collapsed on the ground, shaking with self-pity.

Later, I began to search our house for the spool of wire. Smooth, yellow wire that Dad used for weaving snares. It turned out to be hidden in the barn, under a pile of chaff. One night, I slid out of the house with the wire. I knew where the water below the weir was deepest, between four black boulders. I climbed to the spot, grasped the spool with both hands and threw it into the stream. It didn't take Dad very long to guess who had taken his wire. He always chased me into the corner of the sitting room. There was no way of escaping from there. I stood in Dad's shadow, because the weak light bulb was at his back. He was so big and husky that the wall was full of his dark silhouette. He reached out for me, a leather rein in his other hand. And then I was lying on the wooden floor, biting my fingers so that I wouldn't cry and disgrace myself before him.

And Mother would sob: "You'll kill him, and they'll lock you up."

She was crying, I could tell that she was crying. She picked me up, undressed me, and put me to bed.

I thought of Dad now, of the whipping I was likely to catch when I got back home.

I ran to the willow copse, scared some partridges, and they whirred off in alarm. The copse was about three acres in size, filled with clusters of long, swishing rods. In the spring they were yellow. They grew out of low, clipped stems, which kept on tripping me up. I was immersed in a web of slippery runners, they touched my face, buds, sap, young bark that feels more like skin; it was as if I were touching living fingers. That's what bamboo is like. I imagined that the willow grove belonged to me. I walked around the brick hut in the middle of the property. Grass was growing on the flat roof of the hut, it would be an ideal shelter for a hermit. The hut never had a door. I threw a pebble inside, into the black opening. I whistled. Nothing moved. I walked to the doorway, and peered inside. In the corner I made out a disheveled bundle of straw, nothing new, the straw was there before. I scanned the walls, I kicked the straw, it rustled. At last, I sighed, sat down, almost toppled into the straw.

I knew who had put the straw here, and when. One day we had a district-wide firemen's exercise. Nothing is as stupid and boring as a public display of firemen. Their helmets shone from weeks of scrubbing. Dad was a fireman, too. They practiced for hours on end, unrolling the hoses, spinning the huge spools up the hill from the river. Eight volunteer companies took part in the exercise. We raced along the hose, watching it fill with water. The worn hose ran like a sieve, we caught streams of water in our mouths.

"Don't step on the hoses!" Kudera's dad yelled at us. He was the best scrubbed one of them all. He blew a whistle.

Then there was a lot of excitement, each company tried to be the first to drown the burning effigy of a house. A stream of water gushed out of the hose, but it didn't reach far enough. All of us youngsters ran up and pissed on the fire. But in the meantime they moved up the hoses and I got a good dousing. I fled before Dad could see me. I ran zigzag between the houses, leaving a wet trail behind. When I got to the willow copse, I hung my clothes on the shrubs to dry. My teeth were chattering, I was nude, the sun had set and it was cold. I squatted down, even though they couldn't really see me from the hut. Bertyna was waiting at the side of the hut, wearing her Sunday best, Kudera's dad was coming through the willows, the magnificent helmet still on his head, a trumpet hanging from a strap on his belt.

He was carrying a bundle of straw from the stack. Bertyna's eyes were roving uneasily over the countryside. They were saying something to each other, but I couldn't hear them. I almost stopped breathing; I was lying on my belly in the shrubbery, nose to the ground. They'd gone into the hut, Bertyna laughing.

Helter-skelter, I got into my wet clothes. I forgot my shoes, had to pull down the pants again. In the meantime, old Kudera had come out of the hut, undressed, hung up his jacket on a branch, taken off his helmet and trumpet, and carefully laid them down on the grass.

I pulled three bricks out of the wall, I had them marked. This was my hiding place. Behind the bricks there was just enough space for my wooden box. There they were—Kudera's shining helmet and trumpet, which he had laid down so carefully and then forgotten. I blew the dust off the helmet. There was a lot of other stuff in the box, too. A dismantled alarm clock, a tennis ball with the initials K.K., rubber strips for the slingshot. This is where the new find would go, too: the cigarette case.

I pulled the treasure out of my shirt, first carefully wiping the silver. Then I opened the case, sniffed the cigarettes, took them out and stuck them in my pocket. Just then, I heard a motorcycle, quite near. I put the cigarette case back, replaced the box and the bricks. For some reason, the three bricks now seemed extremely suspicious. I had a feeling that they stood out like red flags. I pried them out again, took the cigarette case, and climbed up on the grassy roof of the hut, to dig a new hiding place in the turf. I wrapped the case in a rag, covered it, tamped down the soil with my palms.

Now I could hear German voices, quite clearly. I was flat on my stomach in an instant, cautiously lifting my eyes over the top of the grass. They were so near! At the edge of the willow copse!

I could see the soldiers. Three of them, a motorcycle with a sidecar standing nearby. They were undressing, throwing away their uniforms and putting on civilian clothes. Hats instead of helmets.

They were in a great hurry, as if every minute counted. They didn't bother with the hats, they were only trying them on, then they tossed them aside. Apparently they didn't like them.

One of them stuck a pistol in his pocket. He carelessly stepped over a machine gun propped against the cycle. One soldier had his left arm in a sling, but he seemed quick and agile anyway. They were peering around all the time, as if they were scared. I slid down from the roof—first, though, I dug up the cigarette case, and once again put it back inside my shirt.

I climbed the haystack to watch the three Germans. They were leaving the willow copse, crossing the open field. One of them went first while the other two watched from the edge of the field. Only after the first one had crossed safely did the others follow. They neither hurried nor walked slowly, they were trying hard not to look conspicuous.

They left the motorcycle in the bushes, as if it were an object of so little value that it could be calmly discarded.

CHAPTER THREE

I followed the Germans for a long time. They struggled from the muddy hollow up the rocky slope, their feet were slipping on the gravel, they were bent forward as they climbed, pulling themselves up by the branches of low shrubs, clutching at rocks, at grass. I saw that two of them were helping the third, apparently he had some other wound besides the busted hand. He could just barely manage, stopping frequently. Then they were lost from sight. They slipped into the thick undergrowth. It seemed that they were aiming for the woods, but wanted to bypass the church.

I got to my feet, stuck a piece of straw in my mouth to chew on. Then I jumped up and down on the haystack, it was like bouncing on a mattress. There was always a breeze blowing across the top of a stack, even when the air was still down below. My hair was in my eyes. I kept searching the spot where the Germans had disappeared. A second plane had climbed into the sky, also a Messerschmitt. The two circled each other, their engines sputtering a duet. The distant gunfire became more distinct. I spat the straw out of my mouth, for I saw a sight that was more important to me than anything else in the war. In the far distance, leaving the church and trudging through a green clover field, I saw the gang, the whole bunch of them, heading for the white, blue, and vermilion village. From where I was they looked like ants. I could even make out the ladder. Somehow they had managed to get out. That made me really mad. I thought it would take them longer. Disgusted, I slid down the short side of the stack. I shook the straw out of my sleeves and pants legs. If I knew anything about those birds, they'd be laying for me, they wouldn't forgive a stunt like that in a hurry. But I wasn't begging them for forgiveness. I didn't need mercy from a bunch of jackasses. If they were laying in wait for me, I knew how to keep them waiting a long, long time.

The big buildings of the manor were straight ahead of me. Several trucks, heavily loaded, were leaving the estate. Their wheels raising clouds of dust, they were carrying furniture. The owner's old-fashioned personal car, a black Mercedes-Benz, was leaving, too.

I stamped my feet to scare a mole, I could see him moving under the soil right in front of me. He stopped burrowing and I knew that he was waiting in the darkness of his little passage until my steps had died away. A mole can sense the slightest vibration of the ground. The departing vehicles circled the sharp-cornered chapel at the end of the fruit tree lane. It was an ancient chapel; the trees were old, too. They had majestic black trunks, the intricate canopy of their crowns could be seen through the small young leaves. The vehicles were racing toward the concrete highway, making sharp turns and swerving around curves; they were in a hurry. Two tractors pulling trailers were also leaving, their loads hidden under canvas covers. The owner was trying to save as much as he could. But I couldn't see his blue Opel. Young Singer generally never used the Mercedes, that was reserved for the old lady whom they called the Countess. She was supposed to have blue blood. I saw her once, and her face really was blue. He was from Bavaria. The estate used to belong to

34

Morris Weiss, but he was a Jew; Singer received the estate from Hitler as a reward.

I dug up the mole's tunnel with the tip of my sandal. The mole had probably run off.

A shot rang out suddenly in the clear air. It frightened me by its power and nearness. I quickly raised my head. Pigeons were rising from the roof of the manor house, circling in a startled white cloud. Then another car came shooting out of the gate. It was the Opel, which had much more zoom than the Countess' big black boat. The entrance to the yard was deserted, the gate wide open, nobody had bothered to close it. I lost interest in moles, and I started galloping toward the manor. When I reached the gate, the sounds of military movement along the road became clearer. The whine of engines, the grinding of metal tracks merged into a single din. I couldn't see the stretch of road near the bridge, but it must have been full of soldiers.

"Selma!" I shouted when I reached the gate. I was calling Singer's mutt.

I whistled a dog signal. No answer, no bark. I whistled a few more times. I was afraid to enter the yard. The estate was a foreign world for me, I had known it only from the outside. Few of the villagers ever ventured inside unless they worked for the Singers. The wall against which I leaned was strong, stony, and ancient.

Lions were sitting on pillars on each side of the gate. I turned to look at the stone beasts with their pointed noses, long tongues hanging out of their open jaws. Pigeons were landing on the eaves of the bulging granary. I peeked inside, my body still pressed to the wall, but the yard was empty and dead. Not a living soul. The atmosphere was oppressive, like after an epidemic. I stayed outside and sat down next to the wall. But then I jumped up—I heard steps in the yard and Cyril Vitlich came striding out the gate. I had no idea what he was doing there, he had never worked for the Singers. He examined the alley, he took in the fields and the stacks. He must have heard my whistling. I bet he heard my signals, he had ears like a deer. He couldn't see me, I was behind his back, flush against the wall. I was glad to see him there, maybe he recognized me when I was yelling at Selma. He looked around for me. I whistled at his back. With two fingers in my mouth. He turned, startled. I burst out laughing, I laughed in Cyril's face.

"Dog's ear, you bloody dog's ear, what are you rummaging around here for?" His voice sounded stern. His old homespun trousers were falling apart at the knees. He wore a rumpled jacket on his bare body; he never believed in shirts. In winter, he would put on a filthy sweater. I looked into his kind, ridiculous face, he had enough wrinkles to have lived through three world wars. I grinned at him, because he was my friend.

"Hey, Cyril," I told him. "I was over at your place to look at the puppies."

"Damn it all, why didn't you stay home!" he said furiously. But I knew Vitlich, I didn't take his anger seriously. "There'll be shooting," he said.

As if I didn't know. He spoke in a squeaky nasal voice, "They'll blow up half the village, and then what?"

"I'm not afraid," I told him. "Are you scared, Cyril?" He sucked a balloonful of air through his nose. Vitlich did this all the time. He must have been born sniffing.

Standing before him, I suddenly remembered an autumn night.

It was cold but light, you could count the trees. I was sitting next to Vitlich's fence, in his house behind the brickyard. Iza got wind of me and started barking like mad.

"Quiet," I said to her, almost begging the silly dog. "Quiet."

Vitlich came through the gate, into the yard, looking around.

Then he saw me. He was wearing pants and a sweater, those were his bed clothes.

"Goddamn it," he said. "Olda, what are you up to? What have you done this time?"

I was holding onto the fence with both hands, teeth clenched, sniveling like Vitlich. I was almost crying.

"I won't stay with him," I said, meaning my father. "I ran away."

I had a hard time keeping my voice on an even keel.

"Oh yeah?" he said, snuffing like a steam engine.

"That's some news!" His sweater was sleeveless, so that his arms were bare. He was never tanned, his body was as white as chalk.

"Goddamn it, this is a hell of a world."

He took me by the hair, knocking off the cap I was wearing, and twisted my face toward him. I pretended that something fell in my eyes, I was rubbing them with my fingers. I didn't want him to think I was bawling when I left the house. I took my escape from home in deadly earnest, and my decision was irrevocable. At that age, all decisions are final. Vitlich saw extremely well in the dark, he knew that I was bawling.

"Stop it," he piped through his nose. "You're a man, aren't you? Are you a panty-waisted piss pot? A man cries only twice in his life, Olda. When they send him into this world, and when they call him to get the hell out of it again. Sometimes, too, when his mama dies. Depends what she was like. You ran away, that's fine, so stop howling about it." While he was talking, he watched me all the time. His face was twitching.

"I am not crying," I lied.

Vitlich understood male pride. "Well, I am glad I had the wrong impression. And . . . you're planning to stay away . . . a long time?"

37

"Forever," I said. "I'm never coming back. I am never going back to him."

"All right then," now he was sniffing without letup. "But what are you going to do here? You're barefoot, aren't you?"

Only then did I look at my feet. Even in the most serious situations, Vitlich didn't miss a single detail.

"He drowned the puppy you gave me," I said. "Would you ever drown a puppy, Cyril? You would never do a dirty, lousy thing like that!" Now I really had to try to keep from blubbering. He watched me silently, rubbing his bare arm with his palm, hiking up the sweater.

"Didn't I tell you your dad would drown it? I told you right away. Why should he feed his own dog, when the neighbor has a mutt, too. In our village, fortunes have always been made by saving pennies. You could have left the pup with me. Why didn't you?"

"He drowned it in a barrel of rainwater!" I shouted my accusation.

Vitlich didn't seem impressed. "In the time it takes to carry a pup to the river and to come back, he could have carted a loadful of beets from the fields. You mustn't hold that against him, Olda. But let's go inside, no use standing out here."

He shot a glance at the sky, sparkling with light green stars. A coolness blew from the sky, over the numb earth. Looking at the vaulted expanse during clear nights, it always seemed to me that the stars were ringing bells. But Cyril Vitlich had hardly any poetic sense.

"In the morning there'll be one hell of a hoarfrost," he said matter-of-factly.

I was still holding onto the picket fence. Right in front of me, behind the giant walnut, the Milky Way was arching down; it was a miracle. It trembled, it was unbelievably bright, so that our figures standing in front of the house almost cast a visible shadow. I wanted to say something about it to Vitlich, but I didn't know what. I never had any words for the really important things.

"Come on, you dog's ear," he said. He was rubbing his arms, clapping his hands. "I'll heat up some soup for you. Would you believe it, I caught five crows yesterday? A crow soup is as strong as an elixir, it's better than beef broth." I was amazed that he could be talking about anything as casual as food, when I was on the verge of making a decision that would alter my entire life.

"I am not hungry," I said. "I have no taste for food."

"I know," he honked through his nose. "All right then."

Once more, both of us trumpeted through the nose. We were already crossing the yard to his house.

I stopped at the doorstep. There was something in his face that put me on my guard.

"Cyril, you're not thinking of calling my dad, are you?" He wanted to shove me into the hall, but I was clutching the door frame.

"Who? Me? Call your dad? What do you take me for, Olda?" he said heatedly.

Sometimes his face looked so sincere it would fool a clairvoyant. I stared at him hard.

"Don't forget, you ran away from home, too, when you were little," I reminded him of an old story he once told me. I was appealing to his sense of solidarity.

He cleared his nose, closing off one nostril with his thumb and blowing hard. He had no need for a handkerchief. He had no need for a lot of things.

"I lied to you, Olda," he said. "That story wasn't true." He grimaced like an actor. "I dreamed it up, the whole thing was made up just to impress you. Do you believe me?"

"Believe what? What you told me then, or what you're telling me now?"

"What I have just finished telling you."

"No," I said. "I don't believe that. You ran away all right. And you came back only when you were twenty. After your dad died."

"Is that what I told you?"

"That's right. I know all that straight from you."

"All right then, come on in." He sighed, breathing like he was trying to turn his lungs inside out. "Let's have a few words about this business of leaving home." He sighed again, even louder than the first time.

He kept at me all night long, explaining, preaching, asking me a million times whether I understood. I said yes. His persistence and storytelling ability were remarkable. He painted the world as a nest of highwaymen. He recounted all the troubles he had undergone and wanted me to avoid. In the morning, he took me back to my house. I was furiously kicking at the stones along the way. As a safety measure, Vitlich led me by the hand. He limped, his right knee had been stiff for many years.

Deliberately, he kept up a steady stream of words. About catching crows; about the stupidity of these birds, they flew into the net and all Vitlich had to do was to pull the string, sometimes catching three or four at one shot.

"You wait here, all right?" he said in front of our familiar house, which now looked so hateful to me. "I want to have a few words with your dad first, all right?"

"I suppose so," I said vaguely. I was itching to turn around and to keep on running till I reached Australia. "You won't fly the coop on me, will you?" He was reading my mind. "You wouldn't do that, Olda. You gave me your solemn."

"Yes, sure, all right." I began to look at Cyril as a bit of a coward.

"Your dad won't do anything to you. He won't lay his hand on you, don't worry. I'll explain everything to him." It was clear to me I could expect Dad to thrash me just a little harder *than usual. But this didn't bother me nearly as much as my disappointment at Cyril. Christ almighty, did he ever get me into a mess!*

I was cold, my feet were freezing, I was sleepy, so I didn't run away. I hid behind a pile of logs, which at that time were stacked high by the side of the house.

Dad opened the door. He didn't even know that I wasn't home. He led Cyril into the hall, and soon I heard him yelling. I knew just what to expect. I took off my cap, stuffed it with dry grass and put it inside my pants. Cyril knew my father from school, but I knew him from practical life. Naturally, as soon as Cyril left, I got the hiding of my life. Dad swatted me with the gusto of a giant threshing wheat.

"Well, tell me, Olda, how did it all come out?" Vitlich asked the next day. "I bet your dad didn't lay a hand on you."

"No. Not at all."

He was truly pleased by the success of his intercession.

"How come your knees are skinned again?" Vitlich was asking me now, in the yard of the manor. He pushed me inside, quickly closed the massive gates. He dropped the bolt into place. He seemed to be in a hurry, but nothing escaped his darting eyes. Actually, even a blind man could have spotted my bloody knees.

"The Germans were in the willow grove," I told him. "They left their motorcycle behind. They were changing their clothes. Just now, Cyril, a minute ago."

"Is that so? Germans?"

"Three of them."

"But I asked you about your knees. You sitting on your ears?"

"I fell off my bike, that's all."

"That's what I thought. You drive that thing like a Tartar. One day they'll have to scrape you off the fence."

But he said that just to keep talking, he seemed to be thinking about something else. I was curious what he was up to. He was nervously hunching his shoulders and craning his neck, as if his collar was too tight or the barber had dropped some hair down his neck. His whole body was twitching, and at times his face too. We looked around the yard, it looked like an earthquake had hit it. They must have left in an awful hurry, that was obvious. Everywhere you looked there were pieces of furniture, crates, old newspapers, sawdust. They seemed to have used whatever they could lay their hands on for packing, even straw. Slivers of glass from broken windows lay on the pavement. A shiny piano was standing under the window of the whitewashed main house, under the inscription ARTHUR SINGER. The piano still had ropes attached underneath, which were evidently used to lower it from the balcony. One leg was broken off.

"Look, they left the piano!" I shouted.

Vitlich wasn't paying attention, he had moved down to the house. He seemed to be shielding something from me with his body.

I rushed up, and peered around him. I saw Selma. She was stretched out on the pavement near the cart.

"Selma!" I cried. "Selma!"

I ran up to her, she didn't move, she seemed to be fast asleep. But she wasn't. On the back of her neck, between her shoulder blades, there was a bullet hole. The hairs around the wound were covered with dried blood. Red smudges on the pavement showed where she had dragged herself from.

"They got her out of the window," said Vitlich, sniffing slightly more heavily and longer than usual. Only now did he stop to pause a moment. "The bastard. He could have let the dog go. I don't know why he had to shoot her, the jackass. Did you see anybody on the road? No procession on their way yet?"

"No," I said. I didn't quite know what he was talking about, his words went right by me. Selma was beautiful, even in death, she had the noblest head and ears of all the dogs I knew. I sat on my haunches by her, I stroked her body, it still seemed soft and warm. She didn't make me queasy. I spoke softly to her.

"You see anybody come through the alley by the chapel?" asked Vitlich.

I didn't understand. "Who do you think might come here? Who are you expecting?"

"Nobody," he said. "Let's find a shovel and bury her. We'll give her a proper funeral. Don't you want to take her collar? That's a fine collar she's got around her neck!"

Selma had a beautiful leather collar in her thick fur, it was probably quite expensive. I knew she'd have no more use for it, but I wouldn't have taken it from her for anything in the world.

"No."

"You're right. Let her take it along to put on a great show. Let's see if there is a shovel around, and get it over with."

I straightened up and followed Vitlich across the yard to the shiny white section of the building, the fancy living quarters. He pushed the door open with his shoulder and went in. I followed behind his huge body. My head was still full of thoughts about Selma, but the inside of the house fascinated me. I never saw anything like it—a hall like that, everything covered with polished wood, the walls, the floor, even the ceiling. I had no idea that somebody could even invent such things.

"Where are we going to bury Selma? Where is a good place for a grave?"

"In the garden," he said. "In the back, by the white wall. The sun shines there all day long. That would be a place I'd choose for my own grave."

Once in a while Vitlich had ideas that would make a pumpkin laugh, but I was not in a laughing mood. I was uncomfortable walking on the shiny floor, where I could see my reflection. I looked shrunk and twisted, my head sat right on top of my knees. One whole wall was filled with Singer's collection of canes. Vitlich never even noticed those sticks. He looked at some papers. On the opposite wall hung a framed photograph. A field tractor, with an eight-bladed plow attached by a steel cable. In the foreground stood Singer. He gazed at the camera, his mustaches turned up.

"Singer had lots of money?" I asked Vitlich. "Millions?"

"You don't know what money means, a lot of money or a little money. You can bet he didn't go around begging, anyway."

I turned a switch, and twenty branches lit up on the metal chandelier. Cyril was climbing upstairs, but he stopped halfway and turned around.

"Do they know in the village that the Germans have flown the coop? Didn't your dad send you here to sniff around a bit?"

"Why . . . ?" I stammered. His questions were beginning to get on my nerves, because I had no idea what he was talking about. "I was with the gang, down at the church . . . What would he send me here for?"

Vitlich often put things in a funny way—it was an answer and it wasn't an answer, it all depended how you took it.

On the second floor I turned another switch. But I was still thinking about what he had said. A light went on under the aquarium, built into the wall. Colored fishes scurried by, some didn't look like fishes at all. I turned to Vitlich. He was pulling some junk out of a box, he was looking for something. When he saw me gawking at him, he put on a mask which he picked up from the floor. The house was full of them, it seemed that rich people liked masked balls. But suddenly he stopped making faces.

44

"You hear something?" His eyes darted around the room. "Somebody banging on the gate?"

"No. Those are the big guns you are hearing." I repeated what I had heard the gang saying.

"Cyril, did you see the planes?" I asked Vitlich.

"No," he said. "Where?"

Once again, he started poking around in the papers.

"Up in the sky," I said. I leaned out the window. You could see both Messerschmitts. "They're still up there."

But Vitlich had already moved into the next room. A writing desk was standing in one corner, small bottles filled with samples of grain were all around. It looked like the office of an agricultural co-op. A map all marked up by numbers and colored lines hung on the wall. It was called a cadastral map. The racks were piled with rows and rows of fat account books. He kneeled and pored over the letters thrown out of the drawers and littering the floor.

"You looking for anything special?"

"No," he said. "I just want to see what I can see here."

"Why?"

"It interests me."

He got up, opened the door for me leading into the next room. That was Singer's bathroom. But what a bathroom! It was full of chrome and shone like heaven. I could see my reflection in all the tiled walls. Cyril Vitlich pointed to the scale, with its built-in measuring rod.

"You want to measure yourself?" he asked. He must have spent a lot of time in this house to know his way around so well. He dropped the shiny metal plate on top of my head. Bemused, he looked at the numbers, but he didn't say anything. He made some kind of noise, you could take it for a laugh. I frowned.

"You've got to eat lentils. You'll grow like a beanstalk. Don't worry! I know what I'm talking about. You're just on the edge. Once your glands start pumping, you'll catch up in a gallop. Anyway, it seems to me you're a bit taller than last time." He wasn't laughing, he said it like he really meant it, to make me feel better. I knew he was only trying to keep me from getting mad.

"Makes no difference," I said—the biggest lie of my life. "I don't give a hoot one way or another."

The bathroom was full of vials and phials, a whole drugstore in itself. I stuck my finger into a little jar, it smelled like something I had never smelled before.

I wiped my finger on my pants, and turned to follow Vitlich. But before I left the bathroom, I stopped before the toilet. I couldn't resist the luxury of pissing into that gorgeous porcelain bowl.

When I went back into the room with all the papers and drawers, Vitlich was again hunting around feverishly, looking unusually preoccupied.

"You looking for money, Cyril?"

Startled, he turned around. Then he laughed, blinking at me good-naturedly.

"Right," he said. "I could use it. Singer's millions!" But he'd stopped looking. He was tearing up a letter.

"Would you buy yourself horses and fields?"

"A steamship," he answered. "I'd sail away to Africa. Would you come with me, you dog's ear?"

I kept silent. His mind wasn't on the small talk, I could see that.

"Come on," he said. "Let's find a shovel. We'll bury the mutt." He made a face in the mirror. I laughed. That was the old Cyril. Nobody could make faces like him.

When we got to the yard he stopped to take off the rubber wheels from Singer's four beautiful wagons. Singer had the most modern wagons of all the farmers, but they were too big and heavy to take along to Bavaria.

"Why are you doing that, Cyril?"

"I'm playing a game," he said. "What else?" He wrinkled his nose, blinked, smacked his lips.

"You're not playing. You are doing something for real."

"Did I ever lie to you, Olda?" He was trying to look as benign as God in Heaven.

"Always," I said. "Every time."

His face changed, but his hands kept working.

"Someday you'll grow into an intelligent fellow, Olda," he said, quite seriously. Sometimes he looked at me as if he was seeing me for the first time in his life, and at those times I never knew how to react.

"You won't be a nobody, believe me, Olda. Now come here. Slide the jack under here!"

The jack weighed a ton, but I tried to handle it like it was all child's play.

"Not too heavy for you?"

"No."

"Just a bit further," he was watching my hands, "by a whisker."

I did as he asked.

"The main thing is to get the hell out of this damn village as soon as you can. If you hang around till you're twenty, you'll rot here forever. Like your old man. Like your grandpa. That was Ondrej. You don't remember him, do you?"

"No."

"It's just as well."

He said it in a way that surprised me. I think my mouth must have dropped a little. The rubber wheel barely missed my knee. I stood in the yard like a dummy.

"Cyril, you knew my grandfather?" I guess my voice trembled, as if I had suddenly penetrated to the heart of a mystery.

"Of course I knew him," he said. "You know what they called him? Satchel. He carried a satchel on his back, summer, winter, the year round. And the loot he brought home! He picked up every apple lying on the ground. If by any chance he didn't see any on the ground, he shook the tree. Your grandpa sure knew how to get along, nothing got by him. And at sixty he could still catch a rabbit on the dead run."

An old, yellowed photograph of Grandpa came to my mind. He was wearing the uniform of an Austrian dragoon, he had impressive mustaches and the eager eyes of a man expecting a great deal from life. Nobody in our family had such a big and firm chin, a chin that showed a determination to make those bright expectations come true. He looked beautiful to me. He certainly looked brave, far braver than my father. It was the only photograph of Grandfather that we possessed. It was over his grave, inside a small iron cross. We always visited the cemetery on All Souls' Day. The autumn trees were already black and transparent, leaves fluttered over the paths, and the three of us would stand at the grave: Dad, Mother, and I. A single, thin candle burned there. It was the thinnest of all the candles that were sold. Father used to say that Grandpa himself would wish to avoid all unnecessary luxury. It burns up, he'd say, and it vanishes in the air, whether it's thin or thick. The main thing was that we were thinking of him. Father traced a cross in the soil over the grave, and then he crossed his forehead, belly, and both shoulders. Mother did the same. He nudged me and I crossed myself, too. I tried to think about Grandpa, but nothing especially dignified ever occurred to me at the graveside.

"Let him be an example to you," said Father, pointing at the photo. "He was always a hard worker and an honest man, to the day he died. People like to remember him." After a while,

Dad bent down, blew out the thin candle, pulled it out of the damp soil and stuck it in his pocket. "We'll bring it again next time," he said. Which meant next year. "Somebody might steal it if we left it here." I half expected some kind of evil miracle, like a rock suddenly flying out of Grandpa's grave or Grandpa's hand clutching my father's leg. But Father was already walking away with my mother, and I tagged slowly behind. They were discussing something or other, I waited till they were out of earshot and then I disappeared among the clusters of people at the cemetery. I wandered among the graves. One had an expensive marble gravestone, and was piled with candles and flowers. It read: JOSEF AND ALOIS KUDERA. Whoever had the biggest house had the biggest gravestone, too. I looked around, everybody was busily praying, I bent over as if to tie a shoelace and pulled a fat candle out of the ground. Josef and Alois had so many of them that I was sure they wouldn't object. I brought it to my mustached grandfather, whom I had never known. I always preferred those relatives who were far away or dead or kept aloof from us. I don't know why, I have often wondered about it.

"He was a tightwad," said Vitlich. "Nobody was such a tightwad as your grandpa. He'd rather fill his pants than fertilize somebody else's field."

Cyril had already taken the wheels off all four wagons. He continued to be very nervous, he was talking with half his tongue, just to keep the conversation going and to keep me from bothering him.

"I could tell you stories about your grandpa from now till morning," he said.

"He wasn't stingy," I protested. Cyril made me mad. I frowned at him, I almost shouted. "It isn't true what you said."

He looked at me carefully, for a moment I felt his concentrated stare. He blinked, sniffed, his whole face seemed to be made up of nothing but nose.

"Maybe you're right," he said. "Maybe I got him mixed up with somebody else. It's possible." He didn't stop looking at me.

"How old are you?" he asked.

"Twelve." I was still mad.

"Could be," he said. "My memory is getting bad."

Vitlich wiped his broad palms on his trousers.

"It seems to me that your grandfather was a bit of a spendthrift. He gave away everything. Come to think of it, they didn't call him Satchel but Empty Pocket."

He blew air out of his nose with vehemence, as if these words had caused some kind of intolerable pressure inside his head.

"You keep changing your story!" I raged. I knew how to rage from my earliest days, especially when something touched me deeply. I found an old bag and I covered up the dead dog. I didn't want to see its open eyes. I knew that Vitlich was watching me. But he quickly moved his head, and looked up at the sky, at the two planes.

"The Germans are watching the bridge," he said, "to keep the Russians from blowing it up."

He turned to me again, shook his finger at the huge electric motor strapped to a wooden platform. "Don't you want some little thing to take home to your father? A motor, or maybe a thresher. Is there anything here you can use?"

"It's not really yours to give, is it Cyril?"

He blinked. "I don't think you'll take after your grandpa. Not after your pa, neither."

"I wouldn't mind the fishes," I said. I pointed back toward the house. "I'd like to have the aquarium."

"What?"

"Fishes," I repeated. "In the glass box."

His eyes floated to the top of his forehead.

"Aquarium? What in God's name for? Your old man'd throw the fishes to the pigs, and use the jar for putting up pickles. I think you're going to take after your mother. She's from Hrdlorezy, isn't she?"

He pissed me off again. "No. My mom is from Bosonohy."

"Oh, yeah, that's right. I always get those two places mixed up." Now he tried to see if he could lift the motor off the platform. It didn't budge.

"We'll never move this thing, not till we're blue in the face." He was obviously disappointed. I couldn't understand why. He examined the windings on the coil, first blowing the dust off so as to see better.

"Your ma will float straight into heaven. Little folks like her don't have to go through purgatory. They've been through it right here on earth."

"My mom isn't little!" I blew the dust off the motor, right into Cyril's face. He could see darn well I did it on purpose. For safety's sake I stepped back. He wiped his eyes.

"You don't know anything about my mom, Cyril!" I shouted. "You don't know anything! Not about Dad, and not Grandpa neither!"

"No," he said. Now he was really angry. "I fell off a tree. Now beat it! Go home! What the hell are you waiting for!"

"You said we'd bury the dog. That's what I am waiting for." I knew that with his bum leg he couldn't catch me, not even if he tried. I have always been pretty smart about certain things.

"I think that first I'll bury my boot." He spat. Maybe the dust got in his mouth, too. "I'll bury my boot right in your behind."

51

"You'd have to catch me first. You'll never catch me on one leg!"

I made a face at him. I was laughing at him. He just stood there and looked at me.

"Beat it. Or you'll be bawling a second time."

Just to make sure, I retreated a few more steps. Come to think of it now—I must have been quite a brat.

"When did I ever bawl? When did you ever see me bawling, Cyril?" I provoked him.

"You were sniveling over that mutt."

"That's a lie."

"Sure, sure."

He lifted a monkey wrench, I thought he was about to throw it at me, and I jumped to one side. But he was only putting the wrench in his pocket.

"It might get lost if we left it here," he said. "I can sell it for good money."

It seemed to sound perfectly logical to him. The tone of his voice was normal again, as if nothing had happened. He knew how to let certain things pass magnanimously. One side of his face was twitching as if he wanted to say something. But just at that moment we both heard voices coming from behind the gate. And the clanging of horses' hooves. "Come on!" whispered Vitlich. He broke into a trot, awkwardly dragging his leg toward the storehouse.

Naturally, I wasn't far behind.

"Hurry, stupid," Vitlich panted. I ignored the insult on account of the extraordinary circumstances. We slid inside the shed, he pulled the door shut and latched the heavy wrought-iron bolt. He heaved a sigh of relief, hissing like a collapsing bellows.

"I was beginning to think they wouldn't show up anymore. I

52

was beginning to wonder if they changed their character," he said. "Yeah, that'll be the day when they change their stripes, those hyenas." I had no idea who he was talking about. Cyril was painfully pulling himself up the wooden stairs, up to the tiny barred window that looked out on the main driveway leading to the closed gate. He peered out carefully, making sure that his face couldn't be seen from outside. I stood up on tiptoe. But even that way, I couldn't see a thing. I noticed a sturdy bucket used for measuring wheat and I climbed up on it. At once I saw four farmers, Kudera, Chumsky, Rez, and Vyska. Honored citizens of our village, good catholics, property owners, free and clear of public or private debt. Now they were standing in front of the farm gates, and I had no idea why. Strangely enough, they had brought their horses along. Kudera was holding the reins, while the three others were trying to open the heavy gate. The horses were carrying full harness. The farmers were continually looking around as if they were still waiting for someone. But maybe they were just scared by the sounds of shooting from the front, which were becoming ever louder.

Kudera was angry. "Damn it, who bolted the gate? Who the hell was here?"

"You sure that Singer left for good?"

"I've got eyes, haven't I," said Kudera angrily. The planes buzzing overhead made him nervous, and he was constantly looking up at the sky. And the deserted fields all around looked ominous. Maybe he thought somebody was hiding behind the stacks. He was scared.

"Who in hell would close the gates from the inside?" wondered Vyska. "If they had left, they wouldn't have bolted the gate."

None of the farmers resembled the conventional image of national heroes.

"We shouldn't stay here too long," said Rez.

Vitlich, crouching by the window, whispered, "You see them . . . ?"

"Yes."

"Remember them. Take a good look and remember them." He spat.

"Why did they come, Cyril?" I asked in a low voice. I had no idea what they were looking for. Cyril knew from the tone of my voice that I was really puzzled. He turned around and scrutinized me quizzically.

"You'll have a pretty hard life—until you smarten up, that is."

Cyril's way of talking in eternal riddles really got my goat. He talked to me like I was just starting kindergarten. I stopped asking him questions, I wouldn't give him the satisfaction. I never begged anybody for anything. I tried to figure the mystery out for myself. Once more I pulled myself up to the window. To see the farmers as clearly as possible.

I had seen the four of them many times riding along in the ceremonial garb of the Rural Guard. They looked like Count Lichtenstein's grooms. The Rural Guard wore broad hats, green jackets, and riding breeches. They practiced riding in the courtyard of the Quality Distillery, Inc. I remember one hot summer day, the white sun was beating down on the dusty yard. They had set up some wicker fences and horizontal bars behind a stack of potatoes, and they were trying to get their horses to jump over the barriers. Kudera sat bolt upright on his nag in the middle of the circle, barking orders like Napoleon Bonaparte. Chumsky, Rez, Vyska were his underlings. Kudera was the type used to giving orders to other people from his very childhood. His shouts reverberated from the distillery walls. That day I was lying on my stomach behind a shrub, and I saw my father arriving through the iron gate to take part in the Rural Guard exercise. He was riding our mare. His legs barely circled Julie's broad back; he sat as if mounted on a huge keg of beer. Like the other farmers, Dad, too, was attired in that ridiculous outfit. The cement sidewalk was hot enough to bake pancakes on. He was drenched with sweat, choking in the tight collar. His hat was too small for him and was constantly on the point of falling off. The farmers saw him and burst out laughing. They reined in their horses, stood in their stirrups and pointed at Dad, again and again giving vent to waves of guffawing. I couldn't quite understand why. Kudera, of course, cackled the loudest. He made out like his belly was aching, he'd point at Dad and then clutch his stomach. Finally he let his body hang limp pretending he was falling off his horse in a faint. To this day I see this degrading scene in all its clarity. I see my father's sweaty face trying to smile at them. When they laughed he laughed, too, even though he knew that he was laughing at himself.

"Oldrich," they shouted, "that nag is dragging its ass!"

This insult to Julie made me angry.

"Why didn't you saddle a cow?" yelled Chumsky. "A cow or a pig?"

"She'll be all right," pleaded Dad. "She's a smart horse, she'll manage."

I stared at Dad with contempt, contempt for lowering himself. I condemned him for his weakness, as never before or since. In his place I would have simply turned around and ridden off.

"It's the only horse I've got," he begged. He was suing for the peasants' favor, he wanted to belong, to be one of them. "Maybe she'll manage . . ." he repeated, wiping his brow and nose with the back of his hand. "Where do you want me to stand, Kudera?"

"First go over to my place," Kudera said graciously. He had laughed enough. "Saddle my Brownie. Go to the barn and throw a saddle on Brownie. Take this nag home . . ." It was a gesture.

55

"Thank you, Gustaf," Father said humbly. In his place I would have never thanked that jerk. "I'll give your horse a good rubdown afterwards," I heard Father promise. He turned our mare as if she was a locomotive. Again, they laughed at Julie.

I pulled out my slingshot. From the day I was born I carried one tucked away in my shirt. And to be ready for all occasions I always carried at least two chunks of metal in my pocket. I let go at Kudera's horse and hid in the thick shrubbery. She threw her rear in the air, she practically did a headstand, Kudera flew into a pile of dirt, there was a loud thud, the beribboned hat rolled on the ground all the way to the brick loading ramp.

Now as I watched the four jackasses climbing the manor gate, I tried to imagine them in their Rural Guard outfit. Vyska and Rez clasped hands, so as to give Chumsky's two-ton backside a boost to the top of the gate. Kudera stood up on the back of his horse and peered over the gate into the deserted yard.

In the end, Chumsky managed to climb the gate after all, and jumped into the yard. Chumsky considered himself an athlete, he landed with his arms stretched out and his knees bent, as if he was performing gymnastics at an Eagle gathering.

I could just imagine him in a pair of tights, his hairy chest nearly bursting out of his gym shirt, muscles working along his massive thighs. I did gymnastics, too, I had always belonged to the Eagles, like every youngster in Moravia: my shorts reached down to my knees, I had a rough linen shirt and an idiotic saucepan hat on my head. The sacristan was our leader, but he was too lenient and couldn't maintain discipline. We kicked and slapped each other, and he pummeled us. The gymnastic drill took place behind the storehouse of the AGRICULTURAL CO-OPERATIVE, with new threshers made by the JEZEK MACHINE WORKS parked on the side.

"Anybody that gets out of line will get a good one," threat-

*ened the sacristan. He never said, "whack," or "boot," he al-
ways said, "a good one." He warned us in a low voice, so as not
to be overheard by the reverend standing on the platform, who
believed in education through kindness. Mom was at the
exercises, too, her dress was too big but she was still the
prettiest of all the women there. Once in a while we looked
at each other and smiled. Dad wore his black Sunday suit, which
made him look severe and menacing. About a hundred people
were watching altogether. The lowing of cows drifted over
from butcher Zita's pen. "One, two, three," prompted the
sacristan. Our part of the program began. We marched toward
the reviewing stand, all wrong from the very first step, the
whole thing out of control. We did it on purpose; the sabotage
was all organized by Jozka, Kudera, and Puma, with help from
Rez, Vyska, and Chumsky. I kicked Chumsky from behind,
pretending it was an accident. I performed with great concen-
tration, as if the future of humanity, fatherland, and agriculture
depended upon precise and correct lifting and dropping of arms,
squatting, kneeling, and rhythmic hopping.*

Chumsky, Sr., was hollering to all corners of the yard: "Any-
body here?" Quickly he opened the gate to let in his comrades,
Kudera, Rez, and Vyska. So he wouldn't be alone. Chumsky,
Sr., is the same kind of hero as his son.

"Hey! Anybody here?" he yelled in the kind of quavering
voice people use when they are alone in the woods.

"Stop hollering," said Kudera. "Cut it out!"

Vitlich and I were craning our necks, our legs buried in grain
up to our knees, we were dying to know what the peasants
would do next.

For the moment they were just standing there, looking around,
the empty yard seemed to discourage them. They left the horses
outside behind the gate. I felt the same anger at them as I did at

their dumb offspring, they were just as conceited and coarse. Some human qualities seemed to slide from one generation to the next. Their children's children will resemble their fathers' fathers, with slight variations, they too will transmit the firm conviction that the whole village belongs to them and that they can do with it as they please.

Kudera suddenly ran over to the wagons from which we had removed the wheels. He shouted angrily: "Where the hell are the wheels, Goddamn it!" He looked up as if wheels could fly through the air. . . . The four of them made a beautiful sight, peering around suspiciously as if the farm was haunted.

"Somebody was here," said Chumsky.

"Or still is," piped up Rez.

"Is anybody here?" Vyska asked softly.

I looked at Vitlich, I was beginning to see the light.

"Cyril," I said to him. "You knew they were going to come for the wagons?"

"I dreamed about it last night," lied Vitlich. I don't think he'll ever stop taking me for a moron.

"I'd like to know what son-of-a-bitch has sniffed this thing out," we heard Kudera ranting. He approached the electric motor.

"Just as I thought," whispered Vitlich, as if talking to himself.

We were watching the farmers. "He's as smart as a bishop," said Vitlich. "Kudera can tell what's valuable and what isn't."

Chumsky pulled a cart out of the shed, an ordinary small cart with iron-rimmed wheels. He noticed Kudera's interest in the motor, and drew near. "So you have found a motor for yourself, Gustaf," he said. "But it's too weak," Kudera answered without embarrassment. "Help me load it." Kudera completely ignored Chumsky's interest. He believed that the world was created mainly for the well-being of the Kudera family. Kudera's three companions looked at one another. Chumsky hopelessly shifted from one foot to the other, with a pitiable expression; he looked like a weeping dog, trying to save what he could.

"I pulled this cart out myself," he said quickly. "It's the only one here. I can sure use it."

"I could use a motor myself," Vyska said to Kudera. "I don't have one."

"I took it and now it's mine," said Kudera; he was in no mood for discussion.

"We'll help you load it and then we can all share it," suggested Rez. "Don't think you can swipe anything you like and hog it for yourself!"

"What possessed me to take you along!" mumbled Kudera. "Why didn't I keep my trap shut!"

But in the end he agreed that they would all share the motor. Not with much enthusiasm, that was obvious. They carried the motor off to the wagon. Each one was holding a corner of the wooden platform. They huffed and puffed, the motor must have weighed a ton or two.

That's how the four of them always carried the purple canopy over our priest on Corpus Christi day. Over the monstrance. They had a broad, violet-white ribbon over their shoulders, like a sash. A shiny sword hung at their side, the tip of the scabbard jingling against the ground. Bells rang out, maidens scattered flowers and green leaves, young birch branches were everywhere. The altar was always in front of Kudera's house, and every year we humbly knelt there.

I now found it hard to square their piety with the greedy speed with which they were carrying off the motor. It all seemed incredible, unreal, as if they were lugging their loot still dressed in their processional garb and walking to the rhythm of church music. I never cared much for any of them, but I didn't think they were thieves—not until that April day. They were all so rich that I did not believe they could be tempted by petty larceny.

"They came . . . they want to . . . they're here to cart those things away?" I asked Vitlich. He looked at me and shook his head.

"No," he said. "They didn't come to steal, they just want to de-Germanize the property. It may seem like the same thing, but sometimes it's a matter of patriotic duty. These people have been looking forward to this moment all through the war, Olda . . . But you're too young to understand. You'll understand by the time your beard starts growing."

I let the insult pass, I just ignored it with dignity. I had to know more about this business.

"But they have their own wagons, Cyril. Don't they?" Vitlich raised his eyebrows, sniffed. Once more, he made me feel like an idiot.

"If stealing was only done by people who needed things badly, you could count all the thieves in the world on the fingers of one hand."

They were now hurriedly trying to pull a huge thresher out of the shed, panting, stretching their tendons to the breaking point. Unity had been restored, they were working as a team, each one straining against a different wheel.

Vitlich and I kept on watching until they had loaded everything they thought they could use and carted their creaking, overloaded wagons out of the yard.

It was only toward evening that Vitlich finally got down to burying the dog. As we shoveled the last clods of earth the sky was dark purple. The rumbling of the guns had become continuous, it sounded like an approaching summer thunderstorm. A rocket floated up somewhere beyond the road, burst into colored sparks which died over the roofs of the manor.

"The priest said that the front will pass right by us, without even stopping," I piped up, just to say something.

"The priest doesn't know a pig from a wheelbarrow," answered Vitlich heretically.

He tapped down the soil with the back of the shovel, leaned forward heavily. "You can tell him at confession. Tell him I said so. You go to confession?"

"Yes."

"Are you a server?"

"He didn't take me."

"You can be proud of that. He only takes real idiots."

He finished the job, awkwardly stamping his bad leg.

"I'll see if I can round up a puppy for you. You won't believe all the tricks I'll teach him. To fetch, to walk on two legs, all kinds of tricks."

Somehow he always sensed my weak moments, when I was on the verge of tears.

"Stop thinking about Selma. Get that mutt out of your head. She wasn't anything special anyway. Just four legs, ears, and a tail."

"She had . . . a pedigree," I defended Selma's memory.

"So? That's nothing. There are millions of dogs with pedigrees."

He put his hand on my shoulder.

"You're not going to bawl over one measly mutt, are you?" I quickly dropped my head so that he couldn't see my eyes. I bent down for a clod of soil. The cigarette case fell out of my shirt. I tried to pick it up, but it was too close to Vitlich and he reached for it first. Naturally, once he had it in his hands he opened it. There was still enough light for him to distinguish the picture of the nude woman inside. I am sure that at that moment all the red blood cells I owned were gathered in my face. He looked at me quizzically; I wasn't sure what he was up to, and for safety's sake took a couple of steps backward. Cyril Vitlich looked at me for a long, long time. He swallowed, rubbed his bulby nose and finally asked, "Is this somebody from your family?"

I shook my head to signify "no."

"That's what I thought," said Vitlich. "I know all your aunts, and this certainly doesn't look like any of them."

He closed the case and handed it back to me—calmly and normally, as if he found nothing extraordinary in my owning such an object. I stuck the silver case back in my shirt.

"I found it. . . . It was lying in the road," I stuttered. Vitlich's lenience really knocked me for a loop. I reached into my pocket, pulled out a handful of cigarettes and offered them to him. This proved too much even for him, his eyes practically fell out of his head.

"You . . . you smoke?" he wheezed.

"Sometimes." It was a moment of triumph. "Only now and then."

He took the cigarettes, examined one of them carefully to learn the make.

"Memphis," he sighed. He lit one, ceremoniously blew out the smoke. His eyes were still hanging on my face.

"If your dad finds this stuff on you," he said slowly and gravely, "he'll knock your block off, Olda!" He blew some more smoke. "If I was your dad, I'd do the same."

That evening, after returning home, a familiar, often-repeated scene took place. I was hidden in the dark, squeezing myself against the wall and watching our door. Mother came out to the threshold, a milky yellow rectangle of light behind her. She peered into the dark.

"Olda!" She sensed that I was there. "Olda!"

I stayed quiet. I loved to watch my mother. She was barefoot, the pins already out of her hair and her beautiful long waves reaching her shoulders. To this day I can see before me the stream of my mother's hair.

"Olda, come home. Time to go to sleep."

I was as quiet as a mouse. I'd stopped breathing. I wanted her to speak some more. I knew exactly what was coming next, I knew our little game, our dialogue, by heart, but I wanted her to pronounce my name just one more time.

"Olda," she said. "Come, it's late!" Her voice was trembling. She was afraid for me. She had to betray me now, but she loved me.

"You hear me?"

"Is Dad home?"

"He's asleep."

"No, he isn't."

"I'm telling you he's asleep."

"You always say that."

"He went to bed early. Hush, now. Come."

"Will I get a whipping?"

"No."

"You always say that."

"Tonight you're safe."

I wanted to prolong this interlude, to postpone what was coming next as long as possible.

"You've only got your shirt on, come on, you'll catch cold!"

I knew I'd get a hiding, I always did, I was never disappointed. I would stand by the door in the snow, without an overcoat, and Mom would call me, her hair already unfastened: "You haven't got your coat, Olda, you'll catch your death of pneumonia." How often have I stood in the pouring rain, water flowing down my face, soaked to the bone. "For God's sake, go inside," she would plead.

"Mom," I'd speak out of the darkness, without really knowing what I wanted to say.

"Now that's enough, Olda," she said. "Come in and stop this nonsense."

I unglued myself from the wall, slowly entered a lighter patch, now she could see me from the door. I heard her sigh. For me? For whom?

"Mom," I said. I was close, on the threshold. "Mom!"

I grasped her hands, touched her hair. She was as tall as I was, maybe just a little bit taller. When I looked at her from up close I could see that her lips were trembling, she had a tiny face, big eyes, hardly any shoulders at all. I was not surprised to find Father hiding behind the door. I was not surprised to feel his viselike grip on my arms. I was expecting it.

"Where were you again? You no-good lout!"

I was no longer aware of where the blows were falling. I tried to think of something else. But Mom did something unexpected. All of a sudden she stepped in, shielding me with her body. "Leave him alone," she said. "I will settle with him myself."

He looked at Mom, then at me. "You'll kill him someday if you keep that up," she said. Dad always had a difficult time stopping, once he got going.

"Get him out of my sight or I'll kill him for sure." He was having trouble getting the words out, as if he was choking on his own breath. Maybe he had wanted to send me for lime or something else, maybe he had been looking all over the house for me and couldn't find me. Mother pulled me into the kitchen; Dad stayed in the living room. I knew that he was sitting on the floor, smoking a cigarette and gazing through the half-open door into the deserted street. But mainly he was listening to find out if Mom was really about to thrash me.

She was standing in the kitchen, shaking, having a hard time to keep from crying. I saw how thin she was, white as chalk and very beautiful.

"Give me a whack, Mom, please, he's listening out there!" I stuck my face out for her to slap. She didn't move, she was trembling.

"Please, Mom, don't be scared! Don't worry, it won't hurt!"

I practically begged her. She slapped me. Her hand never caused any pain to my face, even when she hit hard.

"You going to do it, or do I have to take care of him myself?" I heard father's impatient call from the hall. He suspected that Mom wasn't taking the punishment seriously enough. Mother could never resist the command of his voice. She was slapping me.

I smiled at her to show that I didn't mind. The sound of the slaps calmed Father down, he fell silent.

"Mom, Mommie!"

She beat me, tears running down her face. And then she came to my bed, after the house had fallen dark and silent, I sensed her figure bending over me, her hair falling on my quilt. I lifted my hands, touched her face.

She whispered, so that only I could hear: "Why don't you do as your father says?" But I wasn't listening to her words, I hugged her tightly and gave her a sudden kiss; she straightened up quickly.

"Now go to sleep. And wake up better behaved."

"Yes, Mom," I whispered. And her face was before me until I fell asleep, and then I dreamed of a green field where a white doe was standing sadly, one leg caught in a steel trap. She couldn't move, there was nobody to help her, the air was filled with coarse, loud laughter, as if a thousand people were guffawing. Sometimes I had such terrible dreams!

CHAPTER FOUR

It was bright morning. Flies buzzed and circled as usual in our kitchen, they came from the yard, out of the barn. When I woke up I had to chase them from my face. I watched them give a wide berth to the dried up flypaper.

The rumbling from the front had become stronger than ever, it seemed to come from right behind the windows. I remember that morning quite clearly. The kitchen door was ajar, I turned my head when I heard voices coming from the hall. Dad's and somebody else's. I recognized that it was Vyska's voice. Mr. Vyska always looked a little disheveled, but now he looked doubly flustered, his mouth was trembling, half-formed words sputtered out, he acted as if a bunch of orangutans had invaded our beloved village.

"The Russians will requisition horses," he was anxiously telling my father. "They'll take all our horses for the army."

Father said that it was a mess. He didn't wring his hands, but he looked shaken. It seemed that we, too, had a few hairy orangutans in our yard. Dad shifted from one foot to another, blinked, his big hands hanging lifelessly by his sides.

"That's all we needed," he gasped. "That's the last bloody straw."

"Your Julie isn't safe, that's for sure. They're sure to grab an elephant like her," declared Vyska.

"Who said the Russians will requisition horses, anyway?" asked Dad. "You sure this isn't only some kind of panicky rumor?"

"Everybody is saying it. The priest found out from the Germans. The Russians are moving on horseback. Nothing but horses! All Moravia has been taken over by the Cossacks." Vyska's information sounded plausible.

"What are the others doing? Kudera, Rez . . . ?" asked father.

"They are sending their horses into the woods. All the way back to the rocks, to the game warden's lodge."

"This is all we needed. Just what we needed," repeated Dad.

"We are sending the boys with the horses. They'll all go together, so that they won't be scared."

"Boys . . . ?" said Dad, surprised. "Boys with horses?"

"Who else? We've got to stay home. Suppose there was a fire?"

"But suppose they pull some silly stunt with the horses?"

"What kind of stunt?" answered Vyska. "What can they do?"

"They could get into trouble," Father said, wavering.

"Nobody would hurt the boys. Not one side, and not the other."

"Maybe," said Father. "Maybe you're right."

Then they both went into the yard. I heard their voices, but couldn't distinguish the words. Wagons were rattling outside. I lifted myself up in my bed, but I couldn't see over the tops of the geraniums which Mom always had in the windows. Footsteps again sounded in the hall. At once I pretended to be asleep. Mother opened the door, and I knew she was looking at my bed.

"Olda," she whispered.

I was great at feigning sleep. I could have passed for a corpse.

"Olda," she sat down on the mattress. She leaned over me, and I watched her through the tiniest of slits. To this day, I am not sure whether she knew I was faking or not. She probably did, her breath and voice were so close to me.

"Wake up," she said. "Get up. You are going somewhere . . ."

And then still more quietly, like a conspirator: "He's waiting for you. . . ."

Sometimes she referred to Father only as "he" when she was talking to me. She shook me gently. "Do you hear me?"

I heard Father coming through the hall. "Shall I come to wake up milord?" He had just said good-by to Vyska. Now he seemed to be fixing the harness, I heard the sound of the awl as it went through the leather. Dad seldom needed an artisan's help, he repaired everything himself.

"No," Mother said. "I woke him already. He is up." She must have known that I wasn't sleeping.

And once again I pulled my trick: I suddenly opened my eyes wide, caught a strand of Mother's hair in my mouth, and at the same time I put my arms around her and locked my fingers behind her bowed neck.

She straightened up quickly, so quickly that she pulled me out of my quilt. I had to let go. "What are you doing?" she said, startled. Suddenly she was as distant as a tiny white star.

"Did you cough during the night?" she asked. She would examine me carefully every morning. Her anxiety used to get on my nerves.

"I am not going anywhere with a bunch of kids," I said. That was my main concern at the moment. "I am not going anywhere with those jerks!"

"What happened between you and the boys?" Mother seemed clairvoyant. "What did they do to you?"

"Nothing."

"You're schoolmates. Why do you fight all the time?"

"Nuts."

"Did you sweat during the night?"

"I didn't cough. I didn't sweat. I don't cough anymore, I told you that. I sweat only when I sleep in my nightshirt."

"You know where he wants to send you?" she asked. She was looking at me.

"Yeah. I know. I know where."

"Won't you be scared?" She was looking at me as if she was seeing me for the first time in her life, as if I was a little baby.

"Scared of what, for God's sake? But I am not going with those jerks, I am telling you right now."

"You'd be scared, all alone in the woods."

"I am not scared. Not in the woods, or anywhere else."

I wanted to put on my sandals, she picked them up and examined them. Naturally, she saw the broken strap, I knew what she was thinking, but I kept quiet. She handed me my boots.

"Put on your boots. The woods will be soaking wet."

"I don't want these horseshoes," I protested. There were few things in this world I hated as much as the massive clodhoppers sewn together by a country cobbler. They were made of iron, for three generations of peasants.

"Put them on," she said.

I banged them against the floor, pretended I couldn't get my feet in, arched my insteps, tensed my hands, made faces, until she left the stove and came to help me. But this was an even greater indignity, so in the end I put the boots on myself. I was furious; at that tender age, when I hated anything I did so with all my soul.

"Mom, tell him that I am going by myself!"

"You have to obey him. You have to listen to what he says. You know him!"

"I won't tell that to him, but I'll get away from those jerks! When I feel like it, I'll just take off on my own!" This thought calmed me down. Then Mother and I had breakfast. Father ate early in the morning, he was the first one up, and fed the cattle. He never slept more than five hours, winter or summer. Mother was buttering a slice of bread thickly for me. I was watching her eyes. When Father walked through the hall, she looked at me and I turned the bread upside down, nonchalantly taking a bite, followed by a swig of the chicory brew from the large tin coffee urn. whole gang, hay and oats are on the wagon, Mom will fix me

He stepped into the kitchen, filling up the whole door frame. He held the repaired harness in the crook of his arm.

"He knows he is going," Mother said to Dad.

"Yeah? And you won't fill your pants with fright?"

I lost all interest in further discussion. I stuffed a piece of bread in my mouth, and made faces like I was choking. On purpose I tried to look pitiful. But Dad's mind was obviously full of the war and the Russians.

"I don't know," Mother said. "You really think it's a good idea to send him into those woods? Everything is full of soldiers by now."

"Nobody will hurt the boy," Father said. "Who'd bother with a snot-nose like him?"

He was repeating what he heard from Vyska. He leaned the harness against the wall, reached for a chair and sat down so hard the chair almost burst.

"You'll take the old road." He was looking at me as if I was a complete imbecile. "Over the wooden bridge. They are all going there. It will be a whole gang. Hay and oats are on the wagon. Fix him some bread and bacon," he told Mother.

"How will you go?" he tested me.

"By the old road, the wooden bridge, they'll all be there, a some bread and bacon," I rattled it off like the multiplication table. Very fast. I looked Father straight in the eye. Maybe he understood my attitude to the assignment he was giving me. And the mocking tone of my voice wasn't lost on him. He clenched his hands, the two fists lay on the table before me like a pair of flails. He gritted his teeth, sucked in air as if he was choking. I knew he wasn't going to hit me. Not now, when he needed me. He got up.

"I'll get away from them at the first crossroad," I told myself. I stared Dad straight in the face, without blinking. I had a pretty good idea what I must have looked like. He turned around fiercely to get me out of his sight.

I remember a burning day in the middle of July. I like July. August, too. It was an oppressive, steamy day full of sticky sweat. The sun was white and yellow, scorching my skin like a ray coming from some giant magnifying glass. We were piling up a stack of straw. I enjoy the building of a stack. You can jump into the straw and make beautiful somersaults. Fresh wheat straw is best, it is soft and crumbly, wonderfully elastic, copper yellow, and above all it doesn't have as many bristles as barley. They sent me with the can to fetch water. I was hurrying so as to be back as soon as possible. The metal slapped against my legs. The five-liter can was as heavy as lead, full to the brim. Each time I bumped against it water splashed my feet. I took a rest, watched the swallows flying low. Their white bellies practically touched the stubble, a storm was coming. Ramparts of black cloud were already forming in one part of the horizon. But the stack was still bathed by hot, purple sunlight. When I came closer I could make out Julie. She was harnessed to the wagon. I saw her head, the rest of her was hidden behind the stack. Mom was standing on top of the stack with a pitchfork, leveling the straw. I walked by with my can. And then I saw Father. I froze in my tracks. I didn't know what to do, I held the can in front of me with both hands. Father was standing between the wagon and the stack, where Mom couldn't see him. A woman who occasionally helped out in the fields was with him. They called her Squirrel. She had red hair, a rusty face. They were standing facing each other in the narrow space as if they were trying to get out of each other's way. But neither of them was moving. Dad was holding Squirrel around the neck, as if he was going to choke her, but the bottoms of his palms were lower on Squirrel's dress. Above their heads there was the steady rustling of the stack; Mother was working, spreading bundles of straw. Squirrel had thick white knees; to this day I can still see their doughy surface. I took a few steps back, put the can down on the grass. I could no longer see them. I couldn't think what to do. I squinted into the sun, its rays were breaking against the top edge of the stack, the straw was reflecting its intensity like the surface of a mirror, the searing heat made the air heave and tremble. I watched Mother working above, I thought of Father. She was up to her knees in straw, her whitish kerchief shimmered against the blue. She saw me.

"Olda," she called. "Bring me some water!" A few moments afterward Father and Squirrel came out. She was barefoot. I couldn't lift my eyes, neither to her nor to Dad. She had large rough toes, scuffed like a man's, firm insteps, massive ankles; I can still see her horsy feet before me.

"Where the devil did you go for that water? To America?" shouted Father. His outline as he came closer was blurred by the wavy air. I didn't care what he was shouting at me.

That year, summer ended in a single day. The countryside grew cold overnight, by morning the river seemed strange. In the barely recognizable cold water floated clumps of rusty hay, lost by wagons crossing the ford. It seemed to me that I had suddenly become old, and the change made me sad. I ran uphill to the church, the bells were already ringing. On Sunday, just about everybody in our village went to church. Organ and in-

cense are the sound and smell of heaven. I am sure heaven must be just like that. Mom sat next to Dad in the oak pew; in church, everybody had a proper place.

Dad crossed himself, he'd put on his dark Sunday suit, vest, snow-white shirt. He was tanned, the skin of his neck sticking out of the collar was black. Mom was more beautiful than the Virgin Mary, or Saint Theresa, more beautiful than Saint Anne, too. Those were all the statues we had in our church. When I turned around in my bench, I could see everybody: Kudera, Vyska, Rez, Chumsky. They were all praying. I could watch them from my place up front; we children sat between the altar and the pulpit, a rope ran all around our section. The girls didn't have a rope, only we boys were corraled this way, so that we couldn't pull any tricks. But even in our "prison" we traded marbles and released bugs which we brought in our pockets. Then came communion, the servers were already ringing their bells. Whoever partakes of communion must clasp his hands and prepare himself spiritually for accepting the Lord's body. The priest's fingers shook. In one hand he held the host, in the other the chalice. As he lifted the host and we all beat our chests, the boys deliberately whacking themselves so loud that they sounded like African drums. Squirrel had come to holy communion, too. In her tight dress she seemed to weigh a ton. I bent down and stretched as far as I could, lifted the edge of the red carpet which runs all the way to the altar. This is a trap to trip a certain person who will soon be striding to the altar with her nose piously up in the air. Nobody saw my evil deed. Once again, my hands were folded devoutly.

Squirrel clumped down the aisle like a horse. Naturally, she didn't notice the ridge in the carpet, almost fell flat on her face, looked at the floor and gave Chumsky a resounding slap. I had no idea I would achieve such a splendid, double triumph. With her meaty hand Squirrel could kill a cow.

"What for?" Chumsky yelped. "What did I do?" His loud

profane protests in this holy place were a sacrilege. Even the priest lifted his head. He looked severe. But then the sacristan came, he let Chumsky have another juicy smack. At that moment, my hands were surely clasped with a greater feeling of devotion than those of anyone else in church.

Our Julie was not a mare, but an angel; she didn't resemble any other horse. You would have to know the warm softness of her skin, the salty odor of her mane, the graceful line of her back and the tranquility of her large eyes to understand my admiration. Father honored the mare as a piece of property. I loved Julie as a being. I never came near her without a sweet piece of carrot in my pocket. Not even that morning. It was early, the cocks were crowing all around and people were just beginning to get up.

She was already standing in front of the house, which seemed tiny in comparison to her huge frame. Eastern light was streaming over the rooftops gently enfolding Julie. She stood quietly, tall and fair. She turned her huge head toward me, mighty as a bell, her nostrils were aquiver because she had already smelled the treat. I stretched out my hand, she snapped for the carrot with her silky mouth, narrowed her eyelids sensuously. "You spoiled beast," I said affectionately.

Dad tossed some old hairy blankets into the wagon.

"If they won't take Julie into the barn, cover her with blankets overnight. Don't forget to throw some blankets over her," he said.

"All right. I won't forget."

I watched the houses to see if the little jerks were yet on the way, Kudera and Co. For the moment nobody was.

"She gets two cans of oats, morning and night," Father was taking me for an utter imbecile. I don't know why, but he was always under the impression that I would mutilate whatever I touched.

75

"Mmm," I tried to give him a hint that his advice was unnecessary. But he didn't seem to get the point.

"At noon give her only hay. But as much water as she wants."

"Mmm."

"Are you listening?"

"I am!"

"Take a look at her hooves. See how she is shod." Julie was a circus performer, all you had to do was touch her leg with one finger, a little over her knee joint, and she would obediently lift up the appropriate hoof and even hold it in the air for a while so that you could see what shape her horseshoe was in. In case of the rear leg she only lifted it a little; in fact, she only lifted the rear part of the hoof and leaned on the front, because she couldn't keep her balance otherwise.

Dad went inside the house to get something else. In an instant I was by the side of the logs, where I was standing the evening before when Mom called me. The logs must have been lying there a hundred years, one was completely rotted away. I reached into that one, all the way to my elbow, and pulled out the cigarette case I had hidden there the night before. I quickly stuck it in my pocket.

"What was that?" Mom was standing in the door. She had brought me a package with food.

"Nothing." There are certain secrets we don't entrust to anybody, not even to a mother we love. She looked at me quizzically.

Father tossed a pail into the wagon. "That's for watering the horse. Where are they? What is taking them so long?"

"I'll wait for them by the end of the village," I said. That fitted my plans. I could tell that Mom saw through me, she knew I wasn't going to wait for anybody.

I jumped up on the driver's seat.

"Now you wait for them, do you hear? Don't go off by yourself!" she called.

"Do you remember the route I told you?" asked Father, for about the eighth time. You could bet he was going to ask a few more times yet.

"Yes, of course, Dad. I have a brain." Magnanimously, he ignored the tone of my voice. "And take care of the nag," he said. "Make sure nothing happens to her, or . . ." I knew perfectly well what that "or" was supposed to mean.

"Take care of yourself, Olda," said Mom.

"If you meet any Germans, say *'Ich nicht versteh,'*" yelled Father. But I had already snapped the reins, clicked my tongue, and the wagon creaked forward. Thank God. I was glad to be leaving at last; the last-minute preparations seemed endless. My parents walked after me for a while. I turned around.

"And what if I meet some Russians?" it occurred to me. "What shall I say to the Russians?" I shouted at Father. I knew that this would embarrass him, he didn't know a word of Russian.

"If you do anything stupid, damn it . . . Just remember that if anything happens, you'll get . . ."

"Leave him alone," I heard Mother say. "Let him go." I stood up, snapped the whip, turned around for one more look at our whitewashed house. Now, when I think back, it seems to me that I had no special feelings about it. After all, it wasn't exactly home sweet home.

The lime on the gate spelled out a strangely frightening word: TYPHUS! I noticed gates of the other houses, everywhere I saw:

TYPHUS!
TYPHUS!
TYPHUS!

Everybody had got typhus. Our whole village had become sick. And now the gates opened, a procession of horse-drawn wagons was on the way. Rez was sitting on the nearest one, hunched down and looking as mournful as if this was his trip to the grave. He straightened up only after he saw me. His vehicle was pulled by an old stallion and a gelding, their backs were as lean as a goat's and they could barely drag themselves along. Rez's father had the nickname, "Horsekiller." The stallion neighed at our Julie, and the silly girl answered him. She even turned her head to look at the old stud.

Rez had come to his senses, he threatened me with his whip and gestured with his fist. I thumbed my nose at him.

Rez's dad was still shouting some advice to his son, so I clicked at Julie and gained a sizable lead. I tickled her back with the tip of the whip, and Julie ran along as lightly as a doe, as though she wasn't hitched to a wagon. It wasn't a trot, it was a ballet, her back was in wavy motion, her rump floated up and down, she stretched her neck and stuck her nose high in the air, as if she was about to fly.

We clip-clopped along past the barns, it was a beautiful ride. Now Chumsky was driving out, it was a good thing I got ahead of him. "Chumsky, the Chump!" I shouted. He couldn't catch up with me, he had to go slow, he even had some cows tied to his wagon.

"Chumsky, you forgot your goat!" I screamed. "Get a goat to keep you company in the woods!" His dad made threatening gestures toward me, too. He seemed to be giving some advice to his offspring, probably telling him to give me a thrashing when he caught up with me. The Chumskys were always very courageous against people weaker than themselves. Julie and I flew along like the pony express. I was afraid a wheel might come off, so I leaned over the side but everything was in order.

"Don't worry," I said to Julie. I talked to her quite often, and she understood. "Why should I wait for those jerks?"

The air was full of the sound of cannon, and now it seemed to me I could also hear rifles and machine guns. A plane droned overhead. A two-engine Junkers, with black wings and a paunchy body. I had no time to watch the plane as the road from the village spiraled upward. We were taking the hill in our stride. Julie had enormous endurance, she didn't even seem to be winded. The road was full of yellowish pebbles, and as the wagon bounced over the gravel, I was still standing up looking back over my shoulder. We had left the boys far behind. At this early hour everything was covered by silvery dew, over the stream breathed strands of fog, wheels cut through puddles and splashes of water flew off at both sides. We were at the cross-roads; on our left stood the little wayside cross, on the right a meadow and a row of stacks, I looked them over, ours was among them, too. I got an idea, yanked the reins and said, "hoot," which is horse language for "right." I made a sharp turn to the stacks, where the boys couldn't possibly see me. I drove the wagon behind the fattest and highest stack, which happened to be ours. It was there that the incident with my father and Squirrel had taken place.

"Whoa there." I pulled up the horse.

I jumped off the seat, and put on the brake so the wagon couldn't roll down the slope. The stack was a wonderful hiding place. Now I could hear the approaching caravan, rattling away, those morons yelling so loud that the Russians could have heard them all the way to Siberia. I grabbed Julie by the bridle, pulled her nose toward me and covered her nostrils with my palm.

"Don't you dare answer that old bag of bones!"

First came Rez, his stallion sniffed us and neighed, he snorted and whinnied and carried on as if he had never smelled a mare before. I had a hard time keeping Julie quiet, she would have loved to answer him, it was a good thing I brought a carrot.

Chumsky's wagon came rolling along right behind Rez. The cows tied to the wagon were forced to trot smartly. If old Chumsky had seen that he'd have had a stroke. All their milk spilled out of their bouncing udders.

Then came Vyska, and Jozka brought up the rear. They all had two horses, except Kudera who had a third one tied behind.

I stuffed Julie with carrot until they all passed by. Then I went to see what kind of food Mom had packed away for me. Bread, dumplings, meat. I looked it over just out of curiosity. The can of milk was cold, it had been standing in the cellar. I untied the napkin with the bread; folded it up again. I wasn't hungry. I pulled the top off the milk can and took a swig, sat down in the straw next to the stack and watched the Junkers and the boys, too. I could still see them, they were getting smaller, as if the horizon was made of quicksand and they were slowly sinking, up to the wheels, up to the horses' backs, up to their heads. Then they vanished altogether and I got up. I couldn't see them even when I climbed on the wagon. I got an idea. Actually, I had been thinking about this idea ever since I left home. I tied Julie by a short rein, loosened one of the shafts so that she wouldn't yank at the wagon and admonished her, "Now you behave yourself!"

She lowered her eyelids in agreement. Sometimes she looked more like a human being than a dumb creature. I ran back to the village, the milk can in my hand. I took all the short cuts. A cat jumped into the bushes but I had no time for games, I was in a hurry. For one thing, there was a war on. What's more, I was going to visit the puppies. I didn't even feel like trying for a record broad jump over the flat cobblestones. But suddenly I pulled up to a standstill. I could see the clay road leading across the fields to the manor which was abandoned yesterday by the German, Singer. It seemed as though half the village was swarming over that red road. The banging of the cannons and machine guns made it sound as if the front was within a stone's throw, but the tree-lined road was jammed with traffic. One stream flowed toward the village, another toward the manor. In spite of my haste I stood there gaping, until I realized what was up: They were liberating the Singer estate!

Master bricklayer Petrzela was of course participating in this event, pulling a load of planks on a handcart; they would come in handy, everything always comes in handy. Bertyna pushed the cart from behind, she was strong, she could have pulled the whole load with her father thrown in for good measure. Everything was moving at a brisk trot. Slejha the railwayman, thin as a birch rod, had no trouble propelling a wheelbarrow with three sacks of grain. Obviously, there are moments in life that inspire human beings with unsuspected strength. Under normal circumstances Slejha couldn't even lift the handles of such a heavily loaded barrow. But as I learned later, that morning he had actually completed six round trips. Andula was carrying a harness and a set of empty baskets, Mrs. Slejha lugged an armchair.

The schoolteacher, with his entire brood was moving the piano. The most pious families in the village were present, and as usual they worked with their greatest diligence. The flow of chairs, mattresses, tables, boxes, bags raised swirls of dust and the faces of my fellow villagers were bathed in a pink cloud of abundance. They looked as if some evil spell had come over them, as if they had suddenly lost their principles, as if something supernatural—demonic—had possessed them on the ochre road. This is how I will remember them for the rest of my life.

I took another sip of milk. The figures continued to move in silent, grim urgency, but as I kept on watching, the stream of thieves began to seem comical.

Once, I went with them in a procession to implore the Lord for rain. God filled everybody's mind that drought-stricken summer; they looked beseechingly at the searing skies as dry as the Sahara, they sang a religious song which sounded like human weeping. They crossed themselves, carried ecclesiastical banners, crosses, images of patron saints. A hoarse bell rang out. The soil around the village was bone dry, ready to split open. The grain was thin and stunted, bare soil could be seen through the stalks, the sun never stopped scorching the earth, the nights brought not a drop of dew. Old women fumbled with rosaries.

"Oh Lord, keep us from the devil's cunning, from drought, from eternal damnation, from all temptation, from sensuality, from perdition, deliver us from hate, Oh Lord!" intoned the priest.

I knelt next to Mother, Father was kneeling in his Sunday best, the road left dusty marks on his trousers. Everyone was down on their knees. The sounds of the litany were unreal, shrunken fingers moved the rosaries, bead by bead, I could see all the faces, even Vitlich knelt, his wife by his side. At that time he still had a wife. She was as dark as a gypsy. She was the only one who didn't move her lips, but she was on her knees, leaning her head against Vitlich's shoulder. And then the people brought lighted candles to the wayside cross. Everybody carried his own candle, to make sure his particular field would partake of the rain. The priest stood erect, hands clasped, narrow face lifted to the arid sky. He was praying for water, beseeching the heavens to send dew from above and to embrace the righteous with blessed moisture. Let the heavens open and send down redemption . . . Father crawled to the wayside cross on his knees, carrying a burning candle. Even Kudera lit a candle, but he walked to the crucifix upright. Chumsky, Rez, and Vyska followed him. Their candles were tall, impressive, decorated with wax flowers; expensive candles. They knelt on only one knee, on a hankerchief spread out on the ground. By noon, a hundred candles burned on the wayside cross. The land, sky, and sun were ablaze, the wax melted, ran down the crucifix over the legs of Jesus, dripped over the holy initials INRI. I held onto Mother as she told me, "Pray! Pray, Olda, the good Lord is watching you!"

Now, these very same devout Christians were falling all over themselves trying to clean out the manor. They stumbled under the load of jars, barrels, utensils, tools; one neighbor was lugging away the scale which Singer had in his bathroom. Somebody else had an armful of totally useless canes taken off the wall. They hadn't even overlooked an old carriage lamp and several window frames. One pious grandma was pushing a baby carriage, but the bottom gave way. A set of tin chamber pots came tumbling out, one after another, a dozen in all. Another family was transporting a whole cabinet. The chest was large and unwieldy, they loaded it clumsily, it teetered on the cart, the woman was supporting it, but the piece was too heavy, it fell over on its side and opened, a drawer slid out, a man cursed as he stumbled over it. The woman was distraught, the man was furious, one could see he was dying to give her a good smack. They started pushing the drawers back in, but the whole works toppled over, cart and all, the cart was far too small for such a massive lump of furniture . . .

I stopped watching them.

In the south, behind the blue hills, the cannonade had become continuous, like the rumbling of empty barrels over cobblestones. The sky was clear and deep, the plane gained altitude. Machine-gun fire and rifle shots became more distinct. On the road I could no longer see faces, only legs, the flutter of legs. All the legs of our beloved fellow citizens, of our beloved village.

I remember the day Vitlich and his wife sat in our kitchen. Her fingers were entwined spastically. Vitlich was holding his hat.

"I would love to be able to help you out, Cyril, old man," Father was saying to him, his face as full of sympathy as if he was really anxious to lend Cyril money. "I would like to . . . but this year I don't know myself how I'll pay my taxes . . ."

Vitlich was blinking, there was a long pause. Then Father saw me standing by the wall, listening to the kind of conversation I wasn't supposed to hear. "Go to the stable!" he said. "This talk isn't for you! Go count the hairs in the horse's mane."

"Oldrich, for heaven's sake, are you sure you couldn't . . . ?" I heard Vitlich's voice from the hall. Naturally, I stopped there to listen. I left the door slightly ajar.

"Kudera will have me auctioned off, if I don't pay what I owe him. He is already getting my meadow for a few coppers . . . and everything I own . . ."

Somebody slammed the door shut from the inside, probably Mother. I didn't hear anymore. Until that night, in bed, when I pretended to be asleep.

Mother: You should help Vitlich out. What is he going to do?
Father: I am having a hard time myself. Goddamn it, am I running a bank?
Mother: His wife is sick. She needs to go to a hospital.

Jesus Christ, what a life! Mom was crying. I could hear her in the dark. . . .

Kudera wasn't crying. He was laughing with his whole face. It was an autumn day, lit by thin, shifting sunlight.

"Twenty crowns," yelled Kudera to the auctioneer. The auction involving all of Vitlich's property was in full swing. It was

being held in Vitlich's yard. A crowd of curious onlookers was milling around inside the house and pressing against the fence.

"Twenty once . . . twenty twice . . . any more bids? Sold for twenty crowns."

They handed Kudera a table, old chairs, stools. He motioned for them to be thrown over the fence to where his farmhand was waiting. He chopped the furniture up with an axe and tossed the pieces of wood on top of a wagon. The whole business was really a public humiliation rather than an auction sale. Kudera was getting even with Vitlich; they'd never liked each other even though they were really cousins. Quite distant cousins, probably, Vitlich had nothing at all in common with the conceited Kudera. They led Vitlich's skinny horse out of the barn. Cyril and his wife were standing by the wall, their arms hanging limply by their sides.

"Asking price is five thousand," declared the auctioneer.

"Five thousand one hundred," yelled Kudera. "For glue!" he added, laughing. Somebody in the crowd actually tittered.

And then my father elbowed his way through the crowd and quickly raised his hand. He, too, for all his friendship with Vitlich, was itching for easy gain.

"Five thousand two hundred," he shouted loudly.

Everybody turned around. I, too, but he didn't see me. I can still picture it in my mind, my father standing with his hand raised, not looking at Vitlich; he had eyes only for the horse. It must have been a good bargain measured purely in monetary terms. Kudera remained perfectly calm.

"Six," he said. He rested his contemptuous eyes on my father. Now the farmers were laughing at my father, at his impotence. Vitlich's wife was no longer leaning against the wall, nobody even noticed that she had left. Until somebody shouted. "Vitlich's wife hanged herself! Cyril, where are you!"

All of us ran as fast as we could to the green walnut tree behind the house. Only the auctioneer remained behind, sur-

rounded by all the bric-a-brac. With a slow, deliberate motion he took off his wire-rimmed glasses and began cleaning them with a handkerchief. He had a finely chiseled face, and seemed to be somewhat repelled by his task. Five hens, tied by their legs into a fuzzy ball, tugged and cackled near his feet. Rabbits jumped about in a wicker basket. In the garden, the crowd spread out in a circle. Vitlich's wife was lying on the ground, Vitlich kneeling by her side. There was complete silence, nobody moved. To this day I remember the group of autumnal geese flying high in the air, at a tremendous height. They craned their long necks, maintained a steady arrow formation behind the drake. They were flying toward the bluish southern hills beyond the river.

And then Mrs. Vitlich had a funeral. A fourth-class funeral does not include a black, gilded hearse, but only a plain cart with the boards covered by dark cloth. The coffin was tied with ropes to keep it from sliding off. The cart was pulled by our Julie, and I walked alongside leading her by the bridle up the hill past the wayside cross. All those who had helped to hound Mrs. Vitlich to her grave were solemnly marching behind her coffin. The hole had been prepared near the wall, the pile of dug-up gravel had a dazzling yellow glint. All the dead of our village lie in rocky soil, their chests are weighed down by a ton of stone. The priest did not accompany suicides on their last journey. The mourners quickly dispersed, as soon as they had passed the cemetery gate. I stood outside, holding the mare, but I could see the grave. Vitlich turned around without shaking anybody's hand, he didn't even offer his hand to my father. He looked right past him.

That year the winter was unusually severe, blue snow was knee high, the cold so bitter that birds dropped right out of the air. We found a few of them under a telegraph pole, they were already half-covered by snow. The whole week before Epiphany ice powder whistled through the streets, windowpanes jingled in the wind. I put on Mother's starched chemise, a sheet over my shoulder, on my head a paper crown ornamented with golden strips. My face was smeared with soot. I was supposed to be the third Wise Man, the black one. We were carrying a can full of burning husks, sprinkled with axle grease to give off a thick black smoke. We took a short cut through the beet field. "Hey," shouted Rez. "There's Vitlich!"

Cyril was lying in the snow, motionless. His coat and sweater were rumpled, at one place his bare skin could be seen.

The boys ran away in fright, thinking that Vitlich was dead. "Run," they screamed. "Pinda, run!"

He was frightening, his eyes were closed and his face all bloody; a bottle stood in the snow. I put down the incense burner. The smoke, knocked down by the wind, streamed in his face. His nose twitched. He sniffed, making a whistling noise.

"Mr. Vitlich," I said. At that time I hadn't yet started calling him Cyril.

I was afraid to touch him, but I did. "Mr. Vitlich!"

He sneezed, sat up, leaning against the snow with his bare hands; he had no gloves.

He opened his eyes, examined my black face and blinked. He opened and closed his eyes several times. Perhaps he thought that he was dreaming. He looked around to see where he was. He noticed my paper crown and spat in the snow.

"Who the hell are you, a king or a chimney sweep?" he asked.

"Get up, Mr. Vitlich. Get up or you'll freeze to death."

Now I was running along the back of the gardens, by the pasture and the three beautiful weeping willows that looked like human figures. The Germans were there. They had two trucks and two guns with long, slender muzzles. The soldiers were digging emplacements, they had uncoupled one of the guns from the truck and were pushing it into the leafy willows. This was probably going to be their artillery position from which they'd defend the entrance to our village. So that the Russians wouldn't have too easy a job. Near the bushes I could see two familiar-looking bicycles. I looked around, and sure enough I spotted Kudera and Chumsky behind one of the military vehicles. With a German, an officer. He had a pistol at his side. All three were gesticulating wildly. Kudera and Chumsky spoke German like I speak Abyssinian. I couldn't hear them, I could only see them. The gun was in place, the muzzle lifted to the sky, they were camouflaging it with a net.

Kudera was pulling a couple of tall bottles from under his coat. He looked around to make sure nobody was watching. He seemed satisfied; obviously he didn't see me. Chumsky, too, was pulling out bottles of booze. And a bagful of homemade salami. Obviously, they were trying to bargain with the soldiers, trying to bribe them. The officer seemed to be hesitating. He shrugged his shoulders. Kudera kept pointing somewhere across the woods, toward the road. The officer studied his map. Then he took all the stuff they offered him, stuck the bottles into a knapsack, stowed the knapsack in the cab of the truck. He whistled and shouted sharp orders. The soldiers were startled, they no longer seemed much interested in the war. They lowered the muzzle of the gun, started to hook up the gun to its carrier, prepared to pull out. They must have bribed the officer with meat and liquor to set up the guns in the next village. I hunched down, because Kudera and Chumsky were walking in my direction, to get their bikes. They were hurrying, constantly peering around, they didn't want to be seen. I darted through the bushes, zigzagged among the trees.

When I looked around I could see that the military vehicles were really leaving, the guns bobbing up and down on their carriages.

I ran to Vitlich's house. Iza barked a greeting from the distance. She jumped against the fence. I whistled a signal, and she lay down quietly. The windows and house door were closed. I opened the gate using my special trick.

"Cyril!" I called into the stillness. I tried not to look at the green tree where his wife . . . Even so, I felt uneasy.

"Cyril!"

I was staring at the house, but I was walking backwards to the annex, to the puppies.

I pulled the cork out of the can with my teeth, poured some milk into the dish. The pups whimpered, scrambling over each other. Iza yipped happily, barely missing my nose with her high jump.

"Stop it, you goat," I said to her. "Didn't you get fed?"

"She did," I heard Vitlich. He was standing at the fence, behind my back. He must have come just that instant. He had a way of appearing silently out of the ground.

"Make sure somebody doesn't drive off with your nag," he said. Obviously, he knew that I was hiding the mare and wagon behind the stack. Vitlich knew everything.

"You know what your dad would do if somebody made off with your nag?" He sniffed. "He'd have a stroke."

I watched Vitlich, he bent over the puppies, cradled their bellies with his palm, turned them over, played with them, but I could tell his mind was elsewhere.

"He stopped buzzing," he said. "He got sick of that bridge and flew home."

Now I realized that the sound of the plane was gone. The sky was clear, unblemished, dazzlingly brilliant. The only sound was the morning chirping of the birds. It was like a peaceful paradise. Vitlich was standing with his legs slightly spread, I could see the muzzle of an automatic under his short, buttonless coat. It was the German kind of gun. He noticed me looking at his weapon.

"Cyril, were you in the willow grove? By the motorcycle?"

His face twitched a little, the bags under his eyes stood out as if he hadn't slept all night. He wiped his nose with the back of his hand.

"What did I tell you? I told you to get going!" He blew his nose, it sounded like a siren. And he kept blinking as if a fly got caught in his eye.

"You hear anything . . . ?" he stuck out his head to one side, like a man who is hard of hearing. Whenever I tried to listen very hard, I couldn't help opening my mouth a bit.

"No," I said. "What?"

He hawked and coughed, spat on the grass. "You think that without you the pups would starve to death? If your old man knew how you took care of his nag, he'd tan your hide good and proper." Suddenly, he held his breath.

"Wait. You hear anything now?"

"No."

"Nothing at all?"

"Nothing."

"They've stopped shooting," said Vitlich. "You hear the engines on the road?"

"No, I don't."

"They've gone," he said. "They've pulled out, Olda. The Germans are gone!"

His mouth was open, his expression watchful, as if he was trying to confirm with his ears what he had just said.

"These bastards pull out, the Russians pull in. They'll be here before you can say '*kamarad.*'"

"Cyril . . ." I was at last getting down to the reason why I galloped out of my way to Vitlich's house. "Lend me Iza, will you . . . ? To take to the woods with me."

He became conscious of my presence once more. He laughed. His face had rapid, convulsive changes of expression.

"You scared?"

"No . . ."

"A little bit?"

"Maybe a little."

Strangely enough, it was easier for me to admit it to Cyril than to my parents.

"Iza," he called out. "Off with Olda!"

"Thank you, Cyril, thank you."

I ran out the gate, set it back on its hinges. I dashed along the fence. Now I really began to worry about Julie. The stillness all around me made me uneasy.

"Olda!" he shouted after me. "Olda!"

I stopped and turned. For a moment we looked at each other.

"Take care, Olda," he said. "Take good care of yourself."

CHAPTER FIVE

In the early morning the countryside had all the colors in the spectrum. That day, the air had been warm from early on. But the rims of the gently bobbing wheels, which I touched now and then, were still cool, the metal still showing traces of sticky overnight dew. The grass, bark of trees, soil gave off a pungent odor. I rode through this blessed, still morning completely alone. By now, the idiots must have been all the way to Mongolia, I didn't see hide or hair of them. Even when I stood up, climbing onto the board which Dad had nailed up to serve as a seat, I couldn't see any trace of their wagons. Or Chumsky with his cows. Julie ambled along at a dignified pace, the war didn't upset her at all. I tickled her back with the rein, the leather strip got stuck on a harness hook, I calmly climbed up on the moving horse, freed the rein and seated myself once more on the box. I didn't have to say anything or do anything. When Julie had a road ahead of her, she kept moving in her steady, rolling way until she was told to stop. Behind her broad rear end one could have safely gone to sleep. But I didn't feel like sleeping. I looked at the sky, and the plane had really vanished. Vitlich's dog ran alongside the wagon, now and then sniffing at rabbit holes. In my solitude I wanted somebody to talk to.

"Iza, jump!" At first she was afraid, even when I smacked my lips encouragingly But then she suddenly took off and landed on all fours in the wagon, barked, shook herself. She stood gingerly in the moving wagon, exploring the planking with her snout as if she was scared that the thick boards might crack under her. She stuck her nose in my side. I scratched her neck, pulled a piece of bacon out of my package and stuffed it in her mouth. She could have eaten a hundred more. I gave her a few more chunks, she took them gently out of my palm. "Go catch a mouse!" I told her. And I motioned toward the field, which was full of mice. It was a clover pasture. She understood my gesture as an order to get back on the ground, she jumped off the wagon but walked along the edge of the road like an idiot. If Iza ever caught a single mouse in her life, it was a miracle. We were nearing the churchyard, the steeple on top of the hill shone like a beacon.

For further rewards of bacon, Iza jumped up on the wagon and down again, over and over, like a trained circus animal. Cyril Vitlich had taught Iza many tricks. I pulled on the rein, just a gentle tug, and Julie stopped. From this spot our steeple looked especially beautiful. I loved its weathered walls, the beautiful bare stone with edges eroded by time. I could count all the beams from the foot of the tower to the cornice of the dome. The church fitted so well into the countryside that the two seemed to have been created at the same time. I don't exactly know why, but throughout my childhood I loved to gaze at that steeple. It dazzled me with its majesty.

Now I was standing at the foot of the steeple, having forgotten about the war. I whistled against the walls. I whistled sharply, three times, the sound reverberated through the air, bounced off the walls, roofs and cupola, fragmenting into a train of echoes. Startled pigeons shot out of the windows, the air suddenly full of them. I heard the swishing of their wings, the sky turned pearly pigeon-gray. During the winter it got so cold that pigeons froze right out of the air and fell lifeless to the ground. In the morning we would pass the church and find several of them lying on the stone doorstep. The sacristan held up one of them by a wing tip. "Frost is their bane," he'd say. "By spring not a half of them will be left!"

But now they were beautiful. They circled the steeple in easy curves. They drew together into a flock, then suddenly burst apart. They were wild pigeons; in April they are at their liveliest. I could see their small bodies, suspended on wings like palm leaves. They settled on the plowed brown field. The portals of the church were wide open.

"Wait here," I said to Julie and jumped off the box. "Come on, Iza!" A pile of straw was lying near the church door. It hadn't been there the previous day. I couldn't imagine who'd left it there. A lot of straw, a whole truss. I was a little scared, but curiosity pushed me on. I listened carefully, but everything was quiet. The inside of the church was also full of straw. Cautiously I moved toward the doorstep. "Iza, go in! Go ahead, Iza!" Naturally, Iza wasn't going to do anything of the kind. She stayed glued to my legs, rubbing her fuzzy body against my trousers. I entered slowly, step by step. The church was empty, cool, quiet, the straw rustled under my soles, straw was strewn along both outer aisles, several of the benches were overturned, soldiers must have been quartered there overnight. I stumbled on a gas-mask container. I didn't even cross myself on entering, for the place looked more like a barn than a church. I thought of Sunday mass, the St. Wenceslaus chorale rang in my ears, it's a hymn that everybody sang. Even Mom. And the organist played fortissimo. I waded on through the tousled straw. I picked up a second container, this one actually contained a gas mask. I had never touched one before, it had a long, segmented hose. Naturally I wanted to put it on. It took me a while before I could figure out how it was supposed to fit. I had to stick my skull through a system of elastic bands that were supposed to go around the back of the head. Once it was on, I peered through the yellow glass windows. Or maybe they were made of celluloid. Anyhow, the eyepieces quickly fogged over, I couldn't see anything. I had to tear off the mask, I couldn't breathe. But I didn't throw it away, I laid it aside, intending to take it along to the woods. I also found a pair of old, dilapidated boots. They were useless, and I kicked them aside. The soldiers had broken down the door to the sacristy, the priest's vestments were strewn over the stone floor, cabinet drawers had been pried open. A window-pane slammed shut in the draft, I quicky turned around, Iza started barking and that scared me even more. Inside the church sounds reverberated strangely. "Shut up!" I yelled at her. "Stop it! Quiet!" I spotted the noisy window, swinging on its hinges. Pieces of colored glass made up some kind of Biblical scene, but the most noticeable thing was the inscription FOR THE GLORY OF GOD DONATED BY THE KUDERA FAMILY. The next window was donated by MARIE AND JAN CHUMSKY. We didn't have a window.

The sound of the Sunday service is still in my ears, I can hear Mother's voice, she went to church mainly for a chance to sing. I wandered among the holy pictures and statues, their faces inert. In the painting entitled CRUCIFIXION in place of the two malefactors on the left and right I always imagined Kudera and Chumsky. Suddenly there was a deafening explosion, everything shook, all the windows rattled, the whole church moved on its foundations as if touched by the hand of a giant. I saw that the door leading to the steeple had been blasted open. But first of all I ran outside. Julie was standing calmly where I left her, there was nothing unusual, just trees, the cemetery wall, fields. I cast a quick look at the steeple windows, the pigeons were circling again, terrified. I ran through the iron door up the stairway to the steeple. Iza ran after me, barking, and I let her bark, it seemed calming somehow.

I stood still and listened. If there was anyone in the steeple, he'd have heard the barking.

"Hellooooo!" I called out. In the stone tower the voice sounded cold and clipped. I climbed a few more steps. Now I could see to the top, nobody was there. On top there was a wooden bench, windows, the end of the bell rope dangled in the air. The bell was much higher. But the stairs didn't go up that far, only wooden beams. If I climbed the beams, I could reach the pigeons. I had already done it a few times. Instead, I made for the window where the gang had been the day before with the binoculars. I wanted to find out what that bang was all about.

I tripped over two metal boxes full of ammunition belts. I was scared to touch them. I looked around the cubicle, ashes and cigarette butts were scattered on the floor. In the corner there was an empty can of rations and a German newspaper. I leaned out of the window, there was Julie down on the ground, the wagon, the countryside, the village in the distance. A gentle stream of air brushed my face. "Julie," I called out, just to hear my own voice. And I whistled at the mare. She moved her head, saw me. If I turned the other way, I could even see the road, the bluish hills, the green river.

A row of evenly spaced poplars. From here they looked like a huge living comb. A cloud of smoke was hanging over the bridge. Or rather, where the bridge used to be. The span was crushed, as if it had been crumpled in someone's hand; it lay in the river. But I couldn't see a living soul, the road was completely deserted. Even the road from the manor was empty, the stream of thieves had vanished. It seemed to me that I was the only living being left in the world, that the bridge had blown up all by itself. I had always imagined that war involved immense numbers of people, but now I couldn't find a single human being.

"Come on, Iza. Let's go," I said to the dog, nothing was going on here. Then I got an idea, not a bad one, it was one of those plans I never put off. I pulled out a piece of chalk, which I always carry with me, and wrote on the tin cornice, in capital letters: KUDERA+CHUMSKY+VYSKA+REZ=PIGS! AND JERKS!

I wrote it with great love and care, there are certain writing assignments which I take very seriously. I put the chalk back in my pocket. It is not salt which is worth more than gold, but chalk. I descended from the tower, faster and faster, first jumping two steps at a time, then three. Iza was barking at my heels. I ran out through the iron door, quickly grabbed the gas mask. I ran to the wagon, patted Julie on the nose, jumped up on the box. "Let's go," I told the mare. And we were again rattling on our way, to carry out Dad's orders.

The pines began a short distance ahead of the forest proper. The thin stand of trunks and crowns resembled a transparent stage set. The trees were fresh in the early morning dew. A cuckoo hooted from one of the branches. The bird was yelling at the top of its lungs. The countryside was an idyll, war or peace. The brown road wound among the trees and bushes. The wagon was silent, the road was not much traveled, ruts overgrown by grassy moss, the ride was as quiet as a trip in heaven. Now and then the harness jingled with the gentle sound of the bells. Iza barked at a sparrow or a mouse. I yelled at her to "stop it!" I fooled around with the gas mask on my lap, removing the tin canister at the end of the rubber hose, to let air in, so that I could wear the mask without choking. The canister was useless. Julie's reins were around my neck. I needed both hands free for work. I banged the tin cylinder against the floorboards; the thread was either bent or rusty. Finally! But at the same instant, I heard a horse neighing. It was not Julie. That changed the whole situation, the mask no longer interested me. Where could Rez's undernourished beast be calling from? I could recognize the cracked voice of that nag that seemed to be calling for the veterinarian. All of a sudden I felt surrounded by cutthroats. It was an unpleasant sensation. I felt a stifling pressure on my throat, I seemed to be choking on my vocal cords. I stopped Julie, pulled in the reins. I scanned the roadway, the surrounding trees, the shrubs. And I was no longer sitting on the box, but standing and craning my neck. Nothing moved, but the stallion neighed once more. Julie sniffed the air, she raised her head and flared her nostrils, and responded with a neigh. Now I could see Rez the Fez. He had parked his wagon sideways at a bend in the road to block my way. I tried to figure out the situation, for Rez would never have the guts to do such a thing all on his own.

"Pinda!" he screamed. "We've got you!"

The plural indicated that the others were somewhere nearby. Rez was wearing a gas mask, the same kind as mine. It was perched like a helmet on top of his head, with the straps fastened under his chin. "We've nabbed you, Pinda!" he yelled.

"Who? You . . . ? Not till it rains and the puddle drains!" I screamed. I pretended to be laughing hysterically. I turned Julie and the wagon around on the spot, a hay wagon is not exactly a chariot, I almost broke the shaft, it creaked as if it was about to give up the ghost, but at last I managed to complete the turn.

I could hear them rattling behind me, shouting to their horses. I flicked Julie's back with the whip, just to give her a signal. That's all I needed to tell her. She was off like a cannon ball, and we were tooling it back at breakneck speed. I wanted to get out of the narrow forest road into freer terrain. Unfortunately Vyska the Pisska suddenly came shooting out of a clearing. I hadn't noticed the clearing before, I was too busy playing with that infernal gas mask. Vyska was wearing one too, completely covering his kisser, but this didn't change his expression. He looked just as dumb with the mask on as he did without it. He pushed it up on his forehead.

"Give up, Pinda!"

He lumbered toward me down the middle of the road, he thought I was going to stop, but I got nearer and nearer without slowing down. The distance between was less than a hundred meters.

"Vyska!" I shouted as loud as I could. "Prepare to die!" The barreling hay wagon was a tank, I was plunging ahead implacably.

"Vyska, pull over!" I yelled. There was not much time left. "Or you're dead!"

All I could see was his salami-colored face, he knew I wasn't going to stop, I couldn't even if I'd wanted to. He yanked his horses aside, up the incline by the side of the road. I flew past him, he threw something at me, it hit the wagon, I hunched down. I saw that all his junk was falling off the wagon, sacks of oats, bundles of hay. His panicky outside nag broke its harness and was rearing convulsively on its hind legs. "Prrr!" yelled Vyska. The wagon began to slide down the incline, and almost got creamed by the oncoming Rez.

Iza was hysterical, barking at the top of her lungs. Rez had to stop for Vyska, but I wasn't yet out of trouble. Jozka and fat-ass Kudera were coming out of the clearing. Chumsky was tying his cows to a birch tree, so he could join the chase. I knew what they were up to, they were hoping to trap me in a pincer.

"Chump, Chump, Chumpsky!" I couldn't resist yelling at

him, even in this desperate moment. There must have been a million masks in that church. Everybody in the gang had one.

"Pinda! Stop, you little jerk! When we catch you you'll pay for this!" threatened Kudera.

"You'll catch a bloody rupture first!" I shouted. My voice was a little shaky.

"Yeeeeeeay," I urged Julie on, and smacked my lips as loud as I could. "Go Julie!"

A word was all it took, Julie shifted to high gear ready to break speed records. She was galloping in such long strides, I was afraid she might tear loose from the wagon. She had endurance, six years of experience, imagination, an ideal war horse. I think she was enjoying herself, she hated boredom. I reached open terrain. But they would probably catch up with me, they each had a pair of horses. I veered off into a field covered by a low growth, realizing too late that it was rye.

"Idiot!" yelled Kudera. "You're driving through our rye, Pinda!" They stopped.

"You moron, stop," Jozka joined in. "Can't you see the field is seeded?"

"I can see! I have eyes! You shouldn't have chased me!"

"Turn around!"

"You bet. Right away! This time next year!"

My lead was getting bigger and bigger, they didn't dare follow me. If it hadn't been for such an extraordinary emergency, I wouldn't have driven into a field of rye, either, but sometimes a man has no choice. Julie was careening along like a runaway, but she was enjoying herself enormously, she tossed her head, yanked at the traces. I had to hold on to the sideboards to keep from falling off.

Chumsky had reached the edge of the rye field, and even Rez was there. Whenever I saw the four of them together it always brought out the worst in me. I shifted my weight until I managed to balance myself upright. I held the reins in my left hand, with the right I unbuttoned my pants, dropped them, pulled down my shorts, too. I took a bow, my rear end pointing straight at them. I let them take a good look. Then I pulled up my pants again. I couldn't have humiliated them more. They forgot all about the rye, they plunged their wagons into the field. I tried to evade them in a zigzag line, they followed the same course, leaving a swath of broken stalks behind them. I took a sharp turn. They caught up with me, dividing into two wings, Jozka and Kudera on my left, Rez and Chumsky on my right.

"Pinda, don't bother buttoning up your pants!" they shouted.

I almost tumbled on my back as the wagon hit a deep furrow.

All of a sudden the whirring of engines burst from the sky. Ten planes, maybe more, came swooping over the tree tops, flying just a few meters over the ground, right over our heads. Their jagged shadows flitted across the field.

"Prrrr!" the boys yelled at their horses. So did I. "Prrr!"

Now Julie was bolting in earnest. She was terrified. The bellies of the planes almost touched the trees, engines screaming. And behind them a second wave. I jumped to the ground, held Julie's bridle, she tugged and pulled.

"It's all right," I tried to calm her. "It's all right."

Rez had a hard time keeping his nags from panicking altogether. The saddled one was rearing and kicking.

And still more planes!

They were all flying in the same direction, from the hills toward Jihlava. Our chase had come to a halt, we were all looking at the sky.

"Russians," yelled Jozka. "They're Russians!"

"How do you know?" I asked. A moment ago we were enemies, but that was all forgotten. "Didn't you see the stars?" he answered.

"I saw machine guns," babbled Chumsky. "Four machine guns!"

"You saw a pig's ass," said Kudera. "They were bombers!"

"My God!" yelled Chumsky at Kudera, pretending to fall out of the wagon. It was the only trick he knew, he grabbed his head and pretended to be fainting.

"Where would they stick the bombs, you dummy?"

"You know where . . . ? You want me to tell you . . . ?" broke in Jozka.

"They were headed for Brno," declared Chumsky. "They were pursuit planes."

"That so?" I piped up. "Since when is Brno that way. Since yesterday?" I joined the debate without really meaning to. Now they became aware of me, they remembered my presence. Their faces once more took on their everyday stupid expressions.

"You still here?" said Chumsky. The mask was around his neck, the hose dangling at his knees.

"Hey, let me come with you," I said. I wanted to be part of the gang. Now that such great events were taking place, our quarrels seemed petty.

"Jozka, I'll give you a cigarette case," I thought I could bribe him. I pulled out the case and showed it to him from a distance, he couldn't have seen very much.

"There's a picture inside," I shouted. "A great snapshot!"

"Go snapshoot yourself, Pinda! So's you know what you looked like before we get through with you!" Rez said belligerently.

"And I know about a motorcycle," I offered further ransom.

"Yeah? And what do you know about a ladder? You know anything about a ladder that happened to disappear yesterday?"

"Jozka, come on . . ."

Jozka and I were facing each other, but the others had already climbed on their wagons. I looked from one to another.

"First you'll get a couple of smacks," said Jozka. "That's for sure."

"But not from Chumsky." I wanted to bargain with Jozka.

"No, not from me," said Chumsky. "From me you'll get a kick in the ass."

I jumped on my wagon, flicked the whip over Julie. I had no choice but to fight to the end, if I didn't want to lose face.

The chase began anew. We raced to the edge of the field. My wagon jumped the boundary wall and careened onto the neighboring tract. They were right on my heels, as their wagons rattled over the boundary, they almost broke to pieces.

"Ten smacks, Pinda!" yelled Kudera. "Two from each of us. Stop!"

"Five!" I negotiated over my shoulder at a full gallop.

A second boundary, I almost fell off. It was an obstacle race with hay wagons.

"No, ten!"

"Stop, or it'll be the worse for you!"

I was trapped and they knew it. Rez was chortling his head off.

"Now we've got you!" he crowed. "Pinda, you're licked!"

His croaking was unbearable. Now that I could hear him triumph, I was capable of anything.

"Your father's dingdong!" I screamed at him, making an orangutan gesture.

"Yeeeeay!" I shouted as hard as I could at Julie. And I pulled the reins to the left, to turn her up the bank, which is hard to scramble up even on foot.

"Julie, go!" The mare didn't hesitate, she was a scrapper, she'd climb the Eiffel Tower.

"Pinda, you idiot, you'll kill yourself!" warned Jozka.

"So be it!" I shouted. "It's your fault. Its on your conscience . . ."

The wagon was practically vertical. The bucket, provisions, blanket, bundles of hay, everything slid against the back gate, heaped up in one pile. Two trusses of hay fell over the sideboards. Out of the corner of my eye I could see the gang far below, at the foot of the bank. Julie was struggling for all she was worth, straight up into the sky. That horse could have taken you all the way to heaven.

I heard their excited voices. "Chumsky, you chump!" I yelled, but strictly from habit. I was scared, anybody could see that. I was afraid that Julie would kill herself. "Julie, easy, easy!" I tried to calm her. She couldn't slow down, the wagon would have dragged her down again. But the critical point passed; the top of the incline was covered by thick undergrowth, five-year-old oaks. We went over the top, wheeled through the brush, the branches creaking and snapping like matches, a thick shoot whipped me painfully across the shoulder. A rear strut cracked, but it was minor damage, it couldn't stop us.

We plunged through the undergrowth like a tank. The mare was possessed; rather than slowing down she kept tearing on, to the meadow, and then to the road. Galloping all the way, arching back toward the woods from which we had come. Iza could barely keep up with us. The mare was bathed in thick foam. Broken twigs stuck out from her headpiece and from beneath the straps of her harness. She looked as though she would keep on galloping for the rest of her life, to the end of the world. I yanked at the reins to slow her down, I was afraid she had gone mad.

We were back on the road leading past the pine trees. The gang hadn't got there yet. My escape up the incline was a stroke of genius. The countryside was again as quiet as a mouse. If it wasn't for the planes you would never have known there was a war. I listened: the mare was breathing like a locomotive. I could hear whistles in the far distance.

"Oldaaa! Pinda . . ."

They were shouting somewhere from beyond the rye field, a good kilometer away. They were looking for me. My lip was split, and I wiped it on the back of my hand, I saw blood and spat out a red blob. A little blood wouldn't kill me! The main thing was revenge. I stopped Julie at the clearing. Chumsky's cows were standing calmly under the birches. They gawked as stupidly as Chumsky, three dumpy milk bags. They were pretty dumb, chewing their cud as if nothing else mattered, drooling all over the ground. Quickly, I untied all of them, slapped them on the rump.

"Move," I chased them off. "Run! Move!" I pelted them with cones. Sure enough, they scattered in all directions. I laughed as their udders splashed from side to side.

And then I hopped back on the wagon, and got Julie started again. It occurred to me that all in all, the morning had got off to a pretty good start.

I found just the right hiding place, a small clearing surrounded by thick shrubbery. I unhitched Julie. Nobody could see us, here we could rest securely after the chase. I tried to guess the time; from the position of the sun I figured it must be about nine. The golden disc was floating low over the shrubbery, it touched the bottom branches of the tall trees. When I half-closed my eyes the sun was surrounded by purple rings, it seemed to be spinning. I stuck a pile of hay under Julie's nose.

It so happened that our resting place was near a brook, I didn't have far to go for water. When Julie is thirsty she drinks up an ocean.

I picked out a big flat boulder, lay down on my stomach and took a good drink myself. I was sipping the water right off the surface, I could see myself as clearly as in a mirror. Trickles from my mouth contorted the picture of my face in the water. At this spot in the brook the bottom made a deep dish, diving beetles scurried to and fro. I made faces at myself, I'd got a million of them from Cyril Vitlich. Then I dipped the bucket in for Julie, who was already eyeing me impatiently. A gentle whine was coming from her throat, she kicked up clods of turf and grass against her underbelly, for it was precisely there, where her skin was most sensitive that a swarm of small sucking flies had settled. I brought a full bucket of water, carrying it in front of me with both hands I put it down in front of Julie. She lost interest in hay and flies, bent her head thirstily over the bucket. Her nose was already dipped in the water, when she suddenly snorted and tossed up her head. She hadn't drunk anything. Something wasn't to her liking.

"What's wrong now?" I said, irritated. Julie was a spoiled beast, an aristocrat among mares. I looked in the bucket, pulled out a couple of blades of grass and a dry leaf. "Drink," I said. "It's clean. I cleaned it out for you."

Sometimes I'd love to have swatted her across the nose. Julie looked at me. There were moments when her eyes became human, when I was sure she was about to speak to me in a human voice. She looked at me for quite a while. Then slowly, painfully, as if she was doing it only for my sake, she lowered her long neck, about a millimeter over the surface, spread her nostrils, sniffed at the water, and snorted. Still she refused to drink. She lifted her head hesitantly, as if she was sorry to cause me so much trouble, and once again cast her heavenly eyes at me, as big as the whites of hard-boiled goose eggs. We stared at each other as intensely as a pair of hypnotists.

"What's your problem?" I raged. "Are you thirsty or aren't you?"

In some situations Julie managed to strike an expressive countenance. Now she looked like an equine countess, like a veritable empress of the entire equine race. I knelt down to smell the bucket for myself.

"Smells of bran. Big deal!" I told her. "Your highness!" She listened calmly, moving her ears slightly, then blinking her heavy lids with their long lashes.

"You'll get nothing!" I threatened. "You think I am your servant . . ."

I sat down on the wagon in a huff. I pretended to be going to sleep, to be terribly sleepy, to be completely unconcerned whether she was drinking or not. Julie was intelligent, she had a good-sized brain in her head, my naïve trick didn't fool her in the least. She waited until I really closed my eyes, and then calmly, without any noise, with a deliberate motion of her front foot she knocked over the bucket. The handle clinked against the ground, I could hear the water running out. Julie knew I wasn't sleeping.

"You're too damn much! That's a fact!" I grumbled, raising my head. I frowned, but jumped off the wagon, and picked up the bucket. I couldn't leave her without water, she must have been awfully thirsty after that chase. I went to the brook once more, scooped up some water, rinsed the bucket. To make sure, I rinsed it out a few more times. Only then did I fill it with water, very carefully, to make sure no blade of grass or stray leaf got in.

"If you don't drink now, you beast, I'll give you a good whipping!" I threatened. Again, the movement of her head, neck, nose was quite self-confident, she ignored my threats. Julie sniffed the water, she was satisfied, she had found nothing wrong, and she started to drink.

"That's better," I said in a tone suggesting that she was back in my good graces. "If you hadn't drunk this time I would have thrashed your hide. That's a fact!" It seemed to me she laughed, but perhaps she only cleared her nose. She polished off the bucket as if it was a mere thimbleful, lifted her head quizzically, again turned those lamps on me. She knocked the empty bucket over with her front hoof. That particular gesture didn't bother me, it was a standard signal, I knew what she wanted. I got a second bucketful of water. Julie had more sucking power than a fire pump, the bucket was empty before I had a chance to scratch the back of my leg. I hauled a third bucketful. I stuck my fingers into her horsy belly.

"Your belly is full," I said. "You're doing it on purpose! You can't still be thirsty, I know your tricks!"

Julie didn't answer, except to fix me again with those huge eyeballs. She acted as if she hadn't seen a drop of water in years. I jogged off for the next refill. I was down on my knees, filling up the bucket, when I heard a familiar splashing sound coming from the direction of the wagon. It sounded a bit like a deluge.

Julie was relieving herself.

She looked at me tranquilly. In a few moments she had piddled away everything that I worked so hard to bring her. Now it was my turn to knock over the bucket with a smart kick.

"Is this what I am doing all that lugging for?"

Nothing depresses me so much as the futility of work. But Julie calmly started to chomp away at her hay, she looked totally satisfied.

Then all of a sudden I had no time for quarreling. I heard horses, carts. I jumped up on the wagon, the shrubs were so high, I could barely see over the tangled growth. I scrambled over the traces onto Julie's high, broad back. Now I could see all the way to the edge of the road. I was not mistaken, they were coming, I could see the whole caravan. Chumsky was bringing up the rear. I recognized his cows, he'd managed to round them up, but it must have cost him a lot of trouble. I was content; malicious joy is a balm for many wounds.

They were coming close. I jumped to the ground and held the mare's nostrils, to make sure she didn't start neighing and betray our hiding place.

"Iza, quiet," I whispered to the dog. She had been asleep, but now she, too, was alert, sniffing the air.

Not taking any chances, I grabbed Iza by her collar, pulled her close to me.

Gnats buzzed around my face, the banks of the brook were full of moldering grass, the brake was pleasantly shady, an ideal spot for flies. The sounds of the wagons were drawing nearer. They had reached the spot in the road closest to our hideout. I squeezed the dog between my legs, so that I could hold the horse's nose with both hands. She was full of electricity, because Rez's mangy stallion was up to his tricks again.

I heard Kudera, "Get a move on! He can't be far! The stallion's already picked up that old bag of bones of his!" I was dying to let him know who'd got the most dilapidated nag. But I kept quiet, I only made a face at him. I could hear their whips slashing at the pine cones as they passed the shrubbery.

"Yoooooooo," I heard their voices.

I stuffed Julie with carrots, keeping up a continuous soft conversation with her, until the wagons passed. Then I jumped up on the shaft and up onto Julie's back again. They were already far over on the other side, where the road entered a thick forest. Chumsky brought up the rear, jogging behind the wagon, flicking the cows with a rod.

Then even Chumsky disappeared. I couldn't hear them any longer. They'd vanished behind the brown, green, and yellow wall of spring wood.

I slid down Julie's mane and turned a smart pinwheel in the grass. Then I tried a headstand. That didn't go too well, each time I toppled over on my back. I rested in the cool grass, the horse and dog silhouetted over my head. I stretched my arms and legs in the young ant-filled gold-flowered grass. I blew at a beetle, it hid under a blade. Sometimes I feel wonderful and I don't even know why. I may just watch the sky and feel good. As I watched the sun through my fingers, it shimmered like a tiny piece of multicolored rainbow. A jay came flying out of the bushes, glistening in the sun like hammered metal. Iza barked, growled.

"Stop it," I shouted at her. "It's only a jay." I followed the bird's flight to see where it would alight. The blue and white feathers disappeared in the undergrowth, but the hoarse insistent call kept on. Something must have scared the bird. Iza, too, continued to bark.

I turned around, picked up a stick to throw at Iza. I was afraid that her barking might carry all the way to the boys. She ran off a few steps, barking all the time. I jumped to my feet. Iza was not barking at a bird. She was snapping at three men, who had just emerged from the shrubs. They were right by the wagon, as if they had come out of the ground. They were looking at me. Most probably they had been watching me for some time, without my knowing it. One of them kicked at Iza. She jumped aside, whining in surprise.

"Ruhe!" he shouted at her. "Hold the mouth, stupid dog," he said in broken Czech. She stopped barking, dropped her tail between her legs. Coward. I guessed that whatever might happen, I couldn't count on Iza's help. But I'd known that from the very first. I noticed that one of the men had a bandaged arm. And then it all came back to me—the three men in the birch grove, taking off their uniforms, throwing away their helmets, putting on civilian clothes. I remembered how they quickly walked away from their motorcycle, while I was watching from the top of the haystack.

Now their eyes darted all around. One of them was as thin as a rail, comically frightened. If the situation hadn't been so serious and if I hadn't been so scared, I would have laughed. His colleague, a good-natured, fat type, asked me in German whether I spoke the language.

I shook my head, meaning no. So he tried again in Czech. "This horse . . . yours?" he asked gently. "Yes, it belongs to you?"

I tried to watch the other two as well. The wounded one and the skinny one. They walked around the wagon. Around Julie. They seemed to be mainly interested in Julie.

The skinny one's hand was under his coat. No doubt, he was holding a weapon. In a fit of fear I couldn't seem to move, or make a sound.

"Good . . . horse?" asked the fat man. He wanted to block my view with his body, to keep me from seeing what the other two were doing. I stepped aside to keep them all in my sight.

"Yes, good horse?"

In the meantime, the skinny one harnessed the horse, tightened the straps which I had loosened earlier. His hands trembled, as if a leopard was about to jump on him from the woods. None of them looked too brave. The strap fell out of his hands, then he dropped the reins, stumbled over the trace. The fat man wanted to distract me, he kept on grinning, pulled something wrapped in rumpled foil out of his pocket. His expression was insincerely sweet.

"Here . . . *schokolade* . . . good *schokolade*," he was offering me a bribe. It was now clear to me that they intended to take both Julie and the wagon. I was not in the least interested in chocolate. It was no trick to run away from the fat one; I could have escaped from that tub of lard when I was a toddler. I made a feint to the left, jumped to the right. His outstretched hands grasped at the air, as if he was playing blindman's buff. I think that he fell flat on his face behind my back.

"Halt!" he gasped. *"Verboten!"*

I jumped beside Julie, held her bridle.

"This is our horse!" I shouted. "Leave her alone! Leave me be!" I shouted as loud as I could right in the thin one's face. He shoved me, tried to fling me aside, but I was still holding on to Julie. I ignored his blows, even though they were painful; he was beating me with his bare hands.

"Himmel herrgott! Idiot!"

"AAaouweeee!!!" I screeched for dear life, till my lungs were ready to burst, I shouted to the furthest reaches of the woods. I wanted the gang to hear me. The skinny man pulled the reins out of my hands. He knocked me down, rolled on top of me. I scratched him. It's a good thing I don't cut my nails very often.

"Schwein," he moaned.

I took advantage of a moment when his calf with the rolled up pants leg was near my face. I shut my eyes and bit as hard as I could. It was not a pleasant-tasting experience for me, God knows what those legs of his had been through in the course of the war. But I had no choice. He screamed loudly, caught by surprise. For a moment he was completely stunned and bewildered, a weepy grimace on his face. I used this moment to jump over to the wagon and unhitch the horse. But I barely had time to finish before all three of them were on my back. They pummeled my head as if they wanted to hammer me into the ground. After one especially hard blow, a thousand red wheels spun before my eyes.

At the worst moment of my ordeal I recalled the day we waited for Dad near the wayside chapel to see the new horse. Of course, we had no inkling that it was to be Julie. Mother was wearing a white kerchief on her head, the whole countryside seemed festive, the trees were in bloom, the bees buzzed so loud that the air seemed full of them. Now and then, puffs of wind scattered flurries of white leaves over the ground.

I climbed up on the roof of the chapel to get a better view.

Mom was afraid I might fall off, even though I could climb it with my hands behind my back. She was always worried about me. I saw Dad as he was turning the curve. Way back in the distance, near the edge of the trees. He was leading a horse! "He's leading a horse!" I shouted from the chapel roof. I slid down so fast I skinned one of my knees. I ran to meet Dad. It was a historic moment for our family, until then we only owned cows, now we belonged among the horsemen. If we had suddenly been dubbed knights, if we had been awarded a noble title, it would have meant little in comparison to this rise in economic status. I kept turning around, motioning to Mother to start running, too. She didn't want to, she was shy, she walked at a brisk pace. But then she began to run, after all. She laughed, looked around to make sure nobody was around to ridicule us. She ran awkwardly, she didn't know how to run at all. I had to wait for her all the time. And then we saw Dad quite distinctly, and he saw us. He waved to us, we waved back. He broke into a run, too, the horse trotting smartly by his side. Mom took her shoes off, and then she raced so fast that I could barely keep up with her.

The three Germans continued to beat me. They nearly killed me. Blood dripped from my nose. I wiped it with my hand, my palm and fingers turned sticky red. They stomped on me. My coat was off, my shirt was torn. But I was not crying. I wouldn't cry in front of Germans, not even if they were skinning me alive. That much national pride I have. They were convinced I wouldn't be able to get up. The fat one and the skinny one walked to the wagon. They looked so tall they reached the sky. I lay on my back in the grass, my mouth full of dirt, I spat it out, it seemed to me I was spitting teeth too. I was conscious of nothing but the thumping of my heart. I never heard it beating so wildly. Birds, brook, trees, shrubs, all had vanished; only my heart was left, it was beating in my brain, it was beating throughout my body.

The wounded one had already harnessed Julie. He sat on the box, waiting for the fat one and the skinny one, holding the reins and whip. I raised myself up on my elbows. After the thrashing they gave me they didn't expect me to get up again. But Germans don't understand the Slavic temperament.

Dad was showing us that day how firm and clean were Julie's hooves. He lifted all four legs one after another. He stroked her back, opened her mouth with an experienced peasant hand and showed us her teeth. They were as healthy as steel. He prodded Mom to peek under the horse, he assured her that it was perfectly safe. Mother was scared. I wanted to do it, but she clutched me, she didn't want to let me go. Father laughed. Fully dressed as he was, he lay down in the dust of the road. The horse towered over him, without moving a muscle. Father shouted "yooooo," as a signal for the horse to step over him. Mom shrieked in fear; I, too, gasped. But the mare stepped over Father with an extremely careful, almost ballet-like step. She lifted her legs high, so as not to touch him. He said "prrr." She stopped obediently and tamely, with a perceptiveness that I had never observed in any animal before or since. He laughed at our appre-

hension, he laughed long and heartily. He was happy and exceptionally kind and gentle to Mother. All of a sudden he picked her up in his arms and placed her on the mare's back. Mother was caught by surprise, her skirt was rumpled up. She quickly pulled it back down over her knees. He caught me, too, in his strong arms, set me down next to Mother. Then he took the horse by the rein and jogged with us toward the village. The mare trotted along with noble dignity. I held onto the mane. Mother held onto me. When we brushed against a cherry branch, a cloud of white blossoms swirled around our heads. Mother's sweet laugh rang in my ears.

Now, these memories were only increasing my anxiety. I couldn't let the three Germans out of my sight. They were on their way. Julie turned her head a few times, but in the end she obeyed her new masters. I zigzagged through the underbrush to reach the forest road so as to follow them. They were going faster and faster. I heard the whip and the rattling of the wagon. I ran after them, but I had no idea what to do. I had only one hope; to come upon some grownups from the village who would force them to give up Julie.

I caught up with them. All three were sitting on the wagon, the skinny one was driving. I moved through the shrubbery by the side of the road, where they couldn't see me. Branches tore at my hands, whipped me in the face, as I scrambled over tree roots. I realized that I wouldn't meet anybody from the village, and even if I did, no one would dare stop the Germans. They were trotting at a fast clip; I had to run as fast as I could to keep up. Again, my heart seemed ready to jump clear out of my body. I was gasping for breath.

I had reached a spot only a few steps away from the road. I slipped through the underbrush like a weasel, concentrating on one thing: the kingpin. I almost fell right under the rear wheel. The Germans spotted me, but I had already pulled out the pin and thrown it deep into the woods, where they couldn't find it. They shouted "Halt!" and some German curses. All I could see was their open mouths. They jumped down off the wagon and sprinted after me, the skinny one snapping his whip. It was all like a feverish nightmare. But the important thing was that the wheel had rolled off.

I turned and ran for dear life. I could probably have gotten away from the fat one and the wounded one, they huffed and puffed like a couple of nightwatchmen, but the thin one must have been the champion forest hurdler of Germany. He threw away his whip, his hands were free, and my lead got smaller and smaller. I was terribly scared. I scrambled up a slope, clutching at tufts of grass.

"Iza," I shouted. "Iza!"

But she wasn't anywhere. She wasn't even barking.

"Dad!" I shouted with all my might. "Daddy!"

I saw my father, but that was only another memory. He was leading Julie into our little yard. To get through the door into the barn, the mare had to bend her head. There wasn't much room to spare in width, either; she barely squeezed through. A stall made of fresh boards was all ready for her, lots of hay in the manger, fresh straw on the ground. The cows started to low. Both of them mooed loudly in protest; now they would have to share their stable with a stranger. The arrangement was not very dignified for Julie, but we had no other choice. She behaved beautifully, she gave no sign of disappointment or annoyance, she was very co-operative even though in our low barn her head was practically touching the roof, and was right next to the swallows' nest, full of young birds screeching in fright. Father sent me to fetch some carrots, so that the horse would get used to her new home. I ran down to the cellar, where we always kept some carrots in a mound of damp sand, and dug out several. I rushed back up into the yard, washed the carrots in a tub of rainwater standing under the gutter, shook water off the roots. Everything on the double, so as to get back to the mare as quickly as possible. But in the door of the stable I stopped cold. Father was embracing Mother, lying on a pile of hay next to the mare. That was the first time I saw an act of love, it looked more like a fight. I went out in the yard. They hadn't noticed me coming or leaving. I leaned against the wall of the hen house, at least I could watch the stupid hens scuffling. I tossed a carrot at them. All the sweet carrots that I had prepared for Julie I wasted on those cackling birds.

Now I was at the end of my rope. The German held a knife. I saw nothing but that shiny knife. I was lying on the ground, I couldn't get up, I couldn't run. All I could do was wait. The skinny German's face loomed over me larger and larger until it took over the whole world, the whole universe. Eyes, nose, lips, teeth. His skin had a damp shine. I had never seen such eyes, they were almost motionless, only the lids blinked now and again, the pupils were the color of smoke and glass.

"It . . . is . . . our . . . horse," I whispered. "Please."

He knelt on top of me. He had made some kind of decision. "Please!"

I kept looking at his knife. I didn't want to die. At that moment I was terribly afraid of death. I wanted to pray, but there was no time for that. The German swung his bare, clenched hand.

A swarm of pigeons came flashing before my eyes . . .

Their wings hummed. They swarmed around our steeple, landed on the ledge. They were not white, but strangely black. So it was probably a dream. All of a sudden, I saw winter trees all covered with pigeons. A thick layer of them blanketed the deserted village. The field of the manor, too, was covered by these mournful birds. The ledges of the steeple turned black from their multitude. Then the pigeons vanished, I heard the rattling of our sewing machine. Mother was making me a shirt. I couldn't understand why she was in the midst of this deep forest. She was looking straight at me—she wanted to make sure that I was asleep. And then she started singing an age-old melancholy song.

But I saw Mother only for a moment, my hallucinations moved quickly, I was in Konopany in a large church, the solemn Confirmation ceremony was taking place. Now and then, somebody coughed nervously. An unreal, thin light filtered through the window, the inside of the nave was bathed in stately semi-darkness. The figures of people I knew—for this scene closely resembled reality—stood motionless along the long, cool walls, around massive pillars, under stone statues. In their inertness they themselves resembled limestone statues. Those of us who were about to undergo the ceremony were arranged into two long, convoluted rows. I was standing with the boys, the girls were on the other side. The bishop worked down the winding passage separating us. We all leaned forward, moving a little out of line, looking in the direction from which he came. He was getting nearer, the creaking sound, that was his shoes. Adults, who were pressed behind us, were mumbling prayers. It was a quiet, almost indistinct, plashing sound, like the lapping of waves. The bishop's embroidered vestment did not reach all the way to his shoe tops, it was a little short, or else they had tucked it in too much; dark civilian trousers stuck out from under the edging, his shoes were powdered with dust. Lumps of dried mud stuck to the soles. I wondered how he could perform the office, shod like that; it puzzled me. The end of a white lace flapped from one trouser leg. But nobody was looking at his legs—luckily. Every-

119

one's attention was on his tall half-meter-high miter. With every step it teetered dangerously on his head. I was terribly excited. I peeled the wax flowers off my long Confirmation candle with my nails. Crumbs of wax lay all around me, hot wax dripped on my new short pants, on the tip of my jacket. Mother was standing on the other side, she was giving me some sort of signal, but I didn't understand. Dad was next to her. He wasn't looking at me. I was upset that I couldn't make out Mom's signal. I turned to my godfather, Mr. Vyska. Father of Vyska-Pisska. He'd cut himself shaving, his neck was covered with red nicks. One cut was covered by an adhesive, which was coming off at the corner.

"I was already confirmed," I tried to whisper.

"What?" he asked. "What's that?"

He must be half-deaf or else he wouldn't have spoken so loud. Even the bishop must have heard him. In fact, the bishop stopped, looked in our direction. Suddenly my candle went out. Maybe Kudera blew it out, he was right next to me. I wanted to light it from his, but he pulled his hand away. Old Vyska saw what had happened and pulled out a box of matches. It rustled in his large fumbling fingers. He, too, was excited. The matches scattered over the tiles. Kudera burst out laughing.

But I blew out his candle, too, so that we were even. Godfather boxed my ears. Trying to pick up the matches, I dropped my candle. The bishop was looking at us again. His face seemed to be powdered with flour. All the faces suddenly looked enormous, and all were turned toward me. Across from me, in the girls' line, stood Anna. It was strange I hadn't paid any attention to her before. I could see that she was sympathetic. She had a white dress, white stockings, thin calves, small knees, a garland of roses in her hair.

She gathered courage, quickly ran across the aisle to light my candle from hers. She had a tiny face, with big eyes, red gums, big spaces between her front teeth. It never occurred to me before that she had such large eyes. I will probably always remember Anna. I wanted to tell her something. Something pleasant and affectionate, maybe I wanted to thank her. But she put a finger to her lips, for me to be quiet because of the bishop, so as not to disturb him during such an important ceremony. I was happy that she didn't light Kudera's candle. Now the bishop was actually right in front of me, standing on the scattered matches. He was supposed to slap me symbolically across the face with two fingers. That is part of the Confirmation ritual. He gave me a real slap instead. I didn't mind the pain, but I was ashamed that everybody saw what happened. Our priest was assisting the bishop and was trying to pick up the matches before the bishop noticed. Three other ecclesiastics were also present. Their faces seemed extremely familiar, though I didn't know why. I couldn't remember where I met them. All three were wearing cassocks, black hoods, their faces hidden in darkness. It seemed to me they were trying to avoid my eyes. I tried the harder to remember. Then one of them unwittingly let his broad sleeve slip back, his hand was bandaged, it was the dirty, soaked bandage of the wounded German. Quickly I glanced at his skinny companion. He hid his hand, but I had the feeling that I saw the glint of a knife blade, a knife that was going to kill me—or perhaps had killed me already, I really didn't know. But there was no doubt that these were the three men who stole Julie from me. I ran, I was scared of them. I heard them in pursuit. Chumsky, of course, tried to trip me up even in this desperate situation, but I jumped over his foot. Rez tried to catch me, I broke out of his grasp. The passageway through the crowd was like a labyrinth, it didn't lead to a way out. But then I saw a bright light shining through the wide open church doors. The path through the throng was getting narrower and narrower. As I pushed my way through the crowd, they were inert, I shoved and squeezed past their bodies, which were like a rubbery mass. I hid behind the side altar. I could see my pursuers groping through the crowd, they didn't know where I was. I found a pile of junk behind the altar: vases, glasses, candlesticks, broken statuary, dried wreaths, a pitcher, washstand, and towel. A chair had been prepared there for somebody; standing next to it on a shelf was an ash tray full of cigarette butts. Somebody seemed to like sitting in the chair and smoking. The chair was old, upholstered in red.

Once more, I ran to the door, I reached it but I couldn't get through even though it was wide open. A net made of thin, sharp chains had been hung there to bar my way. I don't know when they put it up, it hadn't been there before the ceremony started. The net was firmly attached to the doorstep and to the stone door post as if it had always been a part of the building.

I stuck my arms through the chains up to my elbows, the whole net bulged out into the sunshine; outside the church, the sun was burning. In the sandy churchyard, lined up along the white cemetery wall, a hundred carriages were waiting, hitched to a hundred pairs of horses. But not a single person was in sight. I couldn't break through the net, my face was drenched in sweat, it ran down my cheeks, my forehead, into my eyes. If they hadn't already killed me in the woods, they were going to kill me now.

But all of a sudden I was home, in my room, lying under a pile of quilts. It was terribly hot, a hundred degrees, I was burning, swimming in sweat. My neck was wrapped in a towel because I had the flu, but it seemed to me that the towel was strangely spotted with blood. Mother sat on my bed, holding a plate of buttered oatmeal sprinkled with sugar. She was feeding me with a spoon, stroking my head. Her hand was rough, I could feel her calloused palm. Strands of my hair kept getting caught, but I didn't complain. She dipped the towel in the basin, wrung it out, washed my forehead and face with the damp, cool cloth. It was soothing. At last I felt at peace.

When I opened my eyes, the first thing I saw was Iza's tongue. It took me a while to realize where I was, what had happened. She was licking my face. She was nudging my cheek with her soft nose, wanting me to move. My immobility frightened Iza, I think she was scared in the woods all by herself. I felt her wet nose traveling over my neck, touching my shoulders, arms, chest, stomach. When she saw me opening my eyes, she barked. Now I knew where I was, I recognized the hornbeam forest. It was an entirely different spot from the place where the German caught me. How had I got all the way there? The sun shone through the dark network of the tree crowns, but it was already quite low, imprisoned behind a wall of massive trunks.

Suddenly I realized everything, what had happened, how it had happened, and why. I chased Iza away, her fawning was annoying, I couldn't forgive the cowardly way she abandoned me.

"You bitch!" I said. "Where were you?"

She looked at me devotedly. Iza knew all about putting on a fantastically pitiful look. "Cowardly stinker," I yelled. I aimed a stick at her, she jumped aside. Then she sat down again, and gazed at me, her half-extended tongue trembled, she whined imploringly, she wanted to get back into my good graces.

Gunfire was very close. I heard a machine gun, the bursts were as clear as if they were firing from behind the nearest clump of bushes. At that moment, though, I wasn't the least bit interested in the war. I felt my mauled body. Every bone and muscle ached, as if I was made of randomly selected, ill-fitting parts. I couldn't bear to touch my face, it burned terribly. I had wanted to sleep, my eyes began to close with fatigue. Iza gathered courage, got up, moved closer, barking; she was trying to tell me something, perhaps an excuse. I was again overcome by pain, what I heard was an Easter rattle, not a machine gun.

Our rattles, decorated with colored ribbons, clattered merrily from morning to night. "The bell flew away to Rome," said the priest. But I wanted to see for myself. Carefully I crept through the iron doors, climbed the stairs to the top, to the steeple. To see with my own eyes. Naturally the bell was there, as always. It didn't fly away. I heard steps behind me, I wanted to get away, but there was no place to run. The sacristan caught me, twisted me roughly by the shoulders, his ruddy face close to mine, he clutched me convulsively, his mouth opened to berate me, but all I heard was barking, it was Iza.

I saw her canine head, for a moment she looked like the sacristan. She was barking her head off. I was wide awake again, in command of my senses. Perhaps I'd only blacked out for a second or two. The sun hung over the forest, it had reddened, a reddish light flowed from the branches and trunks to the low shrubs, flickering like the dying wick of some immense candle. The shooting was continuous, it reminded me of the rattling of dried peas poured from one metal container into another. I stood up, gasping with pain, but when I examined myself I found nothing worse than assorted bruises. That surprised me, I thought I must have at least six broken bones. Iza stopped barking, rubbed herself against my calf. Now she loved me immensely. When nothing was at stake, she really was man's best friend. I could just as well have left her at home for all the good she was in my hour of need. I stumbled around a bit, there were stars before my eyes and a ringing in my ears. "Beat it!" I screamed. "Why didn't you bite them?" My lips were glued to my teeth. I spat out some blood, licked my lips with my tongue —carefully, because certain spots hurt horribly. I must have been an awful sight, I was glad I couldn't see myself, a good thing Mother couldn't see me. I was anxious to know whether the incessant shooting came from the Russians or the Germans. Not that it mattered much from my point of view—it could just as well be the Tartar. Still, I wanted to know. Even in the most desperate situations I am always interested in all the minor details. I scrambled down the birch bank, stumbling, sliding down on my rear end. I didn't seem to have a nose any longer, at least I couldn't feel one on my face. I felt the inside of my mouth with my finger, I touched my gums, my teeth, they seemed wobbly. One front tooth was loose; for sure. The German had revenged himself on me for all Germany. Maybe he was a boxer in civilian life. I pushed through the bushes, even though I could walk around them. Painfully I stumbled against tree stumps which I could see plainly. It was as though I was sleep-walking—one moment my body seemed to be completely weight-less, the next my head seemed to weigh a ton. But I kept on in the direction where I had last seen the wagon and Julie. I found the gas mask, wheel tracks in the grass. That was all. It wasn't a dream, it had all happened. I kicked the gas mask angrily, boot-ing it with all my pent-up fury, nearly breaking my big toe. I hopped on one foot. This explosion didn't calm me in the least. The bucket was lying on the ground, or rather what was left of it; a wagon wheel had crushed it as flat as a pancake. I flung it into the shrubs. Iza, the idiot, ran after it, obediently picked up the handle with her teeth and dragged the flattened hunk of tin to my feet. That killed me. She was so devotedly dumb that I couldn't really get angry at her. I always thought that Vitlich had trained her to perfection, but no educational system can change an individual's basic character. Not even in the case of dogs.

"Julie," I shouted into the woods. "Julieeee!" I ran toward the road, but the road was deserted. I looked in both directions, no trace of anyone. A sputtering rocket whirred over the forest, burst into tiny glowing buttons. Somewhere far away there was the thump of explosion.

"Julieeeeee!" I shouted, almost in tears.

I jogged through the hollow, Iza at my heels.

"Go away! Beat it!" I took out my anger on the dog, bent down for a rock. "What do you want from me? Beat it, stupid!"

I knew I wouldn't find Julie. The thought of the impending catastrophe at home wrung my heart with icy fingers. Frightened, Iza was strolling along the edge of the woods, far enough to stay out of my range. She circled ahead, waited for me on the road, then took off again to make sure I couldn't reach her with a rock. In some ways she was too darned smart. She was holding a piece of cloth in her teeth.

"Iza!" I called to her. "Come here! What have you got there?"

She watched me suspiciously, keeping her distance. She was dragging some sort of rag. She had to keep her nose high in the air to keep from tripping over it.

"Iza!" I clicked my tongue at her. "Don't be afraid! I won't hurt you, silly!"

In the end, my friendly tone convinced her; she let me come near. She was holding the napkin which my mother used for wrapping up my food bundle. It must have fallen off the wagon, evidently the Germans were moving as fast as Julie could carry them. Once more, I started running after them. It was more an expression of desperation than a realistic plan. Even if I caught up with them—which was highly unlikely—I'd only get another thrashing.

When I think about Julie now, I like to recall her visit to the stud farm. Dad unharnessed the mare, led her past the whitewashed buildings down to the corral on the green meadow. Julie was dancing, gaily undulating her back, Dad had a hard time to hold her. When they reached the ramp they were both almost running. Dad laughed at Julie, talking to her as if she could understand: "Take it easy! You'll get there!" An old employee, extremely bowlegged, opened the enclosure. He was tall, so that his legs formed a large O. His riding breeches were held up by stout suspenders; his pants would surely have fallen off without them, for he had no hips at all. He was wearing a bright, striped shirt, and a forester's hat was floating on the back of his head. He laughed with his whole face, spreading wide his almost toothless mouth. He seemed hearty and robust. He shouted to Dad:

"Look at that nag! She can't wait! Lord, will you look at that hurry!"

"Back to the wagon!" Father said to me, when he saw how interested I was in the proceedings. "See if the wheels need greasing."

Both of them kept on laughing, Father and the stud-farm employee, as if the whole thing was some kind of big joke. They must have taken me for a stupid little brat who still thought that foals were brought by storks. Sometimes adults can be quite naïve and ridiculous. Naturally, I dragged my feet willy-nilly.

"Did you hear me?" said Father. "Don't make me help you on your way!"

It made me mad, the way he embarrassed me in front of other people. I walked a little faster, I pretended to be running, I ran like somebody lame from birth. Then I gaped at the dumb wheels of the dumb wagon, dripping with black grease.

I could only watch the corral through the spokes of the wheels. The stallion had already been released from the stable. His vocal chords were going wild. He romped from the stable, reared on his hind legs, danced pirouettes in the air. He was large, steel-gray, the sun glistened on his shiny, metallic back, his high head, sculptured legs. I didn't even notice that I was pressing my forehead against the black hub of the wheel, smearing my face with axle grease. Excitedly I grasped the wooden spokes. I saw the stallion and mare outlined against the blue sky. They were higher than all the roofs. I had the impression that the stallion was standing right on top of Julie, and I was terrified.

On the way home from the stud farm, we stopped to "fortify" ourselves. This was a traditional part of the procedure. Every farmer who took his mare to be bred stopped at the inn on his return trip to drink to a favorable outcome. Dad bought me a pretzel sprinkled with poppy seeds, which for him was an unbelievable extravagance. We each had a plate of goulash soup. He ordered a shot of brandy for the coachman from the manor, and had one himself. They were standing at the bar, both of them holding their whips, and talking about horses. "Well then, to your new colt!" said the fellow. "Here's hoping it's a champ!" "God willing," answered Dad. "Damn it, God willing!" They clinked their glasses, some brandy spilled over their fingers and dripped on the floor.

We went home by field roads, it was shorter than the highway. Dad was singing at the top of his voice. He was belting out songs he had learned when he was in the army. He frightened all the partridges out of their nests. The countryside looked beautiful, the rye was blooming, wheat pollen powdered the air. Trees stuck out of the sea of wheat like green lighthouses. Now and then Father teetered on his seat, almost falling off. Each time, I caught him and held him by his coat. He smelled of brandy.

"Don't worry," he'd say. "Don't worry, Olda."

"Dad, I'll drive. Let me drive."

I reached out for the reins. "You can lie down in the wagon," I said.

He looked at me. "Wipe your nose," he said. "And hold on so you don't fall off."

But when we reached the little chapel at the bottom of the hill, he was lying in the back. He gave in after all. His head kept rolling off the bundle of straw onto the bare boards, and he lifted it again, grumbling. He bumped his head and mumbled: "You going off the road or what? Stay on the road, Goddamn it!"

"Yes, Dad," I said. I drove as best I could. Dad kept his mouth open in his sleep. He looked very big when he was lying there, he filled the whole wagon.

When we reached the well he yelled "Prrrr!" The mare stopped in her tracks. He got off the wagon as if he had only one knee. I was afraid he'd fall and break his neck. He knelt at the well, dipped his hands in and splashed water over his face, his neck, his shirt. Soon he was soaked through and through, and then he began drinking, he drank as if his insides were on fire. He snorted, stood up, but had no sense of equilibrium; he seemed on the verge of toppling over. He looked up, saw my surprised and probably scared expression. He wiped his eyebrows with the hairy back of his hand, which was still dripping water, and kept his eyes fixed on me. He blinked, spat, then seemed to be lost in thought. He always made the same grimace when he was trying to concentrate.

"Doesn't that soup make you sick, too?" he said. "God knows what garbage they put in that stuff!" He thought I would fall for this lame excuse. I pretended to agree with him. Once more, he accomplished the perilous feat of climbing up on the box.

Now I was slumped down on a grassy knoll, I had no breath or lungs left. I stared at a crossroads. All three roads were hard and gravelly, I had no way of telling which way the Germans went.

"Which way did they go?" I asked Iza. But she was no tracker; at most she could scent some chow. She ran along the grass verge sniffing at rabbit holes. I got up, completely at a loss as to what to do. No matter how carefully I looked, I could see no traces.

The sun was getting weaker, it sparked against the tips of the bushes, soon it would reach the ground. The gunfire was incessant. I was no longer aware of my own breathing, the pulsing of my blood. I realized that the shooting was even closer than a moment ago.

There was no point in running. I walked slowly, wearily. I was awfully thirsty, my tongue dry and rough, I made for the brook. At this point the brook ran parallel to the road. I lay down on my belly, propped up on my elbows, my mouth touched the surface, I sucked the water, swallowing in big gulps, the cool water between my teeth soothed the pain of raw gums, it was a wonderfully good feeling. I examined myself in the mirror reflection of the surface, some strange creature stared back at me, I looked ready for the grave. The whole side of my face was covered by a black and blue lump, one eye had disappeared. I closed my good eye, covered it with my palm, I could still see all right. It was only a bruise, then. The dog was drinking, too, she scooped up the water with her pink tongue so lightly that the surface was hardly disturbed. Then she suddenly pressed against my feet, whimpering. She had scented something. Something very near, otherwise she wouldn't have carried on that way.

"What's up?" I whispered. I wanted her to hear my voice. "What is it, Iza?" I tried to give her courage, by showing her that I was not at all afraid. I followed the direction of Iza's head. Carefully, I stepped around the bushes. Immediately, I threw myself to the ground letting only my eyes stick up above the grass. I didn't see three Germans, I saw three thousand Germans! A stream of military vehicles was strung out along the road, all dusty and covered by branches and camouflage nets. There were tanks and guns, but mainly trucks, and several motorcycles with sidecars. There was a battery of mine throwers, a million assorted weapons. Everything stood still, nothing moved. It was strange to see the soldiers sleeping on the ground around the vehicles and guns. They were fast asleep, they must have been terribly tired. The road and the whole side of the hill was full of them. Some were sleeping in cars, behind the wheel, others in motorcycle sidecars, some on top of crates. Only one man was on guard, next to a machine gun, leaning against a tree. His head kept drooping.

There was loud shooting, but none of the soldiers seemed interested. A man with stripes on his collar walked among the sleepers, carrying a carton on his arm. He threw two small white packages to each of the men. Some of them let the packages lie where they fell, others woke for a moment, reached out and stuck the packages in their pockets. Hardly anybody took the packs directly from the non-com. There was no talking. He stepped over them trying to see who had still to receive his share, peered into the carton. Finally he reached the guard, coming close to my bush. He gave him two packages, too. The guard proceeded to tear the package with his teeth, pull out a cigarette and stick it in his mouth.

"*Schluss,*" said the non-com. Both lit their cigarettes. These soldiers were the most frightening of all the ones I had seen, because they slept while there was furious fighting going on nearby. I had never come so close to the inner mechanism of war.

I wriggled backwards on my stomach, holding one hand over Iza's nose. I wriggled all the way to the stream, then I climbed up the bank, crouching low to the ground, so as to give the Germans a wide berth. I didn't know what to do without Julie, but I wanted to get out of the woods at all costs. A shoelace had come loose, it flapped at my feet. The way seemed awfully long, I must have lost my way in the excitement. I thought there would never be an end to all those trees, branches, bushes, roots. But suddenly the forest thinned out, there was more light between the trunks, then I passed only isolated oaks and before I knew it I was in open country. I don't even know how I did it. Behind a wave of fields I could see our church, our steeple. I had to sit down and tie my shoelace before it tripped me up. I examined the countryside. It sounded as if the firing was coming from below, from the river, the bridge. But perhaps it was further away, sounds are deceptive in open country. The surrounding country looked peaceful as if nothing was going on. Nature is not the least bit disturbed by great moments in human history. I saw a mouse, scurrying from hole to hole; she stopped for an instant to look at me, her eyes as tiny as pinheads. I tried to imagine what I looked like from the viewpoint of such a little creature. I have crazy ideas like that so often they no longer surprise me. I should have been bawling, but I wasn't. Then suddenly I was scared again. I couldn't catch my breath, it was as if somebody was squeezing my heart with one hand and my throat with the other. I couldn't sit still, I had to get up. By now shadows stretched far over the ground, the sun was dark red, but it was still there. I started jogging through the acacia bushes, growing so low that they hardly reached my waist. My mind was again full of my tragedy. And of events that happened long ago.

I remembered the day I'd hurried to fetch the veterinarian. His outside gate was locked. I can still see myself desperately ringing the bell. I heard it buzzing inside the house. I jumped on the fence.

132

"Doctor!" I shouted. "Doctor!"

A buzzer sounded in the gate. I had never heard of this American invention before. Instead of pushing the gate open, I just stood there listening to the quiet buzz. Naturally, by the time I realized what to do the buzzer had already become silent. I shouted once more. I was hoping that the veterinarian would come to the door, but it was his wife who appeared. Her first name was Alexandra. She must have come from a real upper-class family. She was always saying things like: Wait here! or Don't touch that, don't lean on that, don't step on that!

"What do you want?" she asked, in a tone that warned me to watch myself. She was wearing slacks, heels that must have measured ten centimeters. Her beauty almost made me faint.

"Our Julie is about to foal," I told her. I could see that she wasn't the least bit interested. Once more I sputtered out the news, which had such crucial import for our family. The lady couldn't seem to care less.

"Just when we're having dinner!" she drawled. Nobody else could have pronounced it with greater scorn and boredom. Now she condescended to amble to the fence and to open the gate. "Wait here," she said. "Wait outside, stay out of the hall!"

"Yes," I said.

I hadn't noticed that the vet was leaning out the window.

"Julie is already on her way?" he asked.

"Yes, doctor."

"All right then," he said. "Wait for me, I have to pick up my tools."

The vet was all right. Veterinarians are usually first-class fellows.

"Are you thirsty?" his wife asked me, in a tone that suggested I should say no. Sometimes she forced herself to be friendly, some of the boys said that she gave them a glass of water.

"Yes, I am," I answered. She seemed sorry that she had asked.

She frowned, but went inside, leaving me standing under the roof of the veranda. I looked around. She had a bowl full of jam on the bench, I smelled its sweet raspberry odor. For a few moments I resisted. It was my misfortune that raspberry happens to be my favorite flavor. I tried to scoop some out with the tip of my finger. But the jam had already stiffened, my fingers left a clear mark. I wanted to fill in the dent, to smooth the surface of the jam but I only succeeded in gouging it even further. I quickly stuck my jam-covered hand in my pocket, just as the vet's wife was returning with a glass of water. I drank the whole glass. The doctor came out at last. He walked to his car. I ran to my bicycle, propped against the fence.

"Thank you!" I shouted toward the veranda, to the doctor's wife. I was in a hurry, I pedaled furiously through the cloud of dust raised by the vet's tires. When I turned around I saw his wife standing at the fence, looking my way. With a menacing and at the same time puzzled expression, she was holding the porcelain bowl. . . .

I remember that the whole time they were in the stable I lay on my stomach on top of the woodpile in our yard, watching. Now and then Mom would run out of the stable to fetch something for the doctor. She seemed worried and preoccupied. Father came out with his sleeves rolled up, his shirt and trousers were soaked with blood and water. He took a thin, coiled rope off the wall. I couldn't imagine what for. I could hardly wait to see the foal.

"Dad, is the foal coming?" He had no time to answer me. Then there was quite a long interval before I heard their quiet, excited voices, I heard Dad talking to Julie. I couldn't make out his anxious tone. But then Mom came out, holding a corner of her apron before her eyes, I saw that she was crying. I heard her, she was weeping aloud, her chest was heaving with sobs. She picked up a shovel, walked over to the wall, and began to dig a hole in the grass. I stood up on the woodpile, I didn't understand the turn of events. The doctor came out, too, Mother followed him. She had prepared a bucket full of water and now she was pouring water over his hands, she handed him soap and a towel. They were silent. He wiped his hands, Mother was still crying. By now I had climbed off the wood-pile and I edged close to them.

The doctor tried to cheer Mother up. "Thank God the mare is all right, anyway," he said. "She had a close call." The veterinarian had a deep, calm, sympathetic voice. "We did what we could."

I followed them through the hall into the kitchen. Mother gave the doctor some banknotes. She kept on sniffing. She had counted out the money earlier. He took it, was about to stick it in his pocket, then he looked at Mother and quickly placed two bills back on the table. He did it at the moment she was turned toward the washstand. He picked up his suitcase and strode briskly toward his car. He was really a fine man. It was said that from some people he refused to take any money at all.

Our yard had become sad and deserted. Only the stupid hens continued to cluck on their manure pile, as if nothing had happened. I stepped into the stable door. It was dark inside. The mare was facing the wall. The dead foal lay on the tiled floor, covered by a burlap bag. Its legs and ears stuck out. Then I saw Father. He was lying on a pile of straw and hay, behind Julie's stall. His face was resting on his arm, his shoulders were shaking. Then he noticed me standing in the door, he turned away so that I couldn't see his face.

"Bring her some carrots," he said. I could tell he had been crying.

"Go bring her a little carrot!"

I don't believe there was a more thrifty family in the world than ours. I never had any burning love for my father, but I must admit that he was capable of depriving himself of practically everything.

I remember his vein-covered, knobby hands resting on our kitchen table. The table top was made of rough, unpainted, carefully scrubbed boards; that's where we had our meals, weekday and Sunday. To this day I can recall all the ridges in that table; the table top always reminded me of a wrinkled familiar face. At one end of the table Dad always used to slice his cigarettes with a razor blade. He bought the cheapest brand of cigarettes, they were called Zory. He cut them into thirds. He would count out five such butts and stick them in his cigarette case. He'd put one in his holder to smoke right away, but then he'd think better of it and blow out the match.

The evening following the birth of the dead foal he was sitting at that table, writing figures in a dog-eared notebook. Mother was sitting next to him. They kept their paper money in the notebook, coins were stored by Mother in a little pot. They were calculating their expenses, writing out a budget. The notebook was their ministry of finance.

"You need a coat," Mother whispered to Dad. They were talking softly not to wake me up, they thought I was asleep.

"I don't need a coat," he answered. "I've got one."

"You can't wear that one anymore," she said.

"Why not? It isn't that bad. I can still get good use out of it."

He was wearing an old pair of wire-rimmed spectacles, one of the lenses was cracked. He put them on only when he was writing or calculating. The only sounds in the room were the *scratching of his pencil and the ticking of the clock. A crucifix hung on the wall at Dad's back, next to a framed inscription MAY THE LORD BLESS THIS HOUSE. I was slowly falling asleep, and long into the night I could hear their worried, whispered voices.*

When I thought about all this and realized that I'd probably never find Julie again, I was on the verge of crying, I sniveled, my chin shook, I had a hard time controlling myself. I had already left the acacias behind, I crossed a plowed field, without really knowing where I was going. I aimed for the church, only because the steeple was plainly visible. There was straw on the floor of the church, perhaps I could sleep there, I couldn't go back home without Julie. Iza was crisscrossing the field, from one mousehole to the next. Her nose was covered with dirt. She was throwing up lumps of soil with her front paws, trying to dig her way into the mouse nests. There are times when a dog is much better off than a human being, I envied Iza's canine life. The firing suddenly stopped. The field was endless, I was in the midst of open, flat country surrounded by gray woods. The hills in the back looked like a dark blue paper cutout, their wavy edge sharply outlined against the dusk.

I walked ever more slowly, wracking my brain, but I couldn't think of anything to do. At one point I seemed to hear the sound of hoofbeats. But that was only imagination, my head was full of pain, fever and hallucinations. If I had stuck with the gang I would have been safe, I would still have Julie, everything would have been fine except for a bit of thrashing from the boys. Now I would gladly trade my troubles for a humiliating whipping by Chumsky and company. I could clearly imagine standing in front of my father, completely swallowed by his threatening shadow, the light bulb at his back would be completely obliterated by his figure, I wouldn't even be able to see his face in the darkness. I'd stand there with that black monocle around my eye, my skinned knees, my torn shirt and trousers. Father would take a step forward—and I knew the rest.

I stopped to examine rows of deep tracks, made by tank treads or armored cars. They led across the field over to the woods. I jumped into one of the tracks, and sank in up to my knees.

Iza was lucky, she finally flushed out a mouse, she chased it over the bumpy ground, but in the end the mouse got away.

All of a sudden I heard a shout. Nobody was to be seen. It didn't sound like any language I knew. *"Stooy!"* I didn't know where the voice could be coming from, there was nobody around.

"Stooy!" shouted the voice again. I turned around, scanned the field and went even faster. I was almost running, really frightened. The calm deserted countryside suddenly became threatening, I didn't know which way to go. Someone jumped out of a hollow and started sprinting toward me.

"Stooy!" I heard. *"Slushai, stooy."* Now I both heard him and saw him. He was wearing a black coat which flapped in the wind. He was not a specter but a soldier. I had never seen such a uniform. On his head he wore something tall and furry; I took to my heels. I didn't need any more black-and-blue marks. I had no idea to which army the soldier belonged, but he certainly didn't look tame. I was pumping as fast as my legs could carry me. I turned around. He was running after me, quite rapidly. And he kept on yelling that word of his. I zigzagged like a rabbit, but it was clear that he was determined to catch me.

I was bent forward from the waist, that's how you can run fastest. I couldn't make out what he was shouting. He was yelling without stopping, not just words but whole sentences.

He was probably cursing, it sounded like curses. I couldn't imagine what made him so angry at me. When a war is drawing to an end there are crazy people all around. Bits of clay were spattering from my heels all the way to the back of my head.

"Iza, sick him! Get him!" I urged the dog. No luck.

She was trying to gather courage, but at the same time she was full of hesitation. At least she was barking like mad. Thank God for that! Then she took herself off in a big circle, barking like three mad dogs. She ran away, because the strange angry man was right at my heels. Through the corner of my eye I made out his odd uniform, the coat with the high shoulders. It was actually a cloak, tied at the neck. At this moment he lost it, it slipped off and he left it lying on the ground. He was wearing high boots, his riding breeches were flapping a bit above his knees. His ruddy face was shining above it all like a flaming torch. I had no doubt he intended to kill me. I couldn't run any faster, and it was useless to oppose his strength. I only hunched down. He jumped on me, pulled me down, pressed my head and body to the ground. I saw his cap, it was a Cossack fur cap, it fell off his head and rolled away. It came to a stop against a rock and I saw its shiny velvet lining. He was lying on top of me, my chin and nose were pushed into the earth. He was choking me. I kicked him; with my last bit of strength I did what I could to save my life. Suddenly there was a machine-gun burst, extremely close. It came as unexpectedly as the soldier had a moment before. Bullets whistled right by us. There was a second burst, then a third. From under his bearish body I saw a lump of clay spattering only a few steps away from us. The soldier's fur cap jumped. The man started dragging me off, surprisingly he didn't beat me. And now another row of shots riddled the ground. But we were already safe behind a wall of trees, where we couldn't be seen from the window of the church steeple. That's where the fire was coming from. I didn't know whether it was a German machine gun or a Russian one, but it occurred to me that I wouldn't be able to stay there overnight if the place was full of soldiers. We were still lying on the ground, spattered with mud, breathing heavily, looking at one another. The soldier's face was dirty, sweaty, he must have had his last shave when the war began. He looked at me, then at the steeple. Finally, he said, *"Nu, malenki, nu, davail Bystro!"*

He got to his feet, lifted me up too, dragged me to the edge of the field where we would be safe. Suddenly he touched the top of his head. I realized at last that he was a Russian, that I was seeing my first Russian. And that actually I was the first in our village to greet him. I couldn't think of anything appropriate to say or to do. Maybe I should sing a national anthem or make a little speech. I was just rooted there like a wooden dummy, I didn't even mumble good day. Naturally, the Russian didn't find the cap on top of his head, since it was still lying in the furrow where it fell when we both hit the ground. He was looking around for it, he seemed to be more interested in his cap than in the machine gun in the steeple. Now he spotted it, but he would have had to cross open terrain where the Germans could riddle him with bullets. It was clear to me by now that it was the Germans who were up in the steeple. Naturally, the Russian did it: He dashed for his hat, was back again like lightning. He dove for it on his belly, bits of earth bursting all around him. I wouldn't have believed that earth could splash this way, like water. But then I would never have guessed that I'd get so close to the war, and that it would leave me so cold. The Russian was back, cleaning the cap with his sleeve. He blew on the velvet lining and set the cap on his bushy head. The Russians apparently have thick beards and hair. He was trying to tell me something, it sounded like melted Slovak, the sound was quite melodious. He was probably cursing a blue streak, he was furious that his cap was so dirty. There was a bullet hole in the cap, too, big enough to shove a finger through. Who knows what that fancy cap meant to him, maybe it was his talisman. I had no time for further deliberations, he shoved me toward the hollow. And now I was truly amazed! Nine or ten saddled horses were standing there! I had never seen such beautiful animals in my life, I couldn't take my eyes off them. Like statues! Compared to those, all horses I had seen before seemed fit only for the slaughterhouse.

"*Shto ty? Konya nevidel?*" You never saw a horse before? he was shouting at me. Now his speech was almost Czech. I was terribly surprised that Russian and Czech were so similar. I figured that there was some resemblance, but I had no idea that it was this close. I recalled our old grandpa saying that all Slavs have one mother.

The Russian lay down on the bank, an automatic with a round drum was resting on the ground, he must have left it there when he took off after me. The soldier pointed at the steeple. "German," he said, as casually as if he had said bread. He made a grimace to indicate that I had a close call, opening his eyes wide and rolling the whites comically. If it hadn't been for my tragic misfortunes, I would have burst out laughing. Anyhow, I kept staring at him entranced. And at his horses even more. "You . . . Slovak?" he asked.

I twisted my head.

His expression changed. "*Germanets?*" His voice became icier.

Again, I twisted my head. "*Neee,*" I said aloud.

"*Austriak?*"

I had no idea what an *Austriak* was.

"Vengrenets?"

The Russian was thinking up fantastic names.

I was silent, looking as forlorn as an abandoned child. Sometimes when I make a certain face I can imagine exactly the kind of expression other people are seeing on me. He started talking to me as if I was a congenital idiot. He pointed at himself.

"Ya Russki. Ty . . . ?" he pointed at me.

"Czech," I answered.

"Nyet." He seemed terribly surprised, he didn't seem to believe me. I don't know why.

"Ty Slovak," he repeated. For some reason, he was trying to turn me into a Slovak at all costs.

"Ne, Slovak," I answered. "Czech! Here is Moravia."

"Shto? Moravia?"

Moravia apparently complicated the whole matter. He started all over again. Decisively. He patted a piece of ground to make it smooth, drew a kind of big balloon with his finger, and labeled it CCCP. *"Sovetski soyuz,"* he said. *"Russia. Ya Russki,"* he repeated. *"Rus."* And he wrote it down *Pyc.* It surprised me that it is pronounced "Rus" but is written *Pyc.* He was drawing some kind of mice around the balloon. Then he pointed at one after another: *"Polsha . . . Vengriya . . . Austria . . . Germaniya."* He drew a long sausage hanging down from the balloon. The picture now resembled a sunflower or the head of a four-eared elephant.

"Czechoslovakia," he said. *"Da?"* He was waiting eagerly for my answer.

A terrible cannonade resounded from the church. Automatics, machine guns, rockets. Like on Corpus Christi.

"Nichevo," he calmed me. *"Nashi. Nemnoshko razgavarivayut s Germantsem. Ty Czech, da?"*

"Hmmm," I answered.

This discussion made me feel like a Turk. The racket from the church rocked the whole countryside. But it didn't bother the Russian one bit. He looked as if he not only grew up on the field of battle, but that he was born there. The Cossack horses in the hollow were also as calm as a bunch of turtles. They were chomping on last year's dry grass which stuck up from the ground like wires. They were unusually undemanding animals, they would have thrived on dry straw; it occurred to me that these would make excellent horses for my father. I couldn't take my eyes away from them. He asked me where I lived, I understood the word *"dom"* distinctly. Or maybe he was asking whether I wanted to go home, or telling me that I should be going home. I shook my head to indicate that it was impossible. I couldn't go home without Julie, I couldn't look Dad in the eye.

"Gde tvoi dom?" That I understood perfectly, he wanted to know where my home was. I shrugged my shoulders. I could have explained it to him in some kind of basic Slavic, but I pretended not to understand. The Russian sympathetically stroked my cheek. He interpreted my hesitation as meaning that I was homeless.

"The Germans killed your parents?" he asked. His broad, flat face was really full of pity. I blinked, which he probably took for an affirmative answer.

"Nichevo," he said, lifting up my chin. "Everything is all right. Don't worry." The shooting from the direction of the church sounded as if some fifty soldiers were exchanging fire. The Russian looked up. His automatic was lying nearby, so that he could intervene in the war any time he chose. He also pulled a hand grenade out of his pocket and placed it next to the automatic. He took an unbelievably casual attitude toward the battle, he still had enough time for chatting with me. In fact, I be-

143

lieve that he was more interested in our conversation than in the war.

"*Kak tebya zavut?*" he asked, while keeping a wary eye on the steeple. I wanted to take a look, too, but he pushed my head down below the crest of the hollow. He did it with all his strength, not at all gently. Then he renewed our sign-language discussion. He buried his thumbs in his soiled jacket.

"*Vasilyi,*" he said. "*Vanusha. Kak tebya zavut? Kak ty?*"

"Olda," I said.

"*Kak?*" He lifted his eyebrows in surprise.

He repeated my name several times, as if he wanted to memorize it. I would have loved to know what was going on at the church. But the soldier burst into noisy laughter. My name must have seemed comical to him. I don't know why. I don't know what's so uproarious about it. But he really guffawed, the sides of his nose were full of wrinkles. His face had a million twists and turns. I could just as easily have gone hysterical over the name Vasilyi, but I kept quiet.

"Olda *Czechia!*" the Russian was muttering to himself.

"Oldrich," I said, to calm him down. The Russian didn't stop laughing. He reached in his pocket and pulled out a small glass bottle. Actually, it looked more like a small test tube, no bigger than a little finger. A bit more globular than a test tube.

"Olda *Czechia, beri!*" He was roaring in his bass voice. The mysterious object was in the palm of my hand. It might have been a bulb for a flashlight, but it had no brass thread, it was made entirely of glass.

He guffawed, realizing that I had no inkling what it was. He touched me on the shoulder, almost knocking me down. In his leisure time he could amuse himself by wrestling elephants. Before I knew what was going on he stuck the bulb in my nose. Into one nostril. After the brawl in the woods my nose was in

144

pretty bad shape, and when he stuck that thing in my nostril it wasn't exactly a sensation of bliss. The Russians sure have some infernal customs! But the soldier was already pulling a mirror out of his pocket. It was actually no more than a sliver of glass, the silver was gone from the edges, only two or three square centimeters reflected like a mirror. I saw that I had a bubble at the tip of my nose, as if I had a cold and my nose was running. It was a fake running nose! The Russian was laughing so hard he was turning blue. Our faces were close to one another, we were lying on the bank of the hollow, between the grass and a tangled net of briar runners. I had to laugh too. I would never have guessed that Russians could be such fun. With my bubble I looked so ridiculous that I could have gone from door to door amusing little children.

I could hear myself hee-hawing in spite of all my troubles. He was the merriest soldier I'd ever met. I tried sticking the silly thing in the other nostril. An invention like that could make a person die of laughter. The village was sure to envy the bubble. Assuming, of course, that he was going to give it to me. Maybe he was only lending it for a little while. He might take it from me and stick it in somebody else's nose. For another minute or two the Russian and I rolled on the ground, screaming with laughter. In the middle of the front, no less! While soldiers were dying all around us!

All firing abruptly ceased. The air became completely still.

Questioningly I pointed at myself, asking whether I could keep the bubble forever.

"*Da,*" he said. I understood he meant yes.

"*Da?*" I pronounced the first Russian word in my life. A whistle as sharp as a whip resounded from the steeple. The Russian lifted his giant body from the grass. He stood at the edge of the field like a peacetime peasant. Another signal. And then a burst from a machine gun.

Vasilyi leaped on a horse, I didn't even notice how he managed to land on the middle one in a group of nine. He sat in the saddle like a gypsy baron. He certainly knew how to ride. He made no fuss, he simply squeezed the chestnut's flanks with his knees, and the horses dashed out of the hollow. He stopped for a moment at the edge of the plowed ground. He whistled at the horses when he wanted them to stop and when he ordered them to move. Each signal sounded different.

"Idi suda!" he said, waving his arm.

I was making rapid progress in Russian, it was clear that he was calling me. He pulled a piece of bread and a big hunk of bacon out of a worn leather pouch. *"Beri!"* he said, and tossed the food to me. *"Beri, beri!"* I still had the stupid bubble in my nose. To my liberator I must have looked like a real jerk. The Russian was once again off to the war, he was streaking across the field toward the church. He wasn't sitting in the saddle, he was almost standing, and he was shouting as loud as he could toward the stone steeple: *"Zdes uzhe Czechia!"* He was doubtless informing someone inside the church that this was Czech country. I tried to make out who was there, and in a while I saw the figures of other Russian soldiers. There seemed to be eight of them, Vasilyi was probably guarding their horses. He continued to shout, obviously pleased: *"Zdes Czechia!"*

I ran after him, the bubble fell out of my nostril, I almost stepped on it, I wiped it and put it in my pocket, I held the bread in one hand, the bacon in the other, I stumbled over clods, Iza right behind me, barking like mad. We were running in the tracks left by eight full-blooded horses, I couldn't get their firm backs, long legs and silky necks out of my head. He didn't have to give me any bubble, or bread, or bacon, I would have settled for just one horse. Maybe he would have thrown in the bubble anyway. Now at last I began to realize that the war was over, that the Russians had come. By the time I reached the church it was all over, nine riders on nine fiery horses were already past the cemetery wall, the soldiers were galloping down into the valley, they were streaking along among the lindens. I put down the bread and meat, and climbed up on top of the cemetery wall to get a better view. I was curious to see where they were going in such a hurry. They were aiming for the manor. The manor yard, too, seemed to be full of horses. In my excitement I hardly breathed; what if they were to give me a gift of a horse? Or else they have so many that I could . . . I dismissed the second possibility; it would be most unfair, they had come here all the way from Moscow and I was thinking of robbing them. All the same, for an instant I saw myself galloping up to our house one fine day, leading a string of eight beautiful horses behind me. No, I revised my dream: four would be enough. In fact, I would settle for two. I would like to come home riding at least one fine horse. An animal as strong and smart as Julie. Maybe even a little stronger. There are many kinds of horses. I'd bring the biggest, strongest, sleekest. Calmly I would knock on the gate. Dad would come out, his eyes bulging. I would show him the animal's hooves, teeth, I would lie down and have the horse step over me. But then a much more likely scene came to my mind, with Dad doing all the performing. Already I could feel stinging sensations in certain parts of my body.

I sat perched on the cemetery wall, I could no longer see the soldiers. The sun was just going down, but it wouldn't be completely dark for a while yet. I turned to the church. Smoke was streaming out of the steeple window, or perhaps it was a cloud of dust. Something must have been going on there, maybe the steeple was on fire. In many places the wall was pitted with shell marks. The beautiful stained glass windows were shot to pieces. I jumped off the wall.

I stood at the crossroads, one road leading to the manor and the other to the village. I tried to make up my mind. After a moment of hesitation I started off in the direction of the Russians. They were my only hope if I ever wanted to return home. And even though my own home was a Sing Sing, strangely enough I did want to go back. At this point the possibility of getting my hands on some horses no longer seemed so hopeless. I set out toward the lindens, the willow copse, in the direction of the red roofs of the manor.

Later on, I found that while I was standing on the cemetery wall live Germans were still inside the church. Two of the six who earlier manned the machine gun in the steeple. They entered the church in the course of the day, while the boys and I were in the woods. After the exchange of fire with the Russians, both of them were mortally wounded, but they were still on their feet. I was told that they came out of the church, leaning against each other, and stumbled toward the woods. One of them had no jacket, only trousers and a shirt. And his back was split wide open, covered in blood, the flesh mangled. They collapsed in the middle of the field and died there during the night.

CHAPTER SIX

Iza was snapping at the bacon. I lifted it out of her reach. Then, holding the loaf of bread between my knees to get my hands free, I pulled out my switchblade, sniffed the bacon, sliced off a piece. I cut a slice for the dog, too. The bread looked like a brick, it was as hard as a brick, too. I made my way down the slope, to the linden tree. It was my tree, the one I always climbed. Rockets were still rattling. Louder and louder. At times it sounded as if something enormously heavy was tumbling to the ground, like a wagon load of barrels. Tremendous rumbling. The sun had vanished, leaving a few light strips across the sky. A fairly decent evening, except for the war. I stumbled across a spool of some kind of wire. It was lying in the grass. I stopped chewing.

I looked around. Nobody. The spool was made of metal tubes, it had straps for carrying on the back. I bent down and turned the drum. It moved quite easily. The piece of wire that was lying in the grass began to wind itself up. First-class rubber insulated wire. Naturally, I had no intention of letting such a fine piece of equipment just lie there, for some stupid fool to pick up. The spool weighed a ton, I could hardly lift it. Behind a barren apple tree grew some briars, close to the ground they were so thick that they made a wall. That's where I dragged the spool, scratching my arms on the thorns. Then I marked the spot. I placed two rocks on top of another rock, and stuck a stick in the ground. So I wouldn't have to search for a month to find the stuff. The briars grew wild. I picked up the bread and meat which I had put on a branch of the apple tree to keep it from the dog, and continued on my way. To the linden.

Remarkably enough, I didn't even have to take a running jump to climb the tree, and I was weighed down by a shirtful of bacon to boot. (I left the bread below, on a stump.) I hoisted myself up like an acrobat. Actually, I paused to admire my performance only after I was safely ensconced up above. I squirreled my way up to the very top, where the branches make their last fork. I sat on one side of the Y, put my feet on the other side. I ate the smoked meat, now and then throwing little pieces down to Iza.

For bacon she had a nose like radar. Whether I threw a morsel right at her feet or far away, she found it at once. When it came to locating chow she was a superb dog. It occurred to me to pull the glass bubble out of my pocket. I had stuck it in my nose, while I was eating. Then I remembered the cigarette case, and hurriedly felt for it all over my body. It was stuck in the back of my shirt, practically under my shorts. I opened it.

I remembered that one side of the case—the one that didn't have the naked woman—was made of shiny metal. I saw myself as clearly as in a mirror. The German had really given me quite a shiner. I stuck the bubble back in my pocket. The case, too. I didn't feel like eating any more. I licked my skinned knees, scraping off flakes of dried blood with my nail.

"You've had enough," I told the begging dog. "Go catch a mouse!"

Once more, I climbed the linden, to the very tip this time.

One thing that's peculiar about a war is that you continually hear shooting, but you never know where it's coming from or where it's directed. The countryside looked quite normal. Bluish. A haze was floating over the land. The sun had gone, but hills, fields, roads, roofs were still visible. I kept gazing longingly toward the manor, it seemed packed full of horses! Behind the stables. Something was moving around there, it just had to be horses . . .

The time when Julie gave birth to a dead foal, I gave her the carrot for which my father sent me. Then I drew near to Dad. I didn't know what to do, but I wanted to do something. He was lying motionless on a pile of straw behind the stall. Right next to the dead foal. But he was no longer crying. He was just lying there. A wave of tenderness swept over me. "Dad," I said. My chin was trembling. I wanted to touch him, though there had never been any fondling between us.

But he had already gotten to his feet. Quite violently. He almost knocked me over. He began stuffing the mare's manger with hay. His motions were rapid, fierce. He was once more his old self.

"You'll have two horses before you're twenty!" he said. It was his credo, the goal of all his striving. He didn't look at me. He went out to fetch water, carrying a pair of heavy metal pails on his shoulders.

Now, again and again, a thought kept coming back to me; when I returned home, I would stand by the wall, swallowed by Father's shadow. I wouldn't be able to see the light bulb behind his head, I wouldn't be able to distinguish the details of his face.

The German had a knife, Dad. He wanted to kill me.

I'll kill you, he'd say.

There was only one occasion in my whole life when I was really happy. The day the ice floed. The morning country-

side was bare, already denuded of snow. Cold. It was a countryside of black poplars and bare, wiry shrubs. The school was
in the neighboring village. We used to cross the bridge. Even
in those days, I had already formed the habit of lagging behind the boys, to keep them from stuffing my schoolbag full
of apple cores and rocks. We stopped just before the bridge.
The air was filled by a quiet, distant scraping.

Then somebody shouted, "Here come the floes!"

We started running to the bridge. The sound of the ice was
getting louder as we neared the river. A pale sun floated
into view. The boys threw down their schoolbags in a heap
and scampered down the bank to the water. A few pieces of
ice were tossed by the river up on the grassy bank. They were
sparkling, melting, their sides were glassy smooth. In the bend
of the river every passing floe bumped against the bank. A
willow bent over the water at that point. They climbed it, then
jumped onto the passing slabs. They tried to pick out the
ones that would be able to carry them. Chumsky almost
sank, his shoes filled with water, but he was afloat. There went
others. They jumped, shouting.

The girls were on top of the bank, standing in a row like a
bunch of hens. Whatever we did, the girls, always just in
the background, nudged each other with their elbows and
watched. I laid down my bag. An irresistible itch to show off
before the gang and the girls came over me. I climbed the
willow. Kudera turned on his floe.

"You better say a prayer first, Pinda."

Anna left the girls and moved closer. She didn't dare come
all the way to the willow, she stopped on the bank, looking
at me. She was wearing a bright kerchief on her head. Her
satchel was on her back. I knew that she was worried about me,
which seemed ridiculous. It spurred me on to take the greatest
possible risk. I jumped, landed on all fours, the floe swayed,
scooped up water, the tip split off. Anna was walking along

152

the bank. At times she had to run, the current was carrying the floe quite rapidly.

"You'll be late to school!" shouted the girls.

They were going across the bridge. Anna stopped, then ran after them. At the next bend the floes hit the bank and the boys jumped to the ground. They dashed back for their schoolbags. Kudera, Chumsky, Rez, Vyska, Jozka, too. A big piece of drift ice was lying on the shore. They were pelting me with chunks of ice, waiting for me to get off. But then their mouths dropped. I didn't jump ashore. The bend gradually straightened, I left the still water for the open, broad river. I was surrounded by a million floes.

"Pindaaaa!" they screamed.

"What are you doing, you crazy fool!"

"You'll drown!"

The voices receded behind me. I was surrounded by the rustle of ice. White birds were wheeling over the river on broad wings. My eyes were full of those birds, their necks and wings. And the distant morning sun. I was floating directly into it. The river was straight and wide . . .

Now the loudest explosion I had heard yet came crashing down on my head. Instinctively I clutched the linden branch with both arms. I turned my head. They'd hit the church! Stones and bricks came tumbling down, smoke and dust rose all the way up to the bell. The air was thick with pigeons.

Quickly I slid down, forgetting the bacon up in the branches, and I had to go back up for it again. At last I was in the grass, next to Iza. I grabbed the dog by her collar, stroking her nose, to make sure she stayed close to me.

I didn't know who was continually sending up colored rockets, in such large numbers. I heard muffled rumbling, like the sound of a train going through a tunnel. Using Chumsky's method, I put my ear to the ground. The only thing my ear picked up was a swarm of ants. My neck was full of them, too. I tried to slap off the stinging little beasts with my hand.

At last I made up my mind which way to proceed. What do you know, three more spools of wire were lying right behind the next bush! It was incredible, all the junk one comes across at the end of a war. I jogged toward the willow copse, along the high-tension wires. Some torn wires were lying across the road. I jumped over them. Or carefully walked around them. I was scared of fallen wires. Two pylons had toppled across the road. There were two huge holes in the ground, and a string of smaller craters.

This surprised me. I hadn't seen any craters yesterday. I picked up a piece of metal, the fragment of a mine or grenade, with jagged edges. I tested the sharpness of the edge against the back of my hand. I felt like stuffing the fragment in my pocket, but it would probably have torn it. Instead I stuck the bacon inside my shirt, against my bare body, and carried the fragment in my hand. I sprinted past the reeds, toward the willows. There was the roar of more giant barrels tumbling to the ground. But I was already squeezing by the willow branches, to a certain spot I had in mind. I peered around impatiently, afraid somebody might have already swiped the motorcycle. But then I turned around and there it was right in front of me. I breathed easier. I circled the machine, after looking it over carefully. Everything was still there just as they'd left it. Even the civilian hats which the three Germans had wanted to put on and then decided to leave behind. I kicked one of the hats, it made an arc in the air. Iza fetched it at once, and laid it at my feet. She thought I was playing games with her. The machine gun was still lying on the ground, too. And a pile of clothes. I examined the cycle and the sidecar from up close, after laying down the grenade fragment. Carefully I grasped the handlebars, stepped on the running board, swung my leg to the other side, warily planted my rear on the leather seat. I must have pressed some button or another, the horn blurted out. My hand jerked back as if it had touched a snake. I almost toppled off the machine, the blare of that horn must have been heard in Mesopotamia. I sat still for a while, nervously, but the willow copse seemed deserted. Under the network of branches there was deep darkness. I pushed the sidecar down with my arm, to test its springs. The sidecar fascinated me, I climbed into it. It had a comfortable seat, but something was lying under my bottom. I loved the shiny yellow tip of the sidecar. I groped around and found what I was sitting on. It was a metal cylinder with a handle. Must be a hand grenade. Carefully I laid it down on the ground. A metal can on the floor prevented me from stretching my legs. I pulled it out, it contained ammunition belts. Moravia was so full of ammunition there'd be enough for two more wars. I stood up, lifted the seat by the springs. It was removable. I shook off the dirt and other junk, put it back in place. It was covered by shiny oilcloth. Smooth, very pleasant to the touch.

I licked my finger to wipe off a muddy spot on the seat. Then I sat down again, stretched out my legs, took a firm grip on the sides. How I would love to have taken such a machine for a spin around the Masaryk Oval! Or to burn up the curves in an endurance race! But nobody was at the controls, I climbed back on the motorcycle. I touched the pedals with the tips of my toes, careful to stay away from the horn button. A pair of goggles was lying on the ground next to the front wheel. They had an elastic strap at the back. I picked them up, put them on. They were big enough for two heads like mine. I was sitting in the willow copse, but mentally I was tearing through our village in a cloud of dust.

It was Corpus Christi day. Fresh grass had been scattered over the road. Maidens were tossing basketfuls of flowers before my motorcycle. Mr. Kelba was leading the band. The firemen were marching carrying a panoply over my head. There were four of them: old Kudera, Vyska, Chumsky, and Rez. As always they were wearing purple sashes, ceremonial swords glittered at their sides. I put on a little speed, the procession drove into a trot. I went faster, and the procession was running at full tilt. The maidens scattered. But I was after the four dumb ministrants—Koo-Koo-Kudera, Chumsky the Chump, Rez-Fez, Vyska-Pisska, I was going to run those idiots over! I yelled at them to run faster. They would if they could, they puffed like locomotives. Chumsky's gown slipped down, his legs got tangled up. All four of them were collapsing to the ground, wringing their hands imploringly. They were on their knees, weeping copiously. But I ran over them all the same, the jackasses!

Or imagine taking the motorcycle to school in the morning. After a heavy rain, I could splash those four little stinkers from head to foot. I'd give a ride only to Jozka . . . Or I could take the family for an outing. I'd put Mom in the sidecar, Dad could sit behind me. I'd give Mother the goggles to keep the dust out of her eyes. We'd arrive at Rosice, on the square, and pull up in front of the store of F. NEBOZES. AUTO-MOTO-VELO—PARTS AND SERVICE. He'd be waiting for us. He'd come out of the store, look the motorcycle over, then reach in his shirt and pull out a wad of bills. A kilo of banknotes. I'd hand them over to Dad, we'd go to the horse market and pick out a mare. One that looked just like Julie.

But this was only imagination and I was alone in the willow copse. I covered the motorcycle with armfuls of dry branches. Behind the brick hut there was a large pile of last year's grass. I hauled armfuls of it till I was ready to drop. I wanted to cover the motorcycle so thoroughly that nobody could guess there was anything hidden under the branches. A light flashed behind the hill. Dusk had already fallen. A rocket burst, and a magnesium ball lit up the sky, giving off a dazzling brightness, as it slowly descended. Every part of the countryside stepped forward out of the darkness.

I started busily storing my new treasures in the hut—the shell fragment, the grenade, the goggles—in my old hiding place with the fireman's helmet, axe, and belt. I plugged up the hole once again with bricks, spaced them out carefully. The bacon and bread were lying in a recess in the wall. I examined the bacon; only a tiny morsel was left from that huge slab the Russian had given me. A stuffed Iza was resting on the floor. She didn't even bother to get to her feet when I stepped over her. She was panting.

A magnesium flare had burned itself out, once again the sky was dark. I stepped outside the hut, Iza crawled after me in a shamefully lazy way. She stretched herself, yawning so lustily that it frightened me.

"Quiet!"

The neighing of horses and the sounds of hooves could be heard quite distinctly from the direction of the manor. But I could not concentrate. I had some urgent business in the bushes, letting down my pants even before I got there.

When I squatted down, over my head there were willow branches and the universe. I had never seen so many stars in the sky before, I had never seen the Milky Way so bright. Everything was calm and peaceful. Not a single shot could be heard.

"Iza," I whispered from the bush. "Iza!"

She ambled over. I wanted to have her near me. I wasn't scared, but in the glow of the sky the bushes took on fantastic forms and shadows, they looked like human figures. I was down on my haunches, trousers hanging round my knees, holding Iza with both hands by her fluffy neck.

Then I really became a bit frightened. Quite a bit. A cloud crossed the sky, the stars disappeared. The night no longer had the tiniest crack, the light vanished from the world. I groped in the blackness, took a few steps then stopped.

The night had its own sounds, grass was growing, dew was falling. I wanted to know where that continuous, barely audible whisper was coming from. I held Iza by the collar, pressed her close to my body. I wanted to feel her beside me, the mutt. She made me feel better.

"Don't be scared," I spoke to her, so as to hear my own voice. My whisper seemed to stick to my palate. "There are no ghosts in the world. Don't be scared." The dog wasn't scared at all. She yawned loudly, practically splitting her jaws. She had a mouth as big as a rucksack. Then she clicked her teeth. Anybody who has ever heard a dog yawning in the middle of the night, when there is complete silence, knows what an awful sound it is. It sounded almost as if something was moaning all around me. Iza always yawned three times. In between she licked herself and smacked her lips. A regular symphony for the mouth.

"Quiet, you mutt." I tugged her collar.

I took a few more steps.

"Lie down, go to sleep."

Of course, I only said it for the hell of it. Ironically, she lay down at once. Certain commands she probably knows, even in foreign languages. She plopped down right on my feet.

"Get up!"

Her intelligence could drive a person crazy. I heard my own breathing in the dark. I still didn't know just where I was. The country is deceptive at night. I pulled her up by the collar to stand on all fours. My eyes scanned all suspicious-looking forms. The bushes had human silhouettes. A rocket burst. It almost made me feel better. The light broke up into a hundred sparks, the shrubs became clearly visible. I saw a stick lying on the ground. It came in handy.

"Shut up," I said to the dog. "I won't use it on you."

And then I almost stumbled over the stick myself. Somewhere far away a single gun was firing, like the hammering of a woodpecker. I broke a useless twig off the stick. Armed this way I felt safer. Nearby shadows looked like a group of four human figures. It was dark once more.

"Nobody's there," I reassured Iza. "Those are just trees."

I felt a clod underfoot, picked it up and flung it into the darkness. In the direction of the shadows. I heard the sound of twigs snapping, a partridge flapped out of the bushes.

"A bird," I said to the dog. "It's only a partridge."

This calmed me down. I started to whistle quietly. But only for a little while. My lips felt as if I had fever. They were thick and dry. I was still moving toward the manor. Suddenly I came upon a road where there really shouldn't have been one.

I stayed rooted to the spot, craning my head all around. The unexpected discovery of a road confused me completely. In the darkness you can go in a completely wrong direction without realizing it. The stars were covered by a black blanket. I couldn't see a thing as long as that damned cloud was around. Iza began to whimper.

"Stop it!" I had no time for discussions. She didn't want to move, I had to drag her by the collar.

"What are you scared of?" I looked around. I couldn't see anything, because there was nothing to be seen. "That thing over there?"

I pointed at a black spot between black trees. The dog continued to whine quietly.

"What would anybody be doing here, you silly mutt?"

But there was a slight quake in my voice. She worried me. I picked up another lump of clay and threw it. But with less assurance. I hunched down. But all I heard was the soothing sound of twigs. Nothing more. I leaned back against a tree, it was full of branches. I lifted my eyes, but I couldn't see the top. It dissolved into the inky darkness.

I pulled a piece of string out of my pocket and tied Iza to the tree. I didn't want her to skip away. I'd had some bad experiences in that regard. Then I climbed the tree, to see what I could see from the top; maybe a light in the window like a fairy tale. But Iza was ruining everything, the stupid ninny. As soon as I started shinnying up the trunk she let out a howl. I hadn't even reached the first branch. I told her in a furious whisper to shut up. She was getting on my nerves. I slid down, comforted her like a baby. You get more out of Iza with kindness than with anger. I scrambled back up. For an instant all was quiet. I reached up for the second branch. Iza barked so loud that it must have been heard in Amsterdam.

"Shut up! Or I'll kill you." I tried to balance myself in the branches. Down below, she was barking like mad. I fell down. She was making such a racket that I lost my grip. As soon as I hit the ground she stopped barking, shifted into an ingratiating whine. I hit my tail end so hard that my whole body was aching. I stood up, kicked at her, she took it as a game. When I untied the rope she tried to lick my face. For a moment there was a break in the clouds, tiny stars dotted the heavens. Now I knew which way to go. I hadn't really drifted too far off course. But Iza was resisting. I had to drag her along. Rockets were trailing across the sky, they all seemed to be coming from the same spot. I watched the luminous scribbles, curious whether they were German or Russian. I dropped into a hole, up to my waist. Iza jerked loose, remained standing at the edge. I was sure she saw the hole, dogs have a much better instinct for getting around in the dark than humans. I scrambled out.

"Those are for planting trees," I explained to the dog, quite unnecessarily. Another dark-blue interval, without rockets.

"Husarek is going to plant apple trees here. After the war." I brushed the mud off my pants. We walked down the slope, avoiding holes. Again I picked up a lump of clay, to toss at nearby shadows of trees. They were probably the reason why Iza was whimpering. Now the shadows looked more like bushes. And there were more and more of them. I reached back, but I never had a chance to toss the clod of clay.

A magnesium flare lit up the sky, making the night as bright as high noon during harvesttime. In no time at all I was lying on the ground, right on top of the dog. A volley of shots resounded from the river.

In front of me, at the other end of the field, was a swarm of soldiers. Germans!

Their helmets were camouflaged with nets holding small branches, like the soldiers I saw sleeping in the woods. I saw the soldiers quite clearly, they were light gray against the dark shrubbery behind them. They were moving in a single file up to the church. I didn't bother to count them. I was crouching with Iza behind a mound of earth, holding tight, trying to merge with the animal and the ground. The light suddenly went out, as if somebody turned a switch. The Germans were passing quite close to me, I distinctly heard their steps, their heavy breathing, now and then the jingle of equipment. Then I saw the silhouettes of men against the sky. They were maintaining an almost identical space between each man. I was holding Iza's nose with both hands. She was usually at her wildest when she was supposed to be quiet. She didn't even realize that lives were at stake. Another magnesium ball came floating down. I could no longer hear or see the soldiers. Maybe it was only a dream. Maybe there were no soldiers at all.

In the stark yellow light the countryside now looked bare. I listened but could no longer hear anything. Only now I began to realize what I was probably lying on. I was almost certain. It was not a mound of earth. In fright a person loses his sense of smell. In April our fields are generally not only full of tree holes but full of manure piles as well. I wiped my hands on the grass. In spring, manure is at its smelliest. I was holding Iza to keep her from dashing off. She was still agitated, I couldn't tell what was bothering her. To be on the safe side I took a careful look around; once in a blue moon she really scents something important. But everything seemed as calm as in peacetime. No doubt, the Germans were already far away.

Then it occurred to me that perhaps those weren't Germans after all. And I realized that the haystacks I saw were right behind the manor wall. There were a million stars in the sky. The moon had risen, too, the countryside was bathed in a white glow. I was no longer afraid. The manor seemed deserted, I could only make out walls and roofs. Not a sign of life. Had it really been full of horses?

I could not see the fence, it was behind the trees. I headed for the stack. Slowly, dragging my feet. Once there I could get a look to see what was going on. But the stack brought up a sad memory.

It was snowing heavily, snow rustled over the stubble. I strode across the field, leaving a zigzagging line of footprints behind me, my schoolbag bobbing on my shoulder. I heard their voices through the white curtain:

"Pindaaa, let's have those caps!"

I had seized three fur caps of the boys. War booty. I was stuffing them furiously with snow and straw.

"Pindaaaaaa!" they shouted from afar. All the way from the road. I walked around the long wall of the stack, to get a better look at them without them seeing me. I gulped. I no longer heard the yelling of the boys. In the snow in front of me was Ludvik's box, his rose-colored puppet theater. It had canvas shoulder straps, and up on top there was a wire loop with bells. Ten little bells. The box was leaning against the stack. Several puppets were hanging on the outside of the box, Ludvik always carried them that way. And then I saw Ludvik's legs, his black socks, his white spats. They were sticking out of the snow. I was afraid to lift my eyes any further.

Then I screamed and ran back across the field, stumbling, shouting. In my rush I lost all the caps.

I can still see Ludvik the Spats before me, alive. It is summer, the sky is blue, the grain is ripening. White, dusty road. We hear his bells. I will never forget them, they had a melody that captured my whole childhood, they sounded like the wings of angels, like all the days forever gone by. We are cavorting in the dry river bed, jumping from rock to rock. Ludvik is on the bridge. We call his name, wave our arms. We are showing him the snake we found. He is watching us, but he never answers. He has a large, sad face, which seems to be made of flour. Yellow eyes. The performance takes place in the tavern that evening. I inch my way to the stage crawling between the chairs. Somebody kicks me, but I don't mind. I am not watching the play, I am watching Ludvik. They can't see him from up front, he is hidden behind a little curtain. But I see him. He is big, beautiful. He moves the puppets, talks for them, smoking a cigarette as if he was swallowing it. He notices me, we know each other. He makes a grimace at me. He knows how to make a hundred faces, maybe a thousand. They are all merry. Later, I wait impatiently in our barn for the hen to lay an egg. She is taking her time. I am in a hurry, but there is nothing I can do. At last she starts to cluck. I stick the warm egg in my pocket, careful not to break it. Ludvik is waiting for me at the bend of the river, under the willows. The pink cabinet is propped against a tree. He was bathing. I had never seen such a skinny fellow in my life. He must have had fifty ribs. I pull six eggs out of my pockets. He taps them open and sucks them up raw. He is "ironing" his pants on a flat rock; they are stretched out, with other flat rocks piled on top of the creases. I sit down, wait. He is combing his thin hair with a piece of comb. I want to hand him the towel sticking out of the pink cabinet, but he reaches for it himself and closes the cabinet. I had always wanted to take a peek into that mysterious box, but I never succeeded. Then he smiles, pulls out a little wooden box. He winds it up with a key, and the box plays music. It was the first real music I ever heard. Ludvik began to dance. His hopping was not comic, but beautiful. After a while he stopped, out of breath. I applauded. . . .

After I found him dead by the side of the stack, a crowd of people gathered in no time. The snow kept falling, it was bitter cold, breath flowed from the mouth and nose like steam. Singer, the owner of the manor, some of his hired help, Kudera, Vitlich, they were all there. They pulled Ludvik out of the straw, placed him on a make-shift stretcher. In death, Ludvik's mouth was open, snowflakes were falling on his lips. Singer opened the pink cabinet with the metal tip of his walking cane. There was the sound of bells. The puppets fell out. Every time Singer touched the cabinet, the bells kept ringing.

"Go on home!" a woman was chasing us away. "This is not for children!" The priest was pushing his bicycle over the frozen *ground, in ear muffs and mittens, wearing high felt boots like a peasant. I could tell he was itching with curiosity.*

"Vitlich," said Singer. "What's in there, in that cabinet?"

Cyril opened the pink doors, pulled out a metal box and handed it to Singer. "An urn!" somebody said in surprise. "How about that, an urn!" They read the inscription KARLA MA-CHOTKOVA. It seemed extremely coarse to me, the way they were prying into Ludvik's belongings. But Vitlich was already shoving everything back into the pink cabinet. Perhaps he was bothered by the same idea. They put the cabinet under Ludvik's feet. Two coachmen from the manor were carrying the corpse, with the white spats sticking out. I stayed on the other side of the stack, crying. A crowd of people was still standing around, blabbing nonsense.

"Don't cry for him," said Cyril. "He is better off where he is."

At last they all started to leave, following the stretcher over the bumpy, stubbly field. The priest was bringing up the rear, discussing the event with Singer and Kudera. Somebody was pushing the bicycle for him.

"He's made it, and we still have to get there," said Cyril.

Now I was standing next to that same haystack. I still couldn't make out anything over at the manor. I stepped carefully, trying not to make a noise in the straw. The complex of buildings looked quite deserted.

But I heard noises, they sounded like the drawing of water. I seemed to recognize human voices. Now and then, when I stopped and listened attentively I heard the jingling of bridles.

"Will you sit quietly?" I whispered to Iza.

I tried to decide which side of the stack would be easiest to climb. Somewhere in the dark space over my head a plane was buzzing. "Will you wait here like a good dog?" The mutt put on her saintly expression. I began to climb up over the ricks.

I threw a suspicious look at Iza. She was following orders, sitting quietly. The drone of the plane was getting louder.

I was great at climbing stacks. I even paused to let go with my hands and wipe my nose.

"Quiet, Iza!" I hissed, just in case. With members of a stupid race you never know what kind of trick they'll pull next. Iza neither whined nor barked, she had lifted her head and seemed to be watching me.

The night had brightened considerably, when I looked up at the inky sky I saw streaming clouds, driven by the wind. But at the stack the air was calm. A loose tile creaked. I noticed soldiers on the top floor. I couldn't make them out distinctly, they were only shadows in the dormer window. There were three or four of them, and they seemed to be clustered around a weapon, probably a machine gun. They were wearing the same caps as the Cossack I'd met. They were Russians. I climbed still higher, now I could see some soldiers in front of the gate, too. I wondered what they were doing, they were stripped down to their shirts digging holes in front of the gate, facing the woods. They worked quickly, silently, their figures merging into the gray night. Now and then I heard the ring of a spade or hoe striking a rock. I was lying on my stomach, the straw seemed to be rustling terribly loud, I hardly dared move. The soil continued to crunch rhythmically under the soldiers' tools. The plane was directly overhead now, although I couldn't see it because in wartime planes have no lights. At last I saw what was happening: the Russians had closed the gates of the manor, but they had dug a trench underneath. They were working in shifts, emerging on the outer side as if they had sprung up out of the ground.

I kept hearing the sound of pumping and the flow of water coming from the yard. I had to stand up to see over the roofs.

And to climb to the very top of the stack. The yard was full of soldiers, a hundred, maybe more. They were gathered around the pump, undressed, some of them stark naked. Their bodies gave off a whitish shine. They were washing themselves. I would have frozen to death, I freeze even without washing. But the Russians seemed to be made for winter. They come from Siberia. They doused each other with bucketfuls of water. The pump turned and creaked. Somebody yelped, started cursing furiously, in their Russian language it sounded quite melodious. It is a peculiar, smooth language, pronounced quickly, one word merging with another.

The sky was again aflame with magnesium. The plane must have been dropping flares. Everybody in the yard dashed for cover, under the nearest roof. In the light I saw clearly that they really were nude, at least some of them. They were covering themselves with their hands, laughing, they found their situation comical. I could see their weapons stacked under the roof with their guns and saddles. I wriggled deeper into the straw, until my body was completely covered. But I could still see. The Russians had closed the wooden shutters over the dormer. The soldiers in front of the gate were spread out on the ground like corpses. One of them moved, sliding into the trench. The greenish fireball sank toward the woods, turning in the air, throwing off small glowing dribbles. The yard was lit up so that the tiniest detail stood out. A thin silver trickle was coming out of the pump faucet. The wheel of the pump was still trembling. A pile of Russian uniforms was heaped up on the bench. But I was looking around to see where they kept their horses. Where could they be . . . ? Calmly I stood up. To hell with the plane. The horses were all the way in the back, I could see them now, they were under the trees, the crowns are so thick over there that they make a roof. I would have to walk around the entire manor in order to get there. Several signal rockets came flying out of the woods, red, white, another red one, blue. The plane had answered with its own rockets, red and white. The magnesium went out. I flopped down in the straw. Two steps away from me a machine gun opened up. At least it seemed to be a few steps away. An unbelievable racket broke out. The Russians were firing at the plane from the dormer. The whole window was lit up by a wreath of fire. It probably lasted only ten or twenty seconds. After the last burst, there was a deafening silence. I felt great pressure in my ears. I turned over on my back, toward the sky. I couldn't see anything. I heard the plane faintly, it had climbed higher. They missed. I lost interest in the plane, turned again toward the yard. Nothing was happening, the machine gun was silent. After a few moments, though, a voice thundered in Russian:

"Who fired?" When I now recall that booming bass voice, I am convinced it could only have come from a direct descendant of Taras Bulba. *"Katoryi durak strelal?"* What idiot opened fire? Somebody ran furiously up stairs. I could hear him clearly, his voice would have been heard in Moscow without a telephone. He was screaming in Russian about the mother of a certain soldier. He must have been in a real fit.

"Who ordered you to shoot? Haven't you got any brains at all? I'll teach you . . ."

"Tavarish litinant," I heard a second, youthful voice. "I only thought . . . I wanted . . . I saw him . . ." he tried to explain.

I couldn't understand why the soldier was apologizing. I would have shot at the German plane myself.

I understood many words. "I saw him clearly . . ."

The tone of voice indicated that the soldier's legs were buckling.

"Davai suda!" the lieutenant bellowed. "Here, quickly! Let me tell you a few things in basic Tartar!" I didn't hear the Tartar part of the conversation. Both voices trailed off. Either they stopped talking, or they went down to the cellar. The plane had become silent, too. Calm reigned once again, the night hummed and rustled. I craned my neck toward the horses. Once again, I heard bridles. And hooves. For me these were the most beautiful sounds of all.

I crawled on my belly to the edge of the stack, then carefully slid down the side. Again I thought I was making a devilish racket. Straw dust irritated my nose, I was dying to sneeze. I squeezed my nose between my palms as hard as I could, it's a wonder I didn't crush it. I was looking for the dog.

"Iza," I whispered. "Iza, where are you?" She wasn't there. I couldn't believe that she ran away. Maybe she was frightened by the machine gun and was waiting somewhere nearby. I had enough to worry about without tiptoeing around the stack like an idiot looking for the mutt. I didn't find her.

That made me mad. I sat in the grass, actually I was almost lying down, propped on my elbows. The Russians were still digging trenches. I didn't feel like going anywhere, a despondent mood came over me again. I might have sulked there for hours, and in the end maybe even gone home, if I hadn't heard a hedgehog moving in the grass. I held my breath. Was he on my left or on my right? He waited, he heard me too. Or maybe he smelled me. Now he was coming closer, he was almost next to my leg. Hedgehogs don't give a damn about the war. I shot up my rear end, got to my knees, grabbed for him. He was one big ball of quills, but I had him. No hedgehog had ever succeeded in getting away from me. I lay down on my stomach before the pincushion, I gently blew into the ball where I thought his nose must be. "I've got you!" I told him. "You're mine!" I took off my jacket, rolled the hedgehog onto it, and lifted him up by the corners. Once again I had company. It's amazing how such a small thing could make so much difference. Carrying the hedgehog I set out to circle the manor. I was walking on tiptoe to avoid making any noise. Naturally, I was aiming for the enclosure. I seized a handful of green alfalfa and threw it inside my coat, for the hedgehog. I tossed in a few crumbs of bread for him, too.

I was going to tear Iza in two when I found her. I kept on looking for the miserable beast, quietly smacking my lips.

"Iza!"

At last I had to forget about her: I mustn't alarm the Russians. I stalked along like an Indian. I covered one stretch so silently that I didn't hear my own footsteps. I couldn't imagine that they'd simply left the horses there unguarded. I am not that naïve. I didn't expect anything of the sort. I stood at the edge of the shadow cast by a growth of brambles. Between me and the enclosure there was an illuminated strip of ground, transparent and treacherous as glass. Now, when I was praying for darkness, the sky was radiant with moon and stars. I darted my eyes here and there, I knew the Russian guard must be around somewhere; he *had* to be. But where?

Behind the bright strip there was another little island of shrubs. From there I'd have the enclosure and the horses in the palm of my hand. Somewhere there was shooting, but I no longer paid any attention to it. Maybe the guard was standing behind the two trees that were so close they were touching each other. If he was, I would never be able to spot him, and he couldn't be anywhere else.

I saw the horses quite distinctly. There was a whole herd of them squeezed into the enclosure, they were standing in groups, barely moving. Even from the distance I clearly made out their uplifted necks, strong backs. Now and then, for no apparent reason, they would break into a nervous run, their hooves making a muffled sound. Then calm would come again. I could have watched them for a hundred years. The advancing night grew colder. I sat down, hedgehog in my coat, coat in my lap, knees under my chin.

Among the horses there were a few light-colored ones, like Julie. I started to count all the horses in the corral. Then the gate of the stable banged shut. I heard voices, and rose to my feet. It was by sheer luck that I didn't give myself away, because only a few steps away, right behind the other side of the shrubs, a muffled voice said, *"Litinant!"*

"Kuda tebe nado?" murmured a second Russian voice.

"Vypuskayet patrol," answered the first.

They entered the strip of light, long, flowing coats, fur caps, guns slung over their shoulders. Their soles must have been made of felt, I couldn't hear the slightest sound. They were crossing over to the enclosure. One of them kept looking warily over his shoulder. I took a deep breath at last.

I don't know how to describe the gray luminosity of that April night, the fairy-tale quality of the silent stride of the two Cossacks, the calm dignity of their silhouettes. I want you to try and put yourself in my shoes as I stood in the uncanny blackness at the edge of the thorny thicket.

I released the hedgehog in the grass. To carry a hedgehog around in my predicament was ridiculous, insane. The hedgehog, chortling with joy, took off for cover. But he'd messed up my coat, the pig. I had to shake it out. I never knew before that hedgehogs suffered from diarrhea.

The Cossack guards were disappearing on the other side of the corral. Hedgehogs leave a terrible stink when they do their business. I smelled like a dog-catcher's bag.

Now I had a chance to cross the bright strip of field. I dashed across it like a rabbit. All the way to the dusky bushes, and a little farther, then again on tiptoe, quietly, to the edge of shadow. The corral was within my reach. I had never seen a group of such beautiful horses, nor such a quiet herd. At times it seemed as if the horses were sleeping, but they weren't.

If you brought a bunch of peasant nags together like that they'd be carrying on like fools—but these animals had real intelligence.

The soldiers were talking softly, I couldn't make out any words. I was more interested in the horses, anyway. But then the soldiers caught my attention. One of them picked up a horse's leg, the way you hold up the hoof for the blacksmith. The second man was winding some rags around the hoof, tying them up at the fetlock with a strip of cloth, like a bandage. The hoof and horseshoe were thus bundled up in a kind of rag slipper. A red and white rocket burst over the woods. The men stopped working, looked in that direction. Then they resumed their whispered conversation.

I could only make out the deep-throated words of one man, a giant. His head was bandaged, he was leaning on a stick—very unmilitary looking.

"No shooting," he told the soldiers getting ready to go on guard duty.

"Just keep your eyes open!" He coughed and spat noisily. "Understand?" he asked. There were four of them altogether, plus two guards.

"*Da,*" one of them answered.

All of them were tall, strong, young. They were yawning unceremoniously, and cursing a blue streak. They seemed to want to go to sleep. They were looking toward the woods, over which a few more multicolored rockets were sailing. Now the Cossacks burst into muffled laughter. I could see that the youngest soldier put a mask over his face, one of those carnival masks lying all around Singer's house. It looked as though it was made of silk, the face was supposed to resemble a princess, golden hair hung down to the shoulders. They were in stitches, even the lieutenant was laughing. But the horses began to shy, so the soldier stuck the mask behind his dark riding coat. The Cossacks' coats were raised high at the shoulders. A scabbard slapped against soft boot leather. The riders were carrying automatics. The guards opened the gate. The Cossacks had swung into their saddles so quickly and silently that I didn't even see them mount. The lieutenant was giving them some orders in an irritated tone, and they muttered acknowledgment. The horses were moving in total silence, and the four riders made no noise either. They hugged the arc of shadow, staying out of the lighted area, one after the other, with an interval of two lengths between. The last one turned to the lieutenant. It was the youthful soldier. "Good night," he said, and put the princess back on his face. The guards guffawed, calling out. *"Sasha!"* The lieutenant good-naturedly shook his cane at them. It was all quite unmilitary. But the young soldier was already catching up with his three comrades. They were riding into the dark in a matter-of-fact way, as if they had been born to carry out night patrols. They were leaning forward, almost touching the horses' manes to keep from brushing their caps against low branches. The black coats covered saddles, boots and the animals' flanks. One of them snapped a twig off a tree, sucked on it in real peasant style. They didn't yield to the rhythm of the horses' pace, they kept their own special, calm seat in the saddle which commanded respect. They sank from view in the undergrowth, they were apparently aiming for the woods showered by sputtering rockets. More importantly, at least for me, the guards were leaving with the lieutenant. He was limping, leaning on his cane. They accompanied him to the whitewashed wall of the manor. A barrage of cannon opened up somewhere in the distance, but it sounded weak and hollow. From where I was standing it was about ten steps to the enclosure. I estimated the distance again, from where I was to the wooden slats. One, two, three. I was trying to build up my courage. I often count to myself when I want to gather courage. I dashed out, I was at the fence post, I slid through. Damn it, I tore something on a knot in the wood. The slat was quivering, droning like a string. I stood stock still, not even daring to breathe. I was praying they hadn't heard me. No. Everything was quiet. And I was in the midst of the horses. I could take a step in any direction and stretch out my arms and touch them. Whichever one I liked. They remained calm, a horse is not a cow. A few big heads turned toward me. Ever so quietly I clicked my tongue, as a greeting. I lost myself among their bodies, I breathed in their nearness, they sensed my presence. Whatever else might happen, this made the night beautiful for me. I was not afraid of the horses, we understood each other. I had to jump up to see over their backs whether the guards were still gone. They were nowhere to be seen. The animals which were closest to me touched me with their soft, mossy noses, inquisitively. A horse is a terribly nosy animal. From their majestic height they bowed down their necks, sniffed at me with their quivering nostrils. None of these strange horses was a stranger to me; I am close to their whole race. I touched them. They became even calmer, surrounding me with big, curious, shiny eyes. Some of them were bandaged up, they were wounded like soldiers. Those were the quietest ones.

One of them was favoring a leg which could not take his full weight. I clicked my tongue at him. I called him, "Lucius!" I knew that wasn't his real name, but I think he was glad that I addressed him. I stroked him. He had an enormously long, wavy mane, shiny jet-black eyes. I went further. They parted to let me through. I clicked at all of them, I talked to them, but I was still looking for the flaxen-colored one, the one that resembled Julie. In the end I did manage to frighten a few of the horses, and they ran off, a wave of unrest sweeping through the herd. I stood still, everything calmed down again, the night resumed its silence. A dim light bathed the plum trees, and the backs of the horses, the roofs of buildings gleamed metallically. Finally I saw him, Blondie, up against the brick wall.

I walked past several other horses, until I stood in front of him. He was so light, he shone. He resembled Julie, in height, width, color. I walked around him, comparing. Even his mane looked like Julie's, his mane too hung like a heavy curtain. His tail almost touched the ground. His expression was a little different from Julie's, less intelligent. But that made no difference in a horse.

Then the most important thing occurred to me: Was he really a he? Or a mare?

I couldn't make out details, even though I hunched down to look under his belly. The horse stood in the darkest spot, right in the deepest shadow of the wall.

"Move over!" I said softly. "Move a few steps."

I slapped him gently, I tried to push him toward a lighter area. After a few moments he yielded. He seemed to be the easygoing type, a bit phlegmatic in fact. A wave of unrest again swept through a row of horses, they clustered together in a bunch. I heard a machine gun, quite close by. But the war no longer interested me.

Blondie moved a few steps, now he was in the light. What a job! His mouth must have been made of cast iron, he didn't even seem to feel the bit. Once more I bent down under the smooth belly, now I could see quite clearly, if anything was there I couldn't miss it. But there was nothing there!

Just to make sure, I lifted up the tail. Yes indeed, she was a mare, an honest-to-goodness mare. Just like Julie!

In spite of all my misfortunes I was pretty lucky. For a long time I kept looking admiringly at the blond mare. She, too, weighed a ton. Thick hairy shanks. Hooves like bread loaves. Surprising that such an elephant wound up with the Cossacks. I nudged her, she moved a little. I lost all interest in the other nags in the corral.

"From now on you're Julie," I announced to the mare.

She took it casually. The christening did not shake her poise.

"You speak Czech?"

She didn't even blink. "I will teach you Czech," I told her gravely. Wartime is no picnic, who knows what this horse had already lived through! I liked her better and better.

"Come here!" I drew her enormous head toward me. Her eyebrows and lashes were as white as those of an albino, her eyes were as red as an angora rabbit's.

"Remember! Your name is Julie! From now on you are Czech."

I began to ponder the question how to get the new Julie out of the enclosure. She had her bridle. I tied my piece of rope to it, so that I wouldn't have to stretch to the tips of my toes. I started looking for the gate through which the Russians had ridden out. I was leading Julie II with me, to avoid the need of coming back for her. At that time—in April 1945—this did not seem like theft to me at all.

"Come on. Don't worry. We will take good care of you."

I talked to her just in case she might have mixed feelings about leaving. She seemed to have no hesitation about following me. I found the gate. But it was bolted so sloppily that the top slat fell off as soon as I touched it. The Russians had taken the precaution of sticking an empty tin can under the gate. Plus all kinds of other noisy stuff. Goddamn it, why didn't I keep my eyes open! The rattling junk started a racket louder than a circus band. The horses, of course, were off in a panic, Julie II, though, stayed calm and cool, proving once more her phlegmatic humor. Such fantastic pandemonium broke out that I skipped through the fence and ran toward the open meadow. There was no question of taking Julie along, the herd was carrying on like crazy. So to be on the safe side I took to my heels. I expected guards to come running from the direction of the limestone wall. But no! Soldiers came after me from quite the opposite side. That took me by surprise. But after all, it is logical that an army as big as the Russians' would have more than two soldiers on guard duty.

"Rrrrrrr!" shouted the Russians to their frightened horses.

"Rrrr!"

Just like our signal "Prrrr," but without the initial "P."

They must have seen me crossing the light strip of ground. What kind of Cossacks would they be if they hadn't seen me!

"*Shto tam takoye?*" shouted one of them. His mustaches reached to his collar bone. At critical moments of my life my brain is filled with idiotic details.

"*Sobaka!*" I heard the second soldier.

I didn't understand what they were saying. The only Russian word I really knew up to that point was "da." And they weren't shouting "da."

A shot rang out. Probably meant for me. I heard it whine overhead, twisting into the air. I fell down on my hands and knees, on my belly. A second bang! That one missed, too. I got to my feet and zigzagged farther.

Maybe they'll pick me off, it occurred to me. They'll kill me, even though I am a fellow Slav. Wars are full of blunders.

"Don't shoot! It's just a boy!" I understood the shout of the second soldier. He must have had better eyesight.

Thank God that the bright stretch was behind me at last. The men digging in front of the manor gates must have joined the hunt, because soon there were as many Russians running around as there are in Moscow. I didn't actually see them all, but I sensed they were there. I got away from one, I hit on two more. I darted for the bushes, shaking them off, and found five more on the other side!

"Stoy!" they yelled at me. Angrily, quite furiously, getting more and more furious. Sure, I'd stop and they'd finish me off! I didn't think I could explain to them quickly enough what I was doing in the corral, so it was better to play dumb. Cossacks are not only terrific riders, but sensational sprinters. A big yellow rocket burst overhead. I must say that every now and then when I am in the soup a bit of luck pulls me out. The soldiers flopped to the ground. The flare must have been attached to a parachute, it kept afloat forever. It wasn't a Russian one, otherwise they wouldn't have been lying on their bellies. I was glad now that Husarek had dug all those holes for his trees. I jumped into the nearest one and lay down at the bottom.

Soon the chase started again, and furious trampling resounded around my hole. And a bagful of Russian shouting, too. I had the feeling that they weren't friendly at all, they were really worked up. Finally all was quiet.

I stuck my head out. I could see one Russian walking through the field, examining the tree holes, one after another.

I hadn't heard him at all, he was stepping as lightly as a sleepwalker, gun in hand. It was too late to take to my heels. But he gave up before he got to my hole, turned and walked away. Only then did I become aware of my heaving chest, my pumping lungs. I was gasping for air, the left side of my chest ached. When my chest hurts like that I always put my hand over it, under my shirt. My face was soaking wet. I could see only the muddy edge of the hole, a strip of sky, streaming stars. In our part of the country the stars are always near. They shine big and pure. Blessed Moravian stars.

CHAPTER SEVEN

For an eternity I lay in the hole. I don't know just how long. Then I heard the sound of footsteps. I listened carefully. Yes, they were footsteps. I held my breath. The crunchy steps sounded unrhythmically, with pauses. They were coming back, I heard them distinctly. Then they stopped. I was afraid. But my curiosity got the better of me. I lifted myself to my knees. When I was kneeling in the hole I was tall enough to see the field. At first I could see nothing.

And then the sound was right behind me. Startled, I turned sharply around. It wasn't a soldier! It wasn't one of the Russians. I gasped in wonder. At the edge of the field stood a big black horse! His head was lifted, he was looking straight at me, as if he knew that I was in the hole. I could clearly see his mane, his nostrils. He was as dark and shiny as coal. I whistled quietly. But for some strange reason the whistle wouldn't come out, my lips seemed to be made of wood. The horse remained motionless. He was standing at the top of the horizon, so that he looked as if his hooves were hardly touching the ground. I licked my lips, puckered them again, this time a quavering whistle came out.

The situation was not funny one bit. I didn't feel like leaving my hole. You don't know what *I* know on the subject of black horses in the night.

My grandma was no longer able to walk, so she used to tie a piece of string to my foot. When I tried to get away, the knot in the string would tighten.

"Stay put on your tail!" she'd scold, without opening her eyes. She used to sleep in a chair in the yard, whole summer days and weeks. One day she was warming her bones in the burning sun. I kept pestering her to tell stories. "I have already told you all I know," she snapped. She had a resonant voice, ten thousand wrinkles. I was getting bored sitting on the ground next to her, playing with sticks and stones. I reached for the knife lying on the bench. (It had a blade which was half honed away, a worn wooden handle, three brass rivets.) I was holding the knife in my hand, hacking at the string. "What are you doing?" Her eyes were old, but she must have had a pair in the back of her head.

"Nothing." At last I succeeded in cutting the string. I crawled away on all fours, quietly, as quietly as I could. Grandma woke up, tried to hook my foot with her cane. She was pelting me with chips of wood.

"You little brat!" she was shouting. "There is a black horse that roams the country at night. I will call him. He'll carry you off to hell!"

The sudden appearance of the horse might have scared me, if I hadn't noticed that he was limping. It was his right rear leg. As he walked, his back was completely collapsing toward that side, he was jerking his whole body, even his head. I watched him for a time. I couldn't understand what he was doing there, or where he had come from. In the shape he was in he couldn't have come from very far.

I climbed out of the hole, I was out in a jiffy. And Mr. Horse came clop-clopping straight toward me! A horse's nose for spotting human beings is as keen as a dog's. He stopped, searched for something on the ground. But the best he could possibly find on the ground was manure. I started walking toward him, with meter-long steps. I looked around nervously, for I couldn't shake the feeling that a platoon of Russians was still lurking in the darkness, ready to pounce on me.

I heard nothing except some distant engines and continual firing. At times a war can be awfully monotonous. The horse waited for me to reach him. Here I was right in front of him. He was so black that axle grease seems pale in comparison. If he was healthy, he could probably kick a man to kingdom come. I had a weakness for this kind of beast. Then I saw his wound. I didn't even have to walk around him to see it. Half his lower leg was gone! He was as bloody as if he had escaped from a slaughterhouse. I circled him, keeping at a safe distance. I could have cried. He didn't even turn his head as I was walking around him.

I moved closer. "Where are you from? Who did that to you?"

I raised my hand and touched his nose. The horse was shaking. He was feverish, drenched with sweat. I felt his matted, damp hair between my fingers. But he was not afraid of me.

"You a Russian, too?"

I couldn't reach all the way to his ears. Not even when I stood on tiptoe. I stroked his mane. I couldn't take my eyes off the terrible wound.

"Does it hurt?"

I only heard his big black velvety nostrils. His breathing was violent, he was laboring to force air out of his lungs. I remembered something, went through my pockets. The cigarette case fell to the ground, I picked it up, shifted the Russian's glass bubble to the other pocket. The horse was standing over me like a silent St. Augustine. He was living with his eyes. His eyes were as big as saucers.

There was a tiny bit of carrot stuck under the lining of my coat. In my childhood, my pockets and my coat lining made a single common receptacle. I handed him the treat on my palm.

"Here. You like carrot?"

He spread his lips, but he didn't gulp it down. He was biting it carefully, as if his teeth were loose. I took a peek underneath. He was a he, all right. I looked for more carrot, but it was all gone.

"That's all there is," I said.

The number 5 was clipped out and branded over his front shoulder blade.

"They call you five?"

I kept on talking to him all the time.

I knew he was a horse that was about to die.

"I'll take you to the brook."

I led him without any trouble, by the head, by the nose. He had neither bridle nor halter. It was like leading a hobbyhorse, but we went. Somewhere an artillery barrage was erupting. It wasn't a pleasant walk, it was the road to Calvary. He stopped after every few steps, I picked grass and brought it to him. He didn't touch it. Not a blade.

But he practically drank the stream dry. He paused a while, then drank again. I sat on my haunches, watching him.

From the manor I heard the neighing of horses. Whenever there was a pause in the shooting other sounds could be heard quite distinctly through the night. I rose to my feet.

"Stay here," I said. "Here you'll be better off." He swayed as if he was about to fall, then regained his balance.

"Here you can take a drink whenever you like."

I nearly cried. I stroked him a few more times. I would have taken him with me, but I knew he was going to die.

I turned to leave. Dripping water, he limped his way out of the stream and up on the bank.

"Stop following me!" I took a few steps. So did he.

I walked back to him. "You can't come with me!" I told him, into his eyes, through which moments of blankness were already passing. I turned him back to the brook. He let me do whatever I wanted, like a toy rocking horse.

Then I broke into a run. When I turned my head, I saw him hobbling after me on three legs. I kept running, over my shoulder I saw that he was trying to follow. My cruelty would kill him. I stopped, sat down, a little miffed; he stumbled nearer, stood over me. The ground was full of rocks, I started picking them up and flinging them into the bushes.

"You're not my horse!" I told him, getting up. "I can't take you home in Julie's place!"

I kicked at a rock, which happened to be buried in the ground. I did a little dance on one foot. Furiously I tore off an acacia branch and stuck it under his nose. To my surprise, he ate the leaves. I broke off armfuls more, he wolfed them down greedily. Red and white rockets lit up the woods.

I led Corpse No. 5 all the way to the willow grove. It took us forever to cover that little stretch of ground from the brook. Dawn was breaking, the countryside seemed steeped in bluish milk. The birds were screaming like mad. Everything steamed, the field, the earth. Five deer were grazing on the alfalfa. He wanted to graze, too, but I didn't let him.

"You can't eat that. It's dripping with dew."

He wobbled after me on his three and a half legs. Mostly we were standing still, I was losing an awful lot of time. I kept telling him that I would take him to the vet, that everything would be all right. Pipe dreams . . .

He was really a goner, but it didn't occur to me that I was

lying to him. I brought him all the way to the brick hut. I was dying of hunger. I crumbled up the piece of Russian bread which Iza and I had left there. Now it came in handy, it tasted like honey cake. I picked out the softest pieces with my fingers and stuffed them in my mouth. The horse was chomping on the crust with such zest that his teeth rattled.

Shreds of fog floated over the willows. It was always damp around here in the morning. I went inside.

The horse couldn't follow me, but he remained standing right by the door. I went out once more and pulled the German coats out of the pile where I had left them. I tossed a pair of them in the corner of the hut, on top of a bale of straw, and threw the third over the horse's back. It was like covering an elephant with a handkerchief. I decided to add another coat, so he wouldn't catch cold before dying. Maybe he didn't even feel heat or cold any longer, but I wanted him to be comfortable. He kept nudging his nose at my palm, sniffing for food.

"I have no more," I told him.

I stretched out on the straw, pulled the German coat over me, turned to the wall.

Whenever I wanted to dream of Mother, all I had to do was to think about her real hard, to picture something that had happened in the past. For instance, the night she was washing laundry in the yard. I got out of bed and came down after her, walking on tiptoe to keep from waking up Dad. She was trying to chase me back to bed. But in the end she threw her warm jacket over my shoulders, covered my legs with some sort of shawl, and let me stay with her a while. I was sitting on a pile of wood, watching her. I loved the way she'd blow her hair out of the way as she was working over the washboard. She'd smile at me.

What are stars, Mom?

Eyes.

Whose eyes, Mom?

The good Lord's.

Why does he have so many?

He has to see all the people.

Me, too?

He has to see you, too.

I climbed under her big tub.

But now he can't see me!

Then she was hanging the wash on clotheslines hung among the trees. In the garden. The night was made up of stars, clouds, distant barking. She was spreading white pieces of linen over the lawn.

It is a vast lawn at night, in my dream. It is already full of outspread sheets and pillow cases. Acres of washed laundry. At the end of the lawn stands Mother's tiny tub, and an immense pile of dirty laundry. A whole stack of dirty laundry. And two more wagons heaped with laundry are parked nearby.

Prrrr! I shouted, because my horse No. 5 came clomping right over my mother's snow-white sheets. His hooves are smearing everything, the white sheets are covered by patches of blood.

And then there is a herd of horses running through open country, a countryside I don't know and have never seen before . . . A thousand horses. Manes are flying, tails are waving. It seems to be a country not yet inhabited by man. A pink sun is rising behind the trees. The horses are running side by side, bodies touching, hooves floating over the ground.

They are making a huge, majestic arc toward the river.

Something woke me up. Noises. I had a feeling it was a horse. Horse's hooves, scraping on the doorstep. For a second I gazed at the bare brick wall. I pulled the military coat more tightly about me. A cold draft was blowing from the willow copse. Then I turned and screamed.

I jumped up and pressed my body into the corner, against the wall. I blurted out something. A huge male figure was standing in the door. I couldn't see his face, the morning light was at his back.

I shouted, "Mom!"

"Damned dog's ear!" said the man, angrily, in a tonsil-choked voice I knew so well. Cyril Vitlich.

"Where in hell's name have you been? What the devil have you been doing?" he shouted. He was breathing heavily, as if he had gills instead of lungs. I was no longer scared. Some smaller companion seemed to be standing in the door next to Cyril.

"Iza!" I shouted with surprise. She was at his feet. "You mutt!" She was yipping happily, as if she hadn't run away from me just a while ago. She ran over to me, I buried both my hands in her fur.

"Cyril!" I addressed Vitlich, in as relieved a tone of voice as I will probably use one day toward Archangel Gabriel.

"I think I'll tan your hide, you little bastard," he said. "I'll knock your block off. Dumbbell! Who the hell is supposed to keep track of you? I've been tearing after you since last night! You get some half-ass idea in your noodle, and you're off and running! Don't you know there is a war on?"

"I know," I said. That dumbbell part made me mad. "I am not an idiot, I know there is a war on." He gave me a juicy smack. It was the first time he had ever hit me. I must say it caught me by surprise. If it had landed on my ear, I could forget about my eardrum.

"I went over to the game warden's to make sure you got there all right. Naturally everybody's there except you! You've always got to be different from everybody else! Where the devil have you been?"

He was squeezing my shoulders so hard they were practically touching in the middle. Iza barked. "Shut up," he said to the dog. The way he was holding me I was hanging in the air rather than standing on my feet.

"What are you hitting me for?" I made an attempt at resistance. Injustice, when it reaches a certain point, can drive a person to extremes. "I don't belong to you, you have no right!"

"You want to catch another one?" he said.

I did not.

"The Russians are already at the manor," he said. "The Russians are here," he repeated in a hushed voice, to emphasize the gravity of the situation.

"Yesterday," I answered casually. "They came yesterday afternoon." I wanted to show him that I wasn't exactly hatched from an egg. "They came just after the Germans swiped Julie," I spilled out.

"They swiped what?" His tonsils quavered.

"My horse. They swiped Julie."

He took a deep breath, and chased the dog away with his foot. So that nothing could distract me.

"You made that up! You're talking nonsense."

There was a minute of silence. And hard looks. In the end he realized that it really happened.

"I am not going back home. Never," I said.

"You better not," he answered. "If I can give you some advice, don't ever show up at home!" Suddenly he dropped his arms. I knew what he was looking at. He sniffed.

"Come here!" he said. "Come here! What's that you got . . . What happened to your noodle?" I imagined that in the early morning light I must have looked pretty ghastly.

"I didn't want to hand Julie over to them." I didn't feel like going into all the details. He rubbed the tip of his nose.

"I didn't go with the boys because they were chasing me," I said. I didn't look at Vitlich, I was looking out into the willows, into the thin fog. It hadn't thickened as yet, it was growing out of the ground in thin wisps. The air was still.

"Sonsabitches!" said Vitlich. "How many sonsabitches were there?"

"Five," I answered.

Vitlich regarded me quizzically.

"Five, or maybe four," I said.

"Does it hurt much?"

His voice now had the gentleness of a patron saint.

"A little."

"Let me see you in the light!"

We went outside. He looked at the black invalid. Naturally, he saw at a glance that this was no longer a horse but a skeleton. The animal was standing in front of the hut like a huge broken toy.

"Where did you come across this mummy?" he asked.

"I found him." Vitlich no longer seemed surprised at anything.

"Don't even show him to your dad. He might shoot the both of you."

"I am not going home!"

"Ah!" he remembered. But he didn't seem to believe me. I repeated, "No, I'll never go home! Don't think you can drag me back there!"

"You sure your nose isn't busted?" he asked, once again focusing on my face.

"No."

"The Germans blew up the bridge. You know that? It's kaput."

"Hmmm." I wasn't the least bit interested in the bridge.

I yelled out, because he touched my nose. He was looking at me with compassion, as if I was about to depart from this world. At this moment, his large worn face was really touching.

"Cyril," I said, to change the conversation. "You know what's wrong with him?" I pointed at the carcass.

"He has a broken instep. Mashed muscles . . . maybe a tendon, too. . . . Where did you find him?"

"On the other side of the brook."

"And he made it all the way here?"

"Uh-huh."

He took another look at the horse's bent hind leg. He was putting hardly any weight on it, and was leaning his flank against the wall of the hut.

As I was watching Vitlich's back, the idea for a great prank came to me. I reached into my pocket for the glass bubble, and stuck it in my nose. The left nostril. A burst of machine-gun fire came from the river, lasted for a few seconds and stopped. Vitlich turned in that direction, toward the manor. Now he was talking to me again as usual, treating me as a grownup.

"Maybe they came too fast," he said. "The vanguard was too far in front. Or they didn't have the right maps." He was analyzing the strategic situation of the Russians.

I felt like pulling out the bubble and saving it for another time, because this didn't seem like the right moment. But it was too late, he had already seen it. In spite of all his worries he couldn't fail to notice a bubble as big as half a thumb.

"Wipe your nose," he said. "Where did they take Julie, after they swiped her?"

"Don't know," I said, sniffing on purpose. "Through the woods. Toward Rynovice."

"Wipe your snoot," he repeated. He was really fooled by the bubble. When he looked at me he was making a bit of grimace as if he himself had a bubble under his nose. I pretended to wipe it.

"Old Chumsky was at the game warden's last night. By now he must have told your dad that you weren't there. For all we know he may be looking high and low for you," said Vitlich. "Damn it, can't you blow your nose?"

"I haven't got a handkerchief," I said. He began to go through his pockets. It was useless. I think the last time Vitlich owned a handkerchief was in 1921.

I was pretending to wipe my nose again, but the wrong nostril.

"The other side," he said.

I turned my face away, pretending to be wiping myself, but I quickly took out the bubble and stuck it into the other hole. Certain situations can lead all the way to madness.

"Can't you blow your nose without a rag?"

He showed me how to do it. He squeezed one nostril with his thumb, blew, then squeezed the other one.

It was a kind of nose-blowing instruction course.

"I don't feel like blowing my nose," I said. I was playing dumb.

"You've got a dripping candle," he said.

"What?"

"A snotty nose."

I felt gingerly around my nose. Then I picked up the bubble with two fingers, slowly, so that Cyril could see it, and put it in my pocket. He was completely bewildered, he looked like he was going to faint.

"You're a card! When it comes to dumb tricks you're number one!" But he reached out his hand. "Let me see that!" I pulled the bubble out of my pocket. It was in his palm, he was examining it carefully.

"Where did you pinch that from?"

"It's a present."

"Who in God's name gives out such garbage?"

"The Russians," I answered. "Tell me, Cyril, what's a *litinant?*"

"A lieutenant? A low-ranking officer."

"*Litinant,* they called him."

"Where?"

I nodded toward the manor.

"You were there?"

"Hmmm."

"There was some shooting," he said suddenly. "A lot of shooting was going on. Is that when you were there?"

"No."

He stuck the bubble in his nose. At first he did it backwards, then turned it around correctly.

"You know what a *'durak'* is? Or *'sobaka'?*" I asked Cyril.

"You have a butt?" he said in reply. I pulled out my cigarette case. I opened it. I no longer looked at the naked woman, I was proud of the shiny, mirrorlike surface. Cyril, too, ignored the photograph. He made a face at me. He was laughing with his whole face. He almost broke out into a guffaw. I started to laugh, too.

"What am I going to do with the puppies, if you leave home?" he asked, transferring the bubble into the other nostril.

"You ought to tell me who to give the puppies to. I can't run a dog pound."

He regarded me quizzically, pulled out the bubble and handed it to me.

I knew what he was talking about. It wasn't so long ago that I brought the puppies to Cyril. I had a tough time getting them, I had to cross a tin roof which made a terrible racket with each step. Even though I was barefoot. I was breaking into someone else's yard, at night. Old Chumsky stepped out the door, wearing only trousers. His chest was bare, suspenders hung at his sides, his face was all lathered up. He spilled out a basinful of water, then went back inside. All was quiet. Their dog ran over, stopped right under the wall on which I was standing. I clicked my tongue at her softly, jumped to the ground. I had a way with all dogs. Then Chumsky's daughter Anna slid out the door. She took me by the hand and led me to the shed, to the puppies.

"He said he's going to drown them first thing in the morning," she whispered.

"There won't be any drowning," I said.

She found a basket, put some straw at the bottom. Anna was just a little sprat, but she acted like a grownup. She had on a nightshirt that fell all the way to her heels. I stuffed the puppies in, climbed the wall, Anna handing me the basket. Everything in quick time.

"They have names yet?" I whispered down to her.

"No."

Chumsky the Chump came out into the yard. It must be hell to have a brother like that. I felt sorry for Anna.

"Anna!" he yelled. "Bedtime!"

Naturally, he lorded it over Anna. That's obvious. I heard him slapping her face. Then he went into the wooden privy. Whistling. I crossed the tin roof on tiptoe. Now I could easily jump down into the road. If I wanted to. But there was something else I wanted to do first. I pulled a carrot out of

*my pocket, set the basket down to get better aim. I cocked
my right arm, aimed my outstretched left arm straight at the
privy. I let go, the carrot banged into the wooden toilet. A real
bomb. Like a drumstick whacking a kettle drum. Now the dog
began a racket. The Chump shot out of the privy, his pants
flapping around his ankles. He made a perfect target. It was
easy to smack him with a second carrot, right in the back. He
was gaping in the air, as if the missiles had come out of the
clouds. Quickly, I jumped off the wall.*

"Dad! Dad!" yelled Chumsky.

Cyril put a flat bottle to his lips and took a good gulp. I, too,
was shaking with cold.

He was about to hand me the bottle, then he realized I was
too young for alcohol. "You hungry?" he asked.

He pulled out a piece of bread wrapped in newspaper. And
bacon. I couldn't bear the sight of any more bacon. I shook my
head to indicate I didn't want any.

"You can ask Jozka, he might like a puppy. Maybe two," I
mused.

He examined the horizon.

"Go lie down," he said. "Catch yourself some sleep. Put on
these coats, too. He won't be cold." He pulled the two German
coats off the horse.

"I've got a motorcycle hidden away there," I told Vitlich,
pointing at the bushes. "A cycle costs more than a horse,
doesn't it, Cyril?"

"Go to sleep," he said. "Off with you. Don't worry, we'll
catch up with your nag someplace. I'll take a peek around
Rynovice. They couldn't have taken her very far. They probably dumped her, by the side of some field she's waiting for us.
With the wagon."

"You think so?"

He shoved me into the corner of the hut, toward the straw. All of a sudden, he asked, "By the way, did your dad say anything about me?" His voice took on a different tone, suspicious, secretive.

"No. What? What would he say?"

"Or Chumsky. Old Chumsky. He comes to see your dad, doesn't he?"

"What would he say about you, Cyril? I don't understand." I was truly puzzled.

"Forget it."

He dropped the subject. He threw the coats over me. They smelled of horse hair, sweat.

"Where are you going, Cyril?" I didn't want him to leave.

He sat down on the doorstep.

"I am not going anywhere. I'll sit right here. Go to sleep." I was terribly sleepy. I pulled Iza toward me. "You won't go over to my house, will you?"

"No," he said.

"Cross your heart?"

"Cross my heart."

He sat on the edge of the milky fog, smoking a cigarette. A machine gun rattled far away. Then he got up, I saw him, he checked to see whether I was asleep, and I quickly closed my eyes. He rustled through the undergrowth, and when he came back he was carrying the machine gun which I had hidden next to the motorcycle. He was examining the mechanism, and tried to pry open the flat metal cover. Overcome by fatigue, I fell asleep.

The herd of horses, which I had been dreaming about, had reached the broad river. The water was shallow, light flickered over the sandy bottom. The animals forded the stream. The sun floated behind the vertical bars of black trees. The countryside still looked strange to me. Some shapes and objects looked familiar, others I was seeing for the first time. Hooves were splashing water on the horses' bellies. Suddenly, the whole herd stopped in the middle of the stream, and eagerly began to drink.

This is an opportune time to note that there is a spot near our village which people to this day call "the dead Russian's place." One of the Cossack patrol that I watched ride off into the night was killed there. It happened in the forest meadow, near the well. Just about the time I was asleep in the brick hut. I didn't hear the shooting at all. Somebody told me the story later. Apparently the patrol was already returning to the manor. In that part of the country birds are always twittering away early in the morning, the bog was steaming, a blue-green haze shimmering between the tree tops. The soldiers saw a doe at the well. She didn't move. She stood still as they circled the meadow, she disappeared behind tree trunks, then they saw her again as they passed a row of pines. They clapped their hands, but she didn't move. They reined in their horses, passed the binoculars to each other. Then one of the Cossacks dismounted and walked to the meadow. The ground at that spot is generally so soaked that it gurgles underfoot. The doe became apprehensive and ran off, but not far. The soldier noticed the broken planks over the well, and looked inside. A fawn was whimpering in the depths. According to the story, the soldier climbed down to rescue the fawn. He took off his shoes and coat, rolled up his sleeves and carried the young animal to safety. Another version has it that the soldier was just getting ready to go down. In any case, a shot rang out. A rifle shot. He sank to his knees, holding both hands in front of his face, for he was shot in the cheek. He managed to crawl a little distance; by then his three companions were furiously firing at the spot where the shot came from.

Later, I saw the dead soldier at the manor.

CHAPTER EIGHT

Before waking up I dreamed that Kudera was vainly trying to cart a heavy load of grain up a steep hill. He was furiously whipping his horses, but to no avail. Right behind him was Chumsky, with an equally heavy load. He too was unable to budge a single meter, and Rez behind him. I had Julie. Calmly, I motioned to Kudera to unhitch his scarecrow nags. Moving with complete assurance, I harnessed Julie, smacked my lips, and we were off. Wheels were rattling, dust flying, and in no time at all we were at the top. Then I came back for Chumsky's load. Rez stealthily unhitched his horses, chained his wagon to Chumsky's. He thought I didn't see him. But this devious trick didn't bother me at all—nor Julie. I smacked my lips, and both wagons were at the top. Festively dressed peasants appeared out of nowhere, surrounded Julie in silent admiration. I stuffed carrots in her mouth. I had pocketfuls of carrots. Koo-Koo-Kudera, Vyska-Pisska, Chumsky, all in ministrant's robes, were solemnly carrying silver dishes piled high with carrots. They were swinging fragrant censers around Julie's head. The mare was completely hidden in a cloud of incense. Farmers were pulling a strong rope around the barn. They said they were preparing a final examination.

"Certainly," I answered. "Conduct any examination you desire."

I hitched Julie to the rope. My father was trying to stop me,

*but I winked at him not to worry. I knew what Julie could do.
Mother closed her eyes; she was scared. I examined Julie's right
rear hoof, Vitlich gave the shoe a few taps with his hammer, just
to make sure everything was in order. Vitlich was on my side.
I smacked my lips, the rope stretched to the breaking point,
the barn teetered, panicky pigeons took off from the roof.
The barn had moved, the mare had pulled the building at least
one meter! If she could manage one meter, she could manage
more! The barn gates were no longer lined up with the road,
but were facing a couple of old trees. I shouted "yooooo" and we
dragged the barn another ten steps!*

*Applause, jubilation, ringing bells, the band playing. People
surrounded Dad, clutching fistfuls of money, they wanted to
buy Julie. To my horror I saw Dad accepting a basketful of
bills from Kudera. The banknotes were spilling over the lawn,
people were trying to pick them up. Quickly, I unhitched Julie,
lifted Mother onto her back, jumped up myself. I couldn't stand
the idea that Julie might belong to Kudera. We went off at a
gallop. They ran after us, but they couldn't catch us. They fell
farther and farther behind. Julie was running with seven-league
strides. The village and woods were below us, the horse was
flying through the air with marvelously silent, long strides, her
mane waving in the wind. I could see the people running
through the village, looking up at us.*

*The farmers were wearing hunting caps, and plinking at us
with their rifles. The priest was standing in front of the church,
he'd got a rifle too, he too was shooting. I always knew he was
on the side of the farmers. I looked around, I saw that Julie's
rear right leg was hurt. The same kind of wound that Horse
No. 5 had. But fortunately we had already reached the poplars;
a rosy sun floated over the green expanse and the gleaming
bend of the river.*

*The herd was still there. That's where we were headed,
toward that last free herd, toward that holy, spotless land.*

I woke up. It took me a while to figure out where I was, the brick wall which I was staring at didn't give me much of a clue. I was lying under a pile of military coats, Vitlich's brown overcoat lay on top of me, too. The brass military buttons were embossed with swastikas. I turned it over, now I knew where I was. But the hut was empty! I tried to piece everything together in my brain.

"Cyril," I whispered. No answer. I got up. I felt cold. April mornings in our part of the country are not exactly tropical.

"Cyril!" I called louder. My nose was running, I sniveled dejectedly.

I stepped out the door. A light fog still floated through the willows. The misty landscape was almost unreal, dreamlike. I tried to blow my nose using Vitlich's method. I closed one nostril, blew. It worked pretty well.

The sun was hanging behind the fog like a light behind a pane of milky glass. The sun was shapeless, it trembled. Its rays did not seem to penetrate, they had no warmth. Firing was still going on, the war wasn't over. An artillery barrage could be heard. I remembered the dog. It had bolted. If a dog is man's best friend, you couldn't prove it by Iza.

"Iza!"

I whistled. But I had to lick my lips first to make any sound at all. I turned around abruptly as I heard a noise at my back. Corpse No. 5 was practically touching me with his nose, he was waiting for me. He probably hadn't slept at all, he waited until I woke up. A neigh rattled deep in his throat. I saw that Vitlich had dressed his rear leg. He'd torn up German military blouses and used the strips for bandages. The motorcycle was still standing undisturbed under the pile of wicker where I had left it. Cyril bandaged the horse's shank and fetlock. The top part of the wound was oozing. It was only now that I saw how horrible the wound actually was. At night it didn't look quite so bad. The horse snorted, his nose practically against my cheek. I stroked him, ran my fingers through his mane. His eyes were almost closed, he felt my presence without actually seeing me. Suddenly he jerked his head. I, too, heard a noise. Hoofbeats! A quiet pounding in the fog. I listened. Yes, hoofbeats! Cautiously I moved toward the shrubs. The sounds became more distinct. I ran through the brush, then stopped. I didn't want to come out in the open. I was in the midst of a thick network of runners, I peered through the tangle. Several Russians were coming down the path. I counted, there were three of them, but they had four horses. Three Cossacks were riding, the fourth horse was tied by a long rope. But the horse's back was not bare, a soldier was strapped across the saddle! His arms and legs were dangling helplessly over the ground, his head, too, was bouncing with each movement of the horse. The soldier was lying on his stomach.

I took a few steps, almost reaching the path, but then I stopped because the soldiers, too, had stopped. Two Cossacks dismounted and adjusted the body to make sure it didn't slip off. Some object had dropped from the lifeless body. I saw it fall, but none of the soldiers noticed it. They were off in the direction of the manor. They dissolved behind a curtain of fog.

I ran to the spot where they were standing, to the object on the ground. I lifted up a silk mask surrounded by a ring of blond female hair. It was smeared with blood. It was the comical mask of a princess which had provided so much amusement to the young soldier the previous night.

I broke into a run, a little farther to the right than the direction taken by the soldiers. I couldn't see the haystack in the fog, but that's where I was headed. That was where there was a corralful of horses. . . .

After a while I slowed to a jog, then to a careful walk. I didn't want the Russians to take another pot-shot at me. The Russians are not the most humorous people in the world. The fog was beginning to lift, the sun was getting stronger, the grass, shrubs, trees glistened with moisture. I walked around the field, with its little piles of manure and tree holes, till I got to the clump of thorn bushes. From there I saw the corral, and the horses, at least two hundred of them. I didn't feel like going any closer. I put one flat stone on top of another, sat down. I was trying to pick out the mare which I had been about to confiscate the night before. Naturally, I was aware that stealing horses from a victorious army is a crime, but I couldn't see the mare anyway. I edged a little closer. If it hadn't been for the lousy fog, I could have seen all the horses quite distinctly. Perhaps I could safely make it to the edge of the thorn bush, step by step. This was where they had spotted me the day before. I recognized the place, I could see the enclosure beautifully. I could even see the gate, with pots and pans hanging from it. I could even make out the *litinant*. I recognized him at once by his cane. He was smoking a cigarette, strolling among the horses. Perhaps he hadn't slept all night, he was walking with another soldier, inspecting the mounts. They lifted a hoof here and there, smeared some stuff on a sore spot, ducked under the horses' bellies. As the *litinant* bent over to examine a hock, another horse nudged his rear, sniffed all over the back of his tunic. The *litinant* cursed, I heard him say something about "the devil," but he pronounced the word in a Russian way.

I sat down on a boundary marker. It was interesting to watch the *litinant*. Then I craned my neck because I had spotted "my" horse. At last! She was behind many other horses, almost at the very back of the enclosure. I stood up on the stone to get a better view. Suddenly I heard at my back:

"Hu! Shto ty?"

I jumped. A Russian with a gun was standing behind me! Another one was emerging out of the shrubbery. I ran for the woods as fast as my legs could carry me.

"Stoy! Slushai! Ty! Stoy!"

He was legging it after me. But he was carrying his rifle in one hand, it didn't look like he was going to shoot. That gave me more confidence. But a third one appeared between the trees. He was laughing at me, spreading his arms, as if the whole thing was some huge joke. I zigzagged away from him, but fell right into the arms of another one. That one wasn't laughing like the others, he was making a threatening face. I tried to jump away from him. But the Russian had the kind of legs that could catch a rabbit. Maybe he was a letter carrier in civilian life and raced all over Russia with telegrams; in Russia distances are tremendous. He almost got me, I fell flat on the ground hoping that he would fly over me. The trick worked! I think he landed on his chin. I dashed in the opposite direction. He got up faster than he fell, I don't know how he did it but he got me firm in his grasp. He'd probably never cracked a smile since the day he was born. He looked like he was about to execute me on the spot.

"Ponimayesh po ruski?" he asked.

"Da," I answered, using the only Russian word which I knew perfectly.

"Shto?" he said, surprised.

I thought it better to remain quiet. He held me by the collar. Soon I was surrounded by half the Cossack army. The soldier was holding me as if he had caught the malefactor who started the whole war. I was choking, sweating and dangling in the air, all at the same time. On several previous occasions in my life, I had found myself in similar circumstances.

One time the priest had also held me by the collar; in fact, it was the collar of my best suit. He held me with all his might, I was thrashing about on the ground in front of the church, then the collar tore and remained in his hand. In the meantime the ministrants were busy chasing a rabbit I had brought to church to make mass more interesting. Another time an Apache chief seized me by the shirt collar, after he caught me crawling past the circus ticket window. He lifted me off the ground with such vehemence that my shirt came clean out of my pants. And my teacher, who looked just like T. G. Masaryk but was far from being a humanist, once dragged me out of my school bench by my sweater, almost choking me to death. A bag full of marbles that was under my sweater had come loose, and hundreds of marbles began rolling to the ground. The whole floor was full of marbles, the whole class was on their knees picking them up and stealing them from me. At least I managed to stomp on Kudera's foot, hard enough for him to yowl with pain. The teacher threw me down on the front bench, but before he had a chance to pick up a ruler I slithered down under the bench.

The same way I was now trying to get away from the Russian, crawling on all fours through the brush. The soldiers were all around, shouting at me. Nobody was crawling in after me, but there was no way for me to escape, they had surrounded me like a hunted animal and I could see their legs through the tangle of creepers and branches.

That day at school I also saw only a tangle of legs—the teacher was trying to pull me out, my miserable fellow pupils were trying to help him. I held onto my classmates' legs, Chumsky kept hitting me with his ruler but I kicked him so hard that he lost interest in the game. At last the teacher managed to pull me out, and dragged me again toward the bench. He wanted me to lie on it with my behind sticking out, but I was turning and wriggling. He finally gave me a good thrashing. I wanted to cover my rear with my hand and he whacked me across the fingers. I got even with him by upsetting a bottle of ink over some notebooks. At an age when a person has only half the strength of an adult, it is difficult to defend oneself against violence.

The Russians were pulling me out of the shrubs. They dragged me by my coat like a criminal, they almost pulled it over my head. I kicked, scratched, thrashed about in a fury. I grabbed branches, bushes, writhing under their legs, they were having quite a time with me. But they were hardened by war, nothing upset them.

I expected them to blindfold me, stand me up against a wall, call an execution squad and shoot me.

One Cossack lost a boot during the struggle, he was hopping in the grass on one foot, his gaiter was coming undone and flapping around his foot like a flag. Another soldier came over to help, but he stepped on his comrade's bare foot and there was a sharp yowl. I had a button from a uniform in my hand. The frowning Russian was holding me, I seemed to have torn off his whole pocket. He was breathing like a bellows. I must have hit him in the nose, because it resembled a squashed melon. His expression was not at all what one might expect of an allied nation. They laid down their guns, to keep both hands free. They vanquished me at last, two of them holding my arms and three sitting on my legs. They were all talking at me at a furious clip. They didn't seem to be saying anything very friendly. It occurred to me that they might tie me to four horses and snap the whip. I read somewhere that this was a favorite amusement of the Czars. I probably didn't have anything pleasant to look forward to. My imagination got the better of me, I started screaming and kicking once more, I tried to get free of their grasp, we were all in one heap again. One of the Russians kept repeating; *"Sobaka, sobaka."* And something about my mother. I couldn't imagine what he could be saying about my mother, whom he had never met. We must have been making a terrible racket, because all of a sudden the *litinant* himself appeared. He walked over all the way from the corral, just to take a look at me. They had practically stripped me down to my underwear, and now I cut a sorry figure for the *litinant*. The officer was frowning, he was obviously angry, my antics were probably holding up the smooth progress of the world war.

"Otkuda?" he asked. I can remember his voice to this day; it was melodious and vibrant, and at the same time deep. The game warden had a similar voice, when he sang in church during Holy Week. The soldiers were no longer holding me, I was standing on my own feet, watching the *litinant*. For a military commander he looked a bit irresponsible. He was laughing. I picked up all my things which were scattered on the ground: my coat, a few silly knicknacks. I wanted to add a couple of shells that were also on the ground, but these had not come out my pockets—they were dropped by one of the Russians. The *litinant* seemed to be all eyes, at the last moment he took the shells away from me. They were already inside my pocket. He rummaged around in my pockets with his fingers, pulled out the cigarette case. He didn't show any surprise, he probably saw a lot more unexpected things in the course of the war.

"Kurish?" he asked me. Russian is not difficult, I could really learn it in no time.

I shook my head to indicate that I didn't smoke. But then I changed my mind and started nodding my head the other way, yes, I did smoke. So that he wouldn't open the case or confiscate it. Which, of course, he did at once anyway.

In certain embarrassing situations I look straight down at the ground. Especially when I know what's coming next. There was a moment of silence. The *litinant* examined the cigarette case, and so did all the other soldiers. I don't know why they gaped at the woman for such a long time, she didn't really seem all that interesting to me at the moment. Finally the *litinant* snapped the case shut, and looked at me with a severe expression. He must have been a schoolteacher in civilian life.

"*Skolko tebe let?*" he asked, sticking up seven fingers. "*Sem?*" That made me pretty angry. But I was not going to argue with our liberators over such a small matter as my age. I merely snorted. To my amazement I saw that he was sticking the cigarette case in his pocket!

"This is not right for you," he said to me. And he looked as if I really ought to be grateful to him for not returning it. "You were here last night, *da?*" he asked, pointing to the corral.

"No."

I was determined to deny everything. But I could see that he knew I was there.

"*Beri!*" he said, and handed me a piece of chocolate, wrapped in silver foil. I took the chocolate cautiously and sniffed it. He watched me. Probably my face didn't show much gratitude, which surprised him. He asked me whether I wanted it or not.

"I guess so," I said casually. I didn't want him to think I was some kind of ninny who had never seen a piece of chocolate before.

The *litinant* then sent one of his soldiers off on some errand, and the others returned to their guard duty. They all disappeared, leaving only the officer and me. I guess he was confident of catching me by himself if I made another break for it. But I was through running. Somewhere in the sky droned a plane, high above the yellow fog. He looked up. I recognized the plane from its sound.

"Messerschmitt," I said.

"*Da,* Messer!" he replied, and glanced at me. I could see I had climbed a little in his estimation. He was walking among the horses. I went with him, I was glad that I could get close to the mare. The *litinant* didn't chase me away, he ignored me completely. Some of the horses were really in awful shape, they must have gone through a fierce battle. Perhaps when they were crossing the Carpathian mountains. People said that the Russians lost more men in the Carpathians than there are trees in those parts. Their horses were probably decimated there, too. He was stooping under the horses' bellies, so that he wouldn't have to go around the animals. I followed him. He threw another glance at me, appeared to be mulling something over. He slapped one animal's rear, the horse let him do it without kicking up. I had eyes only for the mare which I'd almost succeeded in leading off the previous night. I was right next to her. I tried not to act suspicious, so that I wouldn't tip the *litinant* off to my intentions. The mare didn't have a single scratch on her body; she was lucky, or else she hadn't yet been in battle.

The soldier sent off by the *litinant* a while ago came back. He handed me a plate of food, field rations. The plate was steaming hot. He pulled a spoon out of his boot for me. The Russians were kindhearted, and they seemed to be under the illusion that we had been starving throughout the war. But the food came in handy. I was sitting on the top railing, my knees under my chin, the plate in my lap. I was eating soup. There was a piece of meat in the soup the size of a calf's head. I picked the meat up with my fingers, it was soft, hot, greasy. The

209

litinant walked on, examining the horses. But while I was struggling with the meat, he came back, pulled a small cut-glass pepper shaker with a silver lid out of his pocket, and sprinkled a little pepper over the boiled piece of beef. Then he pulled out a second little bottle, a salt cellar, and salted the meat. His pockets must have been full of all sorts of fascinating things.

"Chorosho?" he asked.

I nodded. Then I was left alone again, the *litinant* went somewhere to the other end of the corral. I slid off the fence, put down the plate. It seemed to be a favorable moment, I couldn't even see a guard. I could beat it. I could kiss the whole famous Russian Army good-by. I thought it over, decided not to do it. Cool as a cucumber, I strolled among the horses, to my mare. By day I could take a much better look at her, she was as fine a beast as our Julie. I touched her front left leg, she obediently lifted it up. Her hoof was as clean as marble. To make sure, I examined all four. As if I was about to buy her, rather than steal her. Then I pulled myself up on my toes. "Stand still," I told the horse. "Stop fidgeting!" I opened her mouth. She'd got a set of choppers that could be shown at the world's fair. A really first-class nag. I had the feeling that somebody was watching me. I jumped up, to see where the *litinant* was, to spot him over the backs of the herd. I couldn't see him. I squatted to peep through the corridor formed by the horses' bellies. I turned red, for he was squatting, too, looking straight in my eyes! We both stood up, I started whistling, he started to talk in Russian to the nearest mount, half of whose head was knocked off by shrapnel.

Then the *litinant* got busy sending out a patrol. Again, four soldiers. A map was spread out on the ground, and he showed them something circled in pencil, then he waved his hand in the direction of the church. He knew everything. He knew about the Germans, where they had placed their guns, their tanks. At the time I thought the young Russian must be omniscient. I stood up on the fence, and watched which horses they were picking out for saddling up. I was afraid that they might pick "my" mare, Julie II. But they didn't, they skipped her. A tall beanpole of a soldier threw his flat Cossack saddle over the back of the horse standing next to Julie II, a rather skinny bay. The horse gasped when he mounted. Julie II probably had too heavy a rear to make a good patrol horse, she was certainly no sprinter. The *litinant* called back one of the Cossacks, the one who was in the greatest rush:

"*Andryusha!*"

"*Zdes,*" answered the soldier with discipline, but without enthusiasm.

The *litinant* motioned to him to come back, and to dismount. The officer was staring into the soldier's eyes, as if he was trying to hypnotize him. At the same time, he ran his hands over the soldier's coat, from the shoulders to the belt. He reached under the coat and pulled out a flat, rather large tin canteen. He uncorked it, sniffed, put the cork back. And stuck the canteen in his own pocket.

"*Davai,*" he said. Meaning that now everything was in order, the soldier could now go on duty. He really knew his subordinates to a remarkable degree. I only grasped the full significance of this detail much later. Today, this story of the confiscated alcohol seems quite touching to me.

And then the four riders took off, galloping up the slope, lying almost flat in the saddle. Horses and riders seemed to be floating over the low gooseberry bushes. The *litinant* sat down next to me on the rail. He was smoking a cigarette.

"Olda," he said. "*Gde Brno?*"

I stood up on top of the fence, looked around to get my bearings. The *litinant* was asking the same thing the Germans had asked earlier. Soldiers of all armies, whether advancing or retreating, seem to be mainly interested in directions.

I looked around to figure out north, south, east, west. I pointed in the approximate direction of the Moravian capital.

"*Praga?*" he asked next.

I pointed west, toward Prague.

I learned all this geography during a school excursion I was once on. We climbed all the way up to the observation tower, high above the countryside. A brisk wind was blowing. The teacher was demonstrating the direction of BRNO, JIHLAVA, PRAGUE, PARIS. There were a number of wooden signs in the shape of pointing fingers, with inscriptions such as STRASS-BURG. While the teacher was talking the boys were stuffing apple cores and stones into the knapsack he was carrying on his back. He was wearing a huge black hat that made him look like a Founding Father. He waved his arm, and the hat took off, sailing over the trees, sliding over rocks, the wind at last depositing it on a grassy slope. We ran after it, laughing, screaming, everybody wanted to get there first. We fought over it, and suddenly it was in my hands. They all let go, Kudera, Chumsky, Rez, and Vyska. In the furious tug they had torn off the hatband, and I was left holding the ruined hat. The teacher was already approaching, coming to recover his muti-lated headgear. It wasn't I who did it, I was innocent, but for some reason I couldn't move, I was rooted to the spot, hat in hand, like a lump of wood. I only managed to grit my teeth. But Anna shouted, "It wasn't him! Olda didn't do it! It was Rez!" The teacher, who had always instructed us that justice must be the foundation of all morality, examined the damage and then gave me a juicy slap in the face. I grasped the great and disheartening truth that many people in this world honor justice only in word and not in deed.

"I have a motorcycle," I told the *litinant,* while watching the mare. She had come to the fence, she was standing only a few steps away from us, rolling her eyes. I had the impression that she could live without the army. In fact, to the extent that a horse can express a view of the world, she appeared quite anti-militaristic. The *litinant* looked at me sharply, then at the horse. He was very intelligent.

"*Shto?*"

"Motorcycle," I repeated. I pretended to be holding the handles, I made a grinding noise like a cycle revving up. And I pointed to myself with my thumb. "I . . . me . . . I have motorcycle. *Ya . . . mayu . . .*" I tried out my Russian.

"You?"

"*Da!*"

"There," I pointed to the willows.

"It has a sidecar," I said. Once more I pretended to be grasping the handles, then I drew a kind of egg with my hands to describe the sidecar.

He must have had a fantastic imagination. He grasped everything at once. He jumped off the fence.

"*Idyom!*" he said, striding toward the willows. "*Bystro, bystro!*"

The *litinant* was apparently fascinated by technical things. He kept repeating *machinka, da?* about ten times. He wanted to make sure that I wasn't making fun of him. Of course I would never have dared to do that, especially to a man of his rank.

I brought him to the brick hut. He didn't seem to be very watchful. I noticed that soldiers who had gone through battle were no longer too concerned about personal safety. The hut was deserted. He saw the wounded horse, already lying on her side. The horse sensed our presence, wanted to get up but was too weak. She made several attempts, jerked her whole body, rocked back and forth, finally lifted herself half way on her front legs, and then slumped back on her side.

The *litinant* glanced inside the hut, walked around it, glanced quickly at the roof, jumped up there, gazed all around, jumped back down and returned to the moribund horse. I think he knew the animal. He put his hand on her back, cast an eye at the wounds, everything was clear to him. He noticed the bandage on the rear instep. He looked at me, thinking that I had bandaged the wound. I didn't say anything about Cyril, I would have needed a whole Russian dictionary for that.

"Kaput," he said about the horse. Nothing I didn't know. He pulled out a pistol.

"No!" I shouted. "No!"

"Idi, Olda. *Idi!"* he said. He pushed me aside, gently but firmly. Behind the hut, to the other side so that I wouldn't see anything. He was extremely tactful. I stood there, leaning against the brick wall, slowly sliding down until my legs touched the ground. I closed my eyes, stuffed up my ears. A shot rang out. Only one. My fingers were still in my ears, but I knew there was only one shot. I stayed behind the hut until the Russian came to get me.

The lieutenant began kicking away the brush that covered the motorcycle. He pulled out the iron monster with its sidecar. He examined the various buttons, pushed and pulled at levers.

Then he stepped on the starter . . .

He said it was a *choroshi machinka. Ochen!*

He adjusted something on the engine, and suddenly the engine started up, with a tremendous roar. The Russian beamed. He was soaking wet with pride. If you had had a chance of observing him as I did, from close up, you would realize that his nation is destined to achieve miracles of technology.

"*Davai*," he said, motioning to me to climb into the sidecar. He himself sat down behind the enormous handlebars. When he grasped the handles his arms were practically straight out. We took off like a rocket, right through the shrubbery. Before he got the hang of the controls, we knocked over about eight young plum trees.

At one point a wheel of the sidecar ran up the top of a thick bush, we almost toppled over, but he managed to right us again. He laughed. We were streaking right over the grassy bound, free and easy.

"Olda!" shouted the *litinant*. "*Chorosho?*"

I tried to make out where we were, I could see that we were racing over Husarek's field. A double slalom, weaving among the piles of manure and the tree holes. Rows of holes ran diagonally across the field, too. I hadn't noticed them before. The *litinant* swerved into the underbrush.

We ran right through a stretch of the deepest jungle, easy as you please. And then across the stream . . . a real joyride, and that's a fact! Even the *litinant* was having a grand time, I could see that. He was driving the cycle up a steep incline. He was really enjoying it, the war must have been very monotonous and boring.

"*Charasho, da?*" he asked.

"*Prima!* First class!" I shouted.

"*Shto?*"

"Super!"

"*Charasho!*" he yelled, and stepped on the gas.

We were wheeling down the linden alley, then into the alfalfa field, that endless stretch of land. We were making circles, figure eights, fancy wigwags. He was showing off his tricks.

The Russians are extremely flexible, they adjust quickly to any situation. He was looking for a cigarette, leaned back, steered with his feet, he managed to get a light. Then, to my amazement, he even stood up on top of the cycle!

"Olda, *smotri!*"

The *litinant* kept his balance beautifully, like a bareback rider. Actually, the principle is the same. Then he sat down again, started examining other levers. I stood up in my sidecar, but I had to hold on tight to keep from falling out.

"*Sidi,* Olda!" he said. "*Nyet, nyet sidi!*" I wanted to show him that I could do it, too, I didn't want him to think that we were an inferior people. He climbed up on his seat again, extending his arms like a tightrope walker.

"*Sidi,* Olda, *a smotri!*"

A burst of gunfire. Ta-ta-ta-ta. I turned my head, made out a machine gun. Because I turned, I didn't see what happened, but only heard it. A sharp violent crack, like a barrel bursting. But not in the distance, right next to me! I jerked my head, the *litinant* sprawled over the cycle. At that instant I still hadn't guessed the worst, I thought that he had lost his balance and fallen forward. The motorcycle veered off to one side, the handlebars at a sharp angle. We were falling, falling, all this within fifteen seconds, all around us there was furious shooting. The wheels bounced in the air, we hit the ground. I was lying on my face. The alfalfa was as high as my flat body. Fortunately, the motorcycle didn't run over us, it turned over a few feet away. I was breathing, I was alive. I was breathing into the earth, the leaves of grass, the little bugs crawling in front of my eyes. Shots whistled and rattled over my head, the noise filled the air. I heard loud explosions. It was all taking place somewhere down below, at my back. That's where the manor was and then the road, and behind the road, the river. Scared out of my wits, I still didn't understand what had really happened. I had goose pimples all over my body, my skin rough enough to grate vegetables. All the same, I lifted my head, just a little tiny bit. . . . I could see Germans running from the woods. They were coming toward me, wearing helmets, camouflage-checkered uniforms, huge tanks were lumbering alongside. On the other side, downhill from the church, another German attack was beginning. The top came off the steeple, it fell down on the church, breaking through the roof, bare beams stuck out of a cloud of dust, like ribs sticking out of a carcass. I wanted to be close to the *litinant,* I crawled toward him. I grasped at the mud, it got under my nails. Maybe my nails were broken. It seemed to me the *litinant* should be doing something, giving orders, leading his men against the Germans.

The air was shattered by gunfire, nothing else seemed to exist. There he was, the Russian. He was lying on his side, seemed to be looking off somewhere. I squeezed up against his body, it made me feel safer.

"Germans," I said. "Germans." Several times. I nestled against him. Suddenly he rolled over on his stomach. Only then did I take a closer look at him. He lay face down but he had no back, only a big bloody stain on his shredded field jacket.

"Ahhhh!" I cried out, drawing back. For a few moments I stared silently at his terrible wound.

"Germans," I repeated, just to say something, nothing else occurred to me. But then I realized the truth, though I didn't want to. I wanted to believe that he was still alive. I crawled around his body, to the other side. His arms were spread out, he was clutching a handful of clover. I was afraid of him. Maybe it was stupid of me, but in those days I was scared of dead people, their presence made me feel anxious. I lay on the ground, trembling, I didn't know what to do next.

217

"Litinant," I said. With dry lips. *"Litinant!* Please . . ."* At last I gained enough courage to touch him, to take him by the shoulder and turn him over. I let him go, now I knew that he was dead. I wanted to stand up, I got to my knees. But a tank was firing, heading down toward the buildings where the Cossacks were quartered. I pressed my face into my palms. My cheeks felt my own hot breath reflected back. I lay very still. I had no idea low long I lay there, weeping. Then it occurred to me that perhaps he wasn't dead after all, I came back and instead of looking at his face or wound I felt for his heart. The thought came to me that perhaps his heart was still beating, but there was nothing. I heard my own teeth rattling. Around me a continuous hell of firing, motors, running men, Germans. I no longer cared what was happening anywhere.

"Los! Los!"

"Achtung! Los!"

In his last moments the *litinant* managed to pull out his pistol, but it was lying uselessly next to his hand, with a wallet which fell out of his pocket. Everything was swimming before my eyes, as if I was looking through a rain-spattered window. Around the wallet were scattered some foreign banknotes, a letter folded into a triangle, a photograph of a woman and one of a man in uniform. The man had heavy mustaches, later I realized that it was Stalin. The firing seemed to be coming closer, the explosions were getting louder, as though they would bury me and smother me to death.

It was here that I would die.

Yes, this was the place. Scared and exhausted, I closed my eyes.

CHAPTER NINE

I was dreaming about the time I was one of the beaters in a hunt. The hunt took place on a drizzly day in late autumn. There was a continual noise of shots, dogs were barking all around, and I was dragging two hares to the wagon, where about fifty were already strung up. All the important people of our village were present. Singer, his wife, carrying a gun. The veterinarian, Kudera, the teacher, several Germans in uniform, who were standing next to Singer and his wife, laughing. They seemed to be swapping amusing stories. Boom! It was Mrs. Singer, an excellent shot, a rabbit made a somersault in the air and landed on his back. The priest, too, was killing hares. He wore a hunting cap and kept wiping his glasses with his handkerchief as he walked along. Vitlich was loading Singer's rifle. He had two of them, so that one was always ready. Cyril threw me a handful of spent shells. There was one live shell among them, I knew that Cyril swiped it from Singer on purpose. Cyril was a real pal. I sniffed the casings, they smelled of burned powder. Later I'd dump the powder out of the live shell and set fire to it, it would burn with an enormous flame. The other farmers were lined up in the circle, too: Rez, Chumsky, Vyska.

I carried the hares to Dad, and he loaded them on the wagon. Dad would have loved to shoot but he had no gun. We don't even have a setter, he says we can't afford one. I spot Dad throwing one of the hares into the bushes when nobody is looking, so that he can come back later and pick it up, after

219

the hunt. It makes me angry to see him demeaning himself like
that, I would tell them to take their hare and shove it.

There was as much shooting going on then as I could hear
now, lying in alfalfa next to the dead litinant. This, too, was
a hunt. And I am afraid I am the one they're hunting. There's
no way out. They are hounding me, encircling me just like
the poor squirrels that we used to chase in the woods. There
was always a gang of us. We'd see it jumping in terror from
tree to tree. We had no rifles, but stones and slingshots. We
pounded the trunks with sticks, we made a noise to flush the
squirrel from hiding. And as soon as it started in one direction,
we drove it back the other way. The squirrel dropped to the
ground, half dead from exhaustion. That's the moment we were
waiting for. Kudera would run toward it with a stick in his
hand, I'd close my eyes, just as I was closing them now by the
side of the overturned motorcycle. But the squirrel managed
to slip away at the last second, scrambling up a tree, Kudera
thrashing the trunk in a fury, because the squirrel remained
nestled in a branch, out of his reach.

I opened my eyes, aware again of my real situation. I got
up, and ran away. I just wanted to get away, far away from that
flat field.

I jumped into the nearest clump of bushes, slid down the
slope on my behind. I rolled like a ball. Then, crouching close
to the ground I ran through last year's dry grass. Not far from
me an explosion set up a shower of soil. The shells were landing
so close that I was convinced they were aimed at me. Artillery
shells. Out of the corner of my eye I saw fire somewhere inside the manor, that's where most of the shooting was going on.
One bang was so close that I was again stretched out kissing the
ground. I stuffed up my ears, desperately trying to think about
something else. I was trying to remember something funny, but

nothing came to mind. When your neck is in the noose, it's not the right atmosphere for laughing.

My eyes closed, it was autumn again, the hunt continued. Bertyna Petrzela was there, too. She was pouring tea for everybody. They all sniffed at it in mock seriousness, complaining that it had no bite. Singer had been waiting for this moment, he pulled a bottle of rum out of his bag. The neck of the bottle clinked against the outstretched cups. Everybody was laughing. Then the maid walked around the little group with a plate of fried schnitzels. Everybody got a napkin and a slice of bread. The German overlords of course were served first, the farmers last. We beaters got nothing at all. We were all huddled together by the little chapel, and we were cold. Vitlich got a big fire going for the hunters, they were warming their hands and backs. The guns were still on their shoulders, muzzles facing forward. Two German officers were whispering something to Bertyna. She was laughing her head off, her mouth wide open showing teeth, tongue; the inside of her mouth was pink, hot, her breath was turning to white steam that curled like a veil around her face. She spilled some tea, laughed even harder. In an unguarded moment, one of the young Germans rolled up the sleeve of Bertyna's raincoat and planted a kiss under the elbow of her fleshy arm.

I have no idea why I was thinking of all this nonsense at such a moment, when my life was at stake. I would rather recall one of my few good deeds. Such a memory can give a person strength in times of crisis.

That time in the woods, the squirrel came running straight toward me. And I let her go. I could have caught her easily, I had already taken off my coat to throw over her, I could have killed her. Instead, I let her go. She vanished. Before the boys could get to me, she was gone. Kudera saw my treacherous act, he jumped on me and started pummeling me, they all joined in, there were too many of them. They gave me more kicks than you could count at a championship soccer match. But that wasn't all.

In the middle of this shrub, where I was writhing with fear, I could remember one single funny incident. That's a fact. The ground was green with a new growth of grass. It rustled, I was drowning it in. I held my head in my hands. Again, I heard the pounding of my own heartbeat, my own breathing, I expected them to finish me off at point-blank range. The Germans were just a step or two away, the air was full of sharp German voices, the r's were rattling, the esses and zees were hissing.

It was the same kind of harsh voice the German officer had. During a pause in the chase, he was training his dog. It had to jump over his arm. It had to roll over, fetch sticks. Then it had to lie completely still, feigning death. The German was not wearing a cap, he had beautiful, youthful black hair. Then he sent his dog to fetch Bertyna. The dog caught her by the skirt, careful not to tear it, and started backing toward the officer, growling. Bertyna was letting out little shrieks, but she had no choice except to follow the dog. Everybody around the fire was howling with laughter. Only Mrs. Singer wasn't laughing. She was watching the black-haired youth, her face pale, not a trace of a smile. Then she abruptly turned away. The priest, too, stopped laughing. Father took advantage of the confusion and threw another hare in the bushes. I saw him, I saw everything he was doing. The dog kept on retreating, pulling Bertyna by the teeth, toward the meadow. The officer was pointing toward a thick clump of bushes, the center of which was hidden from view from all sides. A peculiar uneasy laugh continued. Bravo, shouted the second officer. Bertyna had to go, whether she wanted to or not. The officer slapped his boot as a signal. The dog turned his head toward him. Bertyna pretended to be begging him for mercy. That made them burst out into a new guffaw. Suddenly a shot boomed out from the nearest side of the forest. A rifle shot. I could tell it wasn't a shotgun blast. It was totally unexpected. The officer fell to his knees, his body suddenly jack-knifed backward. My mouth was wide open. Everybody stood motionless. The other officer dashed into the woods, Singer right behind him. Singer was yelling hysterically, ordering Vitlich into the woods. They all shouted that it was a bandit. As a matter of fact, there actually was a sign at that time posted on a forest road, which read: ACHTUNG, BANDITEN! That's how the Germans designated partisans. The dog finally released Bertyna. She, too, had her mouth wide open, and she was as pale as Singer's wife. . . . The dead German looked very much like the dead Russian officer in the alfalfa field.

When I am dead, I will look the same as they did, I will clutch at the earth with all ten fingers, both hands will be full of soil and shreds of grass. All my adventures so far in life have ended sadly. That's a fact.

That day in the woods, the boys stripped me naked and tied me to a tree. After giving me a good thrashing, they left. They left me there and went off. I cried, I wept convulsively, I yelled after them, but they didn't care. I wept for several hours, till it got dark, and I couldn't even make out the nearest tree trunks. Then I saw Anna, looking for me, but I was naked. Some kinds of disgrace are worse than death. She was looking for me, calling out my name, but I didn't want to answer, because I had no clothes. Inside of me, manly pride struggled against the fear that I would be left in the woods to die. I

*couldn't break the ropes, my wrists were already sore to the bone.
It seemed that Anna would pass right by me without seeing me.
At that moment I shouted at her, and she saw me. I was yelling
something at her, asking her not to look at me. She was walking
straight toward me. When she realized my predicament, she
walked to the other side, and untied the rope from the back,
from behind the tree. As soon as I was free, I slapped her face!
I have no idea why I struck the only person who showed compassion for me. I picked up my trousers and fled away from
her. I heard her weeping, running after me, but I didn't stop.*

I guess it couldn't have been a good deed that I performed,
after all. True, very little that could be called good has happened to me so far in life, but then I haven't done too much
that deserved credit, either.

I got to my feet, ran to the willow grove; subconsciously,
without thinking, I was aiming for the hut.

Nothing but bare beams!

The hut was demolished. A crater. In place of the brick
structure there was only a hole in the ground, and three more
holes, lined up in a row. I darted to the pile of wicker where
the motorcycle had been concealed. I wanted to hide there myself. I no longer knew who was fighting against whom. I didn't
know where the Germans were or the Russians. I covered my
ears with my hands.

A shower of earth splashed over the pile, spattering me too.
A whole geyser of mud and small stones. Another detonation.
The earth shook.

"Mother!" I called. "Mother!"

I had lost all sense, I was burying myself under a blanket of
dried brush which offered no protection at all.

My teeth were chattering. "Mother! Mom!"

After I die, I will have a grave in the cemetery, next to the stone wall. Children generally have a simple white cross and a tin plaque with their name. I see the inscription quite clearly: OLDRICH VAREKA. There will be a small photograph of me under an oval piece of glass, in that flappy sailor blouse, with anchors on the sleeves. Mother will come to visit my grave. She will bring a small watering can, which she will fill at the pump that makes such an awful squeaking noise. Then she will water the violets which she has planted over my grave. And she will stick one tall candle in the ground. I think it is the same one I got at Confirmation. She will light it, weeping, and go away. And up will jump Vyska-Pisska, who had been hiding nearby; naturally, he'll swipe the candle from my grave . . .

I pulled more of the osier branches over me, and held the top of my head with both hands. Bang. Bang. There was no end to it, it was longer than the Thirty Years' War.

"Ourfatherwhoartinheaven . . ." I hear myself mumbling.

"Someday you will call upon the Good Lord," the priest would always warn us in class. "Someday you will call on him, but it will be too late!"

About ten children were sitting on the benches, two were standing in each corner, and at least fifteen of us were kneeling on the podium, being punished. I was kneeling humbly, because the priest was looking at me. But with the hand which he couldn't see from his chair I was taking chalk out of the cardboard box and stuffing it in my pocket. Somehow he must have seen it after all, he picked up a bunch of keys lying on the table and flung them at me, hitting me in the back.

Now I was again pelted by a rain of dirt. The machine guns sounded like a buzz saw. I was no longer opening my eyes at all.

Once, a long time ago, they were sawing something up-stairs, a rain of sawdust came pouring down into the cellar. There was a huge pile of it, I was making a tunnel for Anna, a little room for her to play in. But as soon as she climbed in, I kicked at the pile and the sawdust came tumbling on her head. I ran off, up the stairs. Maybe God was really watching us, counting up our sins.

Now the big Russian guns opened up. They were positioned right by the river, but were aiming somewhere far ahead. They thundered as if the whole sky was coming down.

The way thunderstorms shook our house at night. I used to pull the quilt over my head. The downpour went beating on the kitchen window, Mother would come out of the hall, and lie down next to me in my bed. I moved close to her, put my arms around her neck. My cheek touching hers, my face full of Mother's loose hair.

"Don't be afraid," she would always say. "A good person has nothing to fear."

"Not even lightning, Mom?"

"Not even lightning. . . ."

A heavy downpour surprised us one time in the field. Mom and I managed to run for cover under a rick of straw. The inside of a rick is as dry as a brick hut. The space was just big enough for two. Wisps of straw clung to Mother's hair. We were panting, drenched to the skin, Mother quickly took off my soaking shirt, took her wool jacket out of her bag and put it on me, and buttoned it up. She herself was so wet that her dress clung to her body. She wasn't even wearing a kerchief on her head, it was folded up, dry, in her bag. She tried to wrap it around my head, but I didn't want it, I wanted her to have it. She wrapped it around my neck, and covered herself with a canvas sheet.

"Are you all right?" she asked. *"Your throat doesn't hurt?"*
"No, Mom, I am fine."

I kept on running. On top of the hill, near the lindens a tank was burning, or maybe a truck. The manor caught it good, even the roof was smashed. The yard was full of horses. I paid no attention, regardless of anything, kept moving on my way—the way home. I plopped through a pile of manure, zigzagged among the tree holes. I jumped over them so as not to lose time. Some twenty horses pranced through the field, I could have taken any one I liked. But I was only thinking of my mother, whether she was all right, I'd never felt such concern for her before. I saw her in all her many guises. Her goodness, her love for me.

Once we had a musical evening at school, we were singing:
"How lovely is God's world to me . . ." I was standing in the
front row, wearing my new sailor suit. The fat teacher was
conducting the chorus, we called her Miss Ton. Mom was look-
ing at me, and I at her. After we returned home, Father yelled
at her: "Who told you to buy new rags for that brat?"

"He needed something for school," I heard Mother an-
swer.

"I work my bloody hands off, and you throw money out
the window. For that dumb brat!"

I heard a slap, several slaps, a common sound in our cozy
home.

"Stop that!" I heard Mother say.

I clutched the door handle. "Father!" I shouted. He'd locked
the door. I yanked furiously at the handle, he was beating her,
I could hear him beating Mother.

"I am not going to take that from you," she said, weeping.
Then she went out, she was carrying a basket with a few bits
of clothing. "Go on!" he shouted after her. "Go to hell!"

He grabbed me, shoved me into the room and locked the door. But he'd no sooner turned the key than I hopped out through the window. I hurdled the geraniums, caught up with Mother on the field path. Dusk had already fallen. She heard me running, turned and waited for me.

"Mom, I'll come with you. I am not going to stay with him."

She drew me close, but she didn't say anything bad about him, and that surprised me a little.

We sat on a stone bench by the church. It was night—moon, stars, white light. I saw Father coming up the path by the chapel, he was looking for us.

"He's coming," I whispered. "Let's run!"

But Mother remained seated, she was holding me by the hand. I wanted her to flee, but she remained motionless.

He stopped at the crucifix. He saw us. He stood there a while, just looking at us. Then he said, "Come on home." He said it quite differently from usual, his voice was strangely soft. I heard him speak like that only about three times in all my life; on two of these occasions, I wasn't even sure whether I might not have been mistaken.

I ran down the tree-lined road leading from the manor to the village. I had to run along the ditch by the side, because the road was full of tanks, trucks, and guns. Clouds of dust were swirling everywhere. Now I was forced to jog through the field, to get out of the way of some Russians changing a tire in the ditch. None of them paid any attention to me.

I was glad it was they who won the battle. They seemed to be in a great hurry, they were chasing after the retreating Germans. A Russian on a motorcycle weaved his way like an acrobat, in and out of the ditch, back onto the road.

A group of trucks was parked on the firehouse lawn, with

soldiers milling all around. A flag was flapping from the firehouse tower. Red, white, and blue. Czechoslovak.

I reached the first houses of the village, and they, too, were full of flags, there were even some red ones. I also seemed to hear the sound of music. It was faint, drowned out by the noise of cars. People were throwing flowers at the Russians like on Corpus Christi day. But the soldiers seemed terribly tired, their faces were black with dust, perhaps they didn't even see the flowers. I jumped over a fence, because I spotted the teacher standing by the side of the road, on a pile of bricks. He was wearing a World War I legionnaire's uniform, his legs encased in military leggings. A ton of medals. He was constantly saluting, shouting: "Hail!" or "Welcome!" In his glorious uniform he looked like the most important man present, as though he'd won the war single-handed. I circled the brick pile from behind, he didn't see me. He had eyes only for the Russians, he was pulling patriotic faces at them. Throngs of people lined the road, there was jubilation in front of all the houses. I threaded my way through the throng of my fellow citizens. Naturally, Slejha's squeaky daughter Andula was there, a wagon-load of girls, all in folk costume. The lady teacher towered over them like Mount Vesuvius, she was sporting the folk costume of a Kievan bride, decked out with a thousand bows and ribbons. She must have been a hundred and sixty years old. She conducted a chorus, which was chanting in unison: "Long live the Soviet Union!"

Andula spotted me. "Pinda!" she yelled. "Your folks are looking for you. The Germans didn't kill you after all?"

"Yeh," I said. "They killed me. How did your pig make out? It didn't choke on you?"

She got mad, the silly goose.

"Get in line, Olda," said the teacher. That'd be the day.

"Long live Marshall Stalin!" the teacher shouted. "Oldrich, get in line, somebody hand him a flag!"

"Long live . . ."

A million flags. It's a fact. . . .

Before I did anything else, I took a drink from the pump. Kelbl's band was playing—that's the funeral-and-festival band of our village. They were blowing their heads off, dressed up in firemen's uniforms with shiny helmets.

"Olda!" Anna called out. She ran after me. I thumbed my nose at her and streaked off. The municipal weighing station had taken a pasting, all the windows were smashed. Farmers were boarding them up.

The veterinarian was wearing a Czechoslovak officer's uniform. It wasn't until 1945 that I found out to my surprise that our little nation had had its own army before the war. A lot of people strolled around with rifles on their shoulders. I have no idea where they got them. Even stationmaster Slejha was carrying one. He'd spent the whole war sabotaging the German war efforts by pilfering from trains. All the hired help from the manor were carrying arms. The sacristan was trying to raise a flag over the rectory, the rope kept slipping, he was loosening a knot with his teeth, then he waved, shouting VIVAT!

I walked to the edge of the village, where the Russians were turning onto the concrete highway. People said they were headed for Prague. The Town Hall no longer carried a German inscription. Instead, there was a large sign which read LONG LIVE THE REPUBLIC!

A red flag and our own flag hung over the sign. I stopped, Bertyna Petrzela was having herself photographed by the side of the road with several soldiers. She was laughing, as merry as she was during the outing with the German officers. Soldiers are soldiers, German or Russian. I turned my head because I heard shouting coming out of a side street, where there was a large throng of people.

I ran over, I couldn't see over the backs of the crowd, so I climbed the wire fence, craned my neck, but somebody boxed my ears. It was Squirrel.

She didn't realize it was me, but when she recognized me, she said, "Olda, have you been home yet? Your people are looking for you!" There was genuine concern in her voice.

"Yes," I shouted over my shoulder and dashed off. I didn't feel like chatting with Squirrel, while the republic was being liberated. Then I froze in my tracks, I realized who it was they were leading in their midst. I scrambled up on a stack of planks, so that I could see over the swarming human anthill. The throng moved like a living wall. Vitlich was in front of them. He was walking as if he was leading them, but actually it was the other way around, they were driving him. He was wearing only trousers and a sweater, he was rumpled and dusty, walking barefoot. I could see that he was in even worse shape than I was. But nobody was beating him any longer, at that moment, nobody was beating him. Then some people standing on the planks alongside of me started throwing stones at him.

He made as if to break into a run, but the crowd behind continued at its even pace. They seemed sure he wouldn't get away. They shouted: "Slowly! Walk!"

He obeyed them, slowed to a walk, and that surprised me. They were following him like a living, threatening wall. I couldn't understand what was going on. My mouth hung open, like a man who suddenly hears a voice calling to him from the sky. I no longer thought of Julie, who was gone, or of the

Germans, who were also gone, or of the Russians, who were here at last. My head was full of Cyril Vitlich, and of mystery.

I ran over the planks behind the crowd, behind Vitlich, to catch up with them. I was pushing as hard as I could, squeezing forward through the multitude.

I understood nothing at all.

CHAPTER TEN

Somebody threw another rock at Vitlich. It missed, and the stone landed behind him, bounced and hit the wall of a building. Vitlich wasn't trying to get out of the way of the stones. Nor was he turning around to look at anybody behind him. I could see Kudera in the crowd, Chumsky, Vyska, Rez. The vet, too, still in uniform, had hurried over. A lot of other people, Puma's father, the game warden, maybe a hundred altogether. A distance of about ten steps separated Vitlich from the crowd. More stones, one hit his leg.

"You bastard of an informer!" the game warden screamed at Vitlich, much to my amazement. One of the farmhands from the manor yelled out: "How much did Singer pay you, you swine?" I knew the man. He was the one who carried Ludvik the Spats from the stack where he died. And he had also taken care of the horses during the hunt, while my dad was busy stowing hares in the bushes.

Everybody in the crowd seemed feverish. The happy music of Kelbl's village band could be heard faintly in the distance, together with the roar of engines from the advancing victorious army.

"How much did he pay you to be his stooge? How many of us did you sell out?"

I got to the edge of the throng, I didn't want to be in the very first row.

"I am surprised the Nazis didn't take you along with them!" mocked Slejha. He ran over, gun in hand. "How many decent people did you betray, you son-of-a-bitch!"

I was so amazed by Slejha's words that I almost stopped in my tracks. Slejha wore a red arm band, a red band on his stationmaster's cap, and a big red-white-and-blue flag was prominently pinned to his jacket. A stick went flying through the air, it whacked Vitlich in the back, a powerful blow. Cyril fell to his knees, got up again without a sound. His forehead was drenched, sweat ran over his brows, rivulets twisted down his cheeks to his chin. Droplets covered his big, bruised face. His sweater was torn, he had to keep hitching up his trousers to stop them from falling. The rain of stones was getting heavier.

"Who brought the Nazis to our house?" yelled Kudera. I didn't think Vitlich heard him.

"Louse! Who gave my name to the Gestapo?"

It was true that one time a black car really did pull up in front of Kudera's house. Vitlich climbed out, with Germans in leather coats. They went inside, and after a while came out with Kudera and took him away in the car.

Vitlich was nervous that day, he was shifting from one foot to the other, looking around to see whether anybody was watching him. The street was empty, everybody was peering out from behind flower pots and curtains—Dad, too. That time, my father said: "Vitlich got even with him for the auction!" Kudera was in custody for approximately four hours (for the rest of his life he proudly referred to this experience in all official records). Singer's car brought him back in the rain, he stepped out self-confidently. Singer himself was behind the wheel, they were laughing, Singer shook his hand. Kudera strutted to his gate, as if to show everybody that he was too much even for the Germans to handle. "*If you have money, you can buy your way out of anything,*" *said my father.*

Now, Chumsky was yelling: "Thrash his hide!"

Others joined in, "A rope around the neck!" "Let's string up all collaborators! Long live the republic!" We had left the village behind, we were walking to Vitlich's house. The crowd was not only behind Vitlich, it had spread out around the sides, like a horseshoe. They were on his left and right, he was in the middle. But they were keeping their distance. They wanted to make sure he was by himself, visible. The stones kept flying. One hit him in the back of the head, blood began oozing down his neck, it soaked into his sweater, but he didn't wipe it, he didn't seem to feel it, he didn't know he was bleeding.

I stopped, to let them pass me, I walked behind them, I didn't want to see any more. The whole scene seemed incredible. The engines were no longer to be heard, only the strains of music. They were playing polkas.

"Don't let him inside the house!" I heard.

"He's got a gun at home!"

They ran on ahead. I was left all alone. I bit my lips, I should go back. Vitlich was now completely encircled. I stood between bodies, I didn't even know who they were. They encircled the garden, a few of them were even standing in the door of the house to keep him from going in.

The puppies were frolicking around the shed, not comprehending anything. Iza skipped over to Vitlich, but somebody flung a stick at her. She whined, and slunk off into the doghouse.

Rocks crashed through the windows of the house. Cyril was standing among the flower beds, he had no place to go. To this day I can remember that moment quite clearly. A few lilac bushes were blooming in his garden, in the back he had a walnut tree which shone with a bright green color from top to bottom. The tree was luminous to its very tip. The sun was sinking, it sparkled through the branches, close to setting.

A rock hit Vitlich in the face, he covered his cheek with his palm. For an instant it seemed that he was about to speak, that he might plead for mercy. But he said nothing. Stupid national jubilation music continued to blare. Sometimes it sounded like a tavern dance and the music carried all the way out into the fields.

"Kneel down, you bastard, and apologize!" screamed Kudera.

Vitlich continued to stand still, without even looking at Kudera.

"To your knees, son-of-a-bitch!"

A rain of rocks and sticks.

A stick hit a puppy, it whined and scampered across the yard. Some of the men were pulling posts out of the fence, looking at Vitlich and screaming at him.

"Don't you know how to apologize, you cur?" I heard Rez. "After what you did, you don't even have the decency to ask forgiveness?"

Vitlich took a step, he was now next to the pump, he was holding the handle, trembling on his exhausted legs. I was not even aware that my face was wet from crying. Somebody pushed me aside, but I found another crack through which I could see. I was terribly afraid for Vitlich.

At that moment Vitlich was standing on the low cement border of the well, he was still holding the handle. The men were coming closer and closer. Cyril's bare foot tripped on the tin cover of the well, the cover rattled and rolled off. The band was playing "Koline, Koline."

He didn't look at his feet. He knew that the well underneath him was uncovered. I can still see his bare, bruised, bloody feet standing on the concrete edge.

The hail of stones stopped.

The men stood still. Some were in the flower beds, others behind the fence, some were even in the midst of climbing the fence, with one leg swung over the top plank. They all froze. Even Kudera turned to wood.

Chumsky's arm was cocked to swing his cane. Slejha looked as if one of his trains had jumped a track. The veterinarian had shouted at Vitlich and at all the men: "Stay where you are!" His voice was anxious. He was the only one who was trying to stop the course of events. Everybody was silent, it was the deepest silence I have ever experienced. Cyril Vitlich didn't see anyone, not even me. I knew what he was about to do. I knew that he was not going to beg. I wanted to scream, I was kneeling up front, face pressed against the fence, clutching the planks.

The veterinarian couldn't stand it any longer. "Don't be crazy! Cyril!"

Cyril Vitlich was probably only aware of the tree, the floating sun, the green lawn. He was staring over the heads of the crowd. Then he moved, I closed my eyes, I heard a metallic impact, the rattle of the steel pipe, the clang of the tin cover which he had bumped against. A muffled thud came from deep within the earth.

Now they all poured into the garden, knocking down the fence, shouting, gesticulating. They wanted to save Vitlich. When I opened my eyes, I saw a puppy. It had run over the fallen fence, and was looking at me.

I turned my back on the house, the people, my fellow citizens. And I ran as fast as I could.

I couldn't think of Cyril Vitlich. I thought of the puppy, of its small, dappled head. At that moment, I envied the poor, dumb life of a puppy; it seemed incomparably more beautiful than the life of a human being.

CHAPTER ELEVEN

I ran along old familiar paths, yet I had no idea where I was going. Objects on both sides of the road merged into a peculiar vague blur, as if I was looking through a murky sheet of glass. Trees, brickyard, houses, flags, faces, band, Russians, signs. My breathing and the slapping of my soles were the only sounds. My heart seemed to be in my brain. In remarkably short time I reached home. Maybe it all lasted only a second.

Here was my house, our house! . . .

Walls, roof, doors, windows, gate, everything I knew, everything I had. I reached for the doorhandle, slumped against the door. I pressed the handle, but the door was locked. I jumped and reached for the key above the ledge where we always kept it when there was nobody home, but the key wasn't there. I lifted the keyhole cover. The key was on the other side, the door was locked from inside. I pounded with my fist, then I beat on the window, on all three windows in a row. I ran to the gate, where the limewater inscription still shouted TYPHUS!

Plus a red-white-and-blue flag, a sloppy flag, hurriedly sewn together, nailed to the brown boards of the gate. I pounded on the gate, put my eye against the round knothole I always used for peering into our yard.

My eyes were still dazed, everything seemed blurred. But then

239

I blinked, and I could see our yard quite clearly. Father was looking toward the gate, he was evidently frightened by the unexpected banging. Mother was in the yard, too. They were unloading furniture from a cart! . . . Yellow cupboards, beds, table, chairs. I recognized the furniture from the manor. The cupboards which I had seen at Singer's house. The furniture was stacked on a flat cart with rubber-rimmed wheels—the same wheels which I had helped Vitlich to remove. Apparently Father had found the wheels which we had hidden in the straw. I was glad that Mother was all right. I wanted to call to her, but I kept silent. I found a bigger knothole, I had to stand on tiptoe to reach it. The cart had horses hitched to it! The horses didn't look familiar, I had no idea where Father dug them up. Two were hitched to the cart, a third one was tied behind. He must have found them somewhere. I banged on the boards again. Father looked at Mother, then he turned to the gate.

"Coming!" he shouted. "Coming!"

Quickly he started unhitching the horses, he didn't know who was behind the gate, I could see that he was trying to think of a way of hiding the animals. Mother started leading them into the barn. Both parents were peering nervously at the gate—at me.

But I was no longer pounding, I was no longer looking. Rocks banged against the gate. I turned my head, the wagons of the gang were rattling straight at me. I couldn't imagine how I'd failed to hear them. They were coming back from the woods, the same caravan that set out yesterday morning. Yes, it was only yesterday morning, but it seemed like a year ago. A million years ago.

Koo-Koo-Kudera, Chumsky the Chump, Rez-Fez, Vyska-Pisska. The biggest jerks in the world. Chumsky still had cows tied to the back of his wagon.

They were flinging rocks at me, yelling threats and they

were jumping off their wagons to settle the score with me. It took me a while to orient myself, before I grasped the situation. But then I had no more time for thought, I had to run for my life, to keep them from giving me a thrashing on the very first day of national independence. That's probably what they were after. I got whacked with a stone, they were racing after me, past our house, into the fields, toward the barns. Jozka was chasing me, too. I was running as hard as I could, but I knew they would catch me. They always did. I had never managed to run away from Jozka.

One of them was already on my back. They were pounding me, I didn't fight back, they were rolling over me but I couldn't defend myself, I had no strength left in my body. I don't know what they were shouting, I knew they were cursing me, they were stepping on my hands, but I no longer cared. Maybe they wanted to kill me.

But suddenly they stopped beating me, they were standing around me, over me, I could hear music from the village, a festive melody, our national anthem. They weren't going to kill me, they were doing something much worse, they were pissing on me.

I was lying on my face, holding my hands over my head.

They were roaring with laughter, the bastards, then they left me lying there and ran off.

I didn't cry. I lay on the ground for a long time, a whole eternity. Then I got up, reached inside my shirt, for my slingshot. A small stone was lying at my feet, just the right kind. I set it in the leather pouch, drew the rubber bands tight.

They were already past the barn, out of my range. But the roof was covered with pigeons, they always sat there. I let fly at them, for no particular reason, almost without aiming.

They took off.

One pigeon was sliding down the roof, his wings spread out. . . . He reached the edge, tumbled into the grass. I watched the flock, as they climbed into the sky like a white corkscrew.

I lay down on my back, without tears, looking straight up. I wanted to die.

The pigeons rose so high that I could barely see them any longer. The tiny dots floated through the wide, free sky.

The earth under them must have looked infinitely far away.

I, too, must have seemed like an insignificant dot.

One person, no matter who he may be, is nothing on such a large earth.

CHAPTER TWELVE

This is what I never found out:

A few days after the events which I have been recounting for you, a wagon was standing in front of the railroad station of a certain German town, the roofs of which were bedecked with white flags. A wagon, and a horse.

For many long hours, for a whole day.

The Germans had other worries. Only here and there somebody noticed the horse, mainly children.

Trains whistled from the station, the street was full of soldiers, victors and vanquished.

The children were standing silently around the horse, examining her shyly. Then a little girl gathered courage, stretched out her hand, and stroked the horse across its soft nose.

The horse let itself be petted.

It was my Julie.

Jan Procházka who died in February 1971 was one of Czecho-slovakia's most popular novelists. LONG LIVE THE REPUBLIC, which has been translated into several languages, won the 1966 Jugendbuchpreis.